A CASE FOR CHRISTMAS

THE LORDS OF BUCKNALL CLUB

J.A. ROCK

LISA HENRY

A Case for Christmas

Copyright © 2021 by J.A. Rock and Lisa Henry.

Edited by Susie Selva.

Cover Art by Mitxeran.

ACKNOWLEDGMENTS

Thank you, Bridget, for all your amazing help.

ABOUT A CASE FOR CHRISTMAS

He loves no-one and never will.

Lord Christmas Gale is a genius and a misanthrope, and, quite to his disgust, adored by all of Society for his capacity to solve mysteries. When a man approaches him seeking help in locating a lost dog, Gale rebuffs him. But what begins with a missing dog ends in murder and intrigue--two of Gale's favourite things, if it weren't for the orphan that comes attached to them. Oh, and Benjamin Chant.

He has sworn to never love again.

The Honourable Mr. Benjamin Chant isn't sure how he got swept up in Gale's mad investigation, but there's something intriguing about the man--a vulnerability that most of the world doesn't notice, but which captures Chant's interest, and his sympathy, from their first meeting. After a disastrous love affair in the past, Chant has sworn to never give his heart away again. Especially to a man who does not want it.

But it isn't just their hearts at stake.

When their investigation takes a dangerous turn and their lives are threatened, both Gale and Chant are forced into the realisation that perhaps two imperfect men might fit perfectly together--that is, if they can outwit the killer who is intent on seeing them both dead.

A Case for Christmas is the second book in the Lords of Bucknall Club series, where the Regency meets m/m romance.

CONTENTS

In 1783, the Marriage Act Amendment was introduced in England to allow marriages between same-sex couples. This was done to strengthen the law of primogeniture and to encourage childless unions in younger sons and daughters of the peerage, as an excess of lesser heirs might prove burdensome to a thinly spread inheritance.

CHAPTER 1

*L*ord Christmas Gale, youngest son of the Marquess of Shorsbury, walked along the river, hating his name nearly as much as he hated the fact that people now knew it.

The sky was a soggy, bloated-looking mass of peach and grey as the sun began to set. If he didn't hurry home, he would miss the family carriage to the Harringdon ball. O tragedy. O despair. He needed to attend the Harringdon ball like he needed a paper knife forced up his nose—an act he was fairly certain several individuals at last night's salon would have enjoyed. But he had promised to chaperone one of his seemingly limitless supply of sisters this evening, and while he was an absolute ass, he still retained a nominal sense of familial duty.

A young couple actually stopped in their tracks to stare at him. He cast them the darkest of glares. He had never wanted the *Gazette* to do that piece on him. And he had certainly never asked for the sketch that had accompanied the write-up. Rendered in pencil, he'd looked like some tormented William Blake deity, all hollow cheeked and martyr eyed. Good Lord, if that was how he appeared to the world, no wonder nobody at the salon ever offered to stick a paper knife up his nose. Or stick anything else anywhere. Disappointing, but he had his molly boys, one of whom he'd engaged in a short but invigorating encounter only moments ago. No paper knives, alas—but a rather inspired use of the crested helmet of an Athena bust.

The vestiges of pleasure had seeped away once he'd found himself back on the street, imagining that everyone who glanced his way had read the *Gazette* article declaring: "Lord Christmas Gale, though less radiant in looks, manner, and accomplishment than his elder brother, has discovered a means to shine this Season. The savvy investigator has just wrapped up yet another case…"

Investigator. Bah. As though he asked for the mayhem he stumbled upon every third day. And did they have to call it a case? He *looked into things*, that was all. He was hardly the embittered hero of some gothic novel.

Dalliances had been much simpler back when everybody looked right through him—including his own father, who often started in surprise when he found him in a room, as though he were a burglar he'd caught in the act rather than his own son. That was likely his own fault, though, as he spent as little time at his family home as possible, so Gale considered it quite probable the old man had forgotten what he looked like. With the unfortunate advent of his celebrity, Gale actually had to consider where he went and who might see him there. He'd begun using molly houses south of the river in an attempt to retain his anonymity, but that didn't always work. Even his molly this evening—a fellow who looked as though he'd never read a news sheet in his life—had asked how he'd been so clever as to discover last month that Lady Carstairs's diamond brooch had been stolen and replaced with a fake, and that her second son's tutor, who was not the son of a parson as he claimed to be, was to blame.

In truth, Gale did not know the answer. He was not "extraordinary," as the *Gazette* had stated. His mother rarely described him as clever, and perhaps he was not, compared to her. Nor did his father, from whom Gale seemed to have inherited a world-weary countenance without any of the man's quick-tongued charm. Nor had his tutors, who'd found him difficult and dull. Even his belief that his thick auburn hair and the surprisingly soft eyes set amid the sharp angles of his face lent him a sort of dark appeal had proved ill-founded when the only person to dance with him at the Wilkes's ball last Season was Miss Emily Tulk—a terribly shy, droop-eyed girl who'd looked on the verge of tears as he'd whirled her about.

"'Ey you!" someone called.

Gale hurried onward, determined not to look up. Unlikely he was the "you" being addressed.

"You there! Lord Christmas Gale!"

All right, yes, well.

He paused, sighing, and tapped his cane once against the cobblestones, then turned.

The approaching man was lumpy and grey as a bowl of porridge, his clothes filthy and a couple of sizes too large. His eyes gleamed like two snail shells as he hobbled toward Gale. Gale glanced upward and around as though hoping someone or something might rescue him from this encounter, but he was forced to turn his attention back to the man.

"I heard about you," the fellow said. "My little girl saw your picture in the news sheet. She said you was a handsome devil."

If she bore any resemblance to her father in visage, her standards were probably quite low. But he'd take flattery where he could get it.

"I told her, you're seven years of age, you! You have no business thinking about handsome men!" The man scratched his backside, and Gale noticed that his left hand had six fingers on it. "She can read, she can. Clever with words. Oh, she'll make games of 'em. Run rings around me."

The sun had sunk lower. If Gale stood there long enough, listening to this old drunk blather about his daughter, mayhap he'd miss the ball entirely. A comforting thought. Clarissa would have his head, sure, but he could buy her a book tomorrow and all would be forgiven.

"She read me the story. 'Bout you, uh… uh… exposing that charlatan parson's son. Good on you, I say."

"Thank you." Gale refrained from saying anything cruel. He didn't know why the urge to hurl barbs overtook him so strongly at times. He recalled, with a rush of humiliation and an even deeper, more visceral rush of pleasure, Teddy's hand cupping his face one night at the salon. Their harsh, boozy breaths mingling. And Teddy had said—what was it exactly? That perhaps the fear of going through life unloved masked an even greater fear of going through life *unseen*. Draw blood with your words, and you'd have immediate proof you existed. In that instant, Gale had experienced a surge of the very fear Teddy described, drawn through his body like a long, cold ribbon—followed by a drunken, bubbling excitement. He'd liked what a preening idiot Teddy was, and he'd liked that Teddy was touching him. The man's words were so simultaneously foolish and true that Gale suddenly wanted to ride the heat of that nonsense as he'd ride a prick.

But then Teddy had taken his pretentious twaddle and the swelling at the front of his breeches and gone off to stroke the cheek—and much more—of a French *artiste*, who, if the violent slashes of rouge on her cheeks were anything to go by, lacked even basic skill with a brush.

The man rambled on. "When I saw you just now, I could scarce believe me old eyes. What would Lord Christmas Gale be doing in these parts? Why, it's fate, I should think, sir, that our paths should cross like this. Me out of Jacob's Island, and you out of…" He looked Gale up and down. "Out of wherever it is you come from. Are you solving your next case?"

Gale sighed and muttered, "Please don't call it a case." Jacob's bloody Island? Gale only knew of it because he made it a point to know everything. Supposedly one of the most wretched slums in all of London. A place that no gentleman with any claim to even a sliver of decency would set foot in. And this poor bastard *lived* there. He made a show of checking his pocket watch. "I'm so sorry, but I am running late for an engagement."

"Right, right. I don't mean to take up your time. The name's Howe. I was wonderin' if you might help me find me dog."

"Your... dog?" Gale repeated.

"Right, well, he went missing this morning, see. I'm quite fond of the old bugger, as is me girl. I work here, you see, at the Quays, and this great hairy fellow—the dog I mean—come bounding up to me one night. Skipped right off a ship, probably!—not more than a few days past. And with no missus—God rest her soul—and the girl and me lonesome sometimes, it seemed a miracle when he came to us. So, seeing as you're good at detecting, I thought—"

"I will stop you there, my good man." Gale tempered his tone as best he could. "I am not available for hire. And I certainly don't have the time to waste tracking down missing dogs."

Well, he had to admit to himself, if he were going to embark on a new investigation, he'd certainly prefer one that involved a dog to one that involved humans. He was never sure whether to admire or pity dogs their blind loyalty. The mere idea of craving another soul the way dogs craved their masters was enough to make him sweat. But there was something touchingly simple about that love, and as he strode away, the six-fingered drunkard shouting behind him, "Wait! Don't go!" he thought how much better off that dog must be, freed from a life with that shabby man and his daughter who could run rings around him with words.

～

The Harringdon ball was every bit as horrid as Gale had been imagining. Clarissa quickly found a couple of her friends, and they'd gone to get punch. Another sister of his, Maryanne—Hartwell insisted she was Anne-Marie, but Gale had his doubts—was in attendance, though she had come with some cousins and an aunt who was acting as her chaperone. Gale found himself stranded on the outskirts of the Harringdons' drawing room, trying to look as though he were casually taking in his surroundings rather than preparing to be executed. But his palms sweated, and the air in the room felt very thick. And what a room it was. As though somebody had taken the most ostentatious aspects of Oriental and Gothic design and beat them together with a broken whisk. He did not know whether he was in more danger of having the ghost of a murdered bride beseech him to bring her killer to justice or of tripping and impaling himself on a truly egregious amount of bamboo. He was earning glances from people who'd never had a glance to spare for him before. He'd hoped the sheer sternness of his visage would be enough to deter anyone from speaking to him, but one by one, Society's finest were darting in and taking bites of him, as though he were a wounded beast marked for death by a thousand cuts.

Lord Abel wished to know details of his confrontation with Lord Balfour—Gale thought it prudent to keep those details to himself as they would compromise his friend William Hartwell and the sulky little addle-pate Hartwell had wed not even a week ago, Joseph Warrington. Mrs. Crayston claimed her neighbour had been acting suspiciously, and asked if he might stop by on the morrow to investigate. Miss Karina Bellborough said he must be very brave to go around confronting jewel thieves and forgers. And Lord Thurston wondered in a low voice whether making people disappear—as opposed to finding them—was a service Gale offered.

Gale attempted an escape, but somehow found himself even closer to the dance floor where the crowd thickened. He was glad of his black coat despite the sudden heat of the crowd, for his underarms were sweating excessively.

A young lady bumped him into the path of a young man, who jostled him into a small group. He stumbled away, and two young ladies walking side by side parted neatly to pass around him. His breath became harsher. Where was Clarissa? He'd lost track of her, and it seemed at once that everyone in the room, or none of them at all, might be Clarissa. A voice behind him said, "Excuse me, I was wondering if I might ask you—"

"No," he barked, closing his eyes as his anger reached a boiling point. "I am not going to find your sister's missing necklace, or cleanse your opera house of its roving spirit, or locate your missing dog. I have had quite enough questions for one night, and I will thank you to *leave* me *alone!*"

Though the *ton* went on chattering around him, and music still played, it seemed as though his words had landed in a horrible silence. Surely the force of his anger and frustration should have cut through the gaiety of the ball. But nobody seemed to have noticed his outburst. Nobody except for the man who had spoken and whose presence Gale could still feel behind him.

He whirled, prepared to give the fellow an earful, then froze.

The man he faced was a few inches shorter than himself. Large boned and well built, wearing silk knee breeches that fit snugly, and clung wonderfully to the shape of his thighs. His black coat was well fitted, yet his cravat was tied loosely, almost sloppily, which set him quite apart from all the men here who looked as though their cravats were strangling them. Just seeing the looseness of the knot made Gale breathe a little more easily.

But it was the man's face that truly held his attention. There were lines at the corners of his eyes, and slight furrows running from his nose to the corners of his lips as though he spent a great deal of time laughing. Personally, Gale hated laughter, but it was oddly pleasing to think that this man enjoyed it as a pastime. The fellow's eyes caught the light of the room and held it. They were a deep blue, narrow but tremendously alive. And the corners of his well-shaped mouth curved upward just slightly as though he were privately amused by everything he saw. He had a sharp widow's peak, and wore his gold hair—for that was its colour; not wheat or flaxen or ash or any such thing, but a pure and shining gold— longer than was fashionable, tied at his nape with a ribbon.

As Gale stood and stared mutely, the gentleman spoke. "I was going to ask if you would like to dance?"

Now Gale was well and truly frozen to his spot. This man actually wanted to dance with him? *This* man? He reminded himself sharply that the whole thing was likely a ploy. Perhaps the man had recently had a priceless family heirloom stolen or a younger brother kidnapped by bandits. Once he got Gale on the dance floor, he would request his aid; nobody spoke to Gale unless they wanted something from him.

Yet his initial shock at the request was so great, and his confusion so complete, that he dipped his head in a manner that probably looked to the stranger like a nod. It most certainly did because the stranger said, "Wonderful" as though it truly were wonderful, and took his hand to lead him onto the dance floor.

~

The Honourable Benjamin Chant wondered if Lord Christmas Gale planned to ask his name at any point. They did not know each other—well, Chant knew *of* Gale from glimpses here and there at Bucknall's, and more recently, from the *Gazette*—and while he had intended to do the polite thing and introduce himself right away, he had become a bit lost in Gale's eyes, which were soft and dark as a hound's. He found that an absolute delight since the rest of the man was so sharp. Long limbs, bony elbows poking at the fabric of his coat, cheekbones like blades. A cravat he wore as if it were a bandage keeping his head attached to his long, slim neck. But oh, those eyes were an agony of softness. As was his hair, from the look of it. Thick, shiny. A dark red when the light hit it just right. Brown when the light couldn't quite catch it.

Yes, Chant had spent a good bit of time admiring Gale before approaching him. The sketch in the *Gazette* did not do the man justice at all.

Gale moved with a rigid determination that was echoed in the set of his jaw. *It's as though he's never danced before,* Chant thought, hiding a smile. Ah, well. Chant would continue his relaxed, happy turns about the floor and hope his companion might soon uncoil.

"Aren't you going to ask me whatever it is you've got to ask me?" Gale's tone was weary but with a hint of belligerence that made Chant's brows lift. "What is it? Did your grandfather leave behind a box of mysterious letters? Do the doors in your house open and close by themselves? Does your portrait of the queen have a treasure map hidden behind it?"

"I have already asked you to dance," Chant replied. "Which was what I wished to ask you. Do you wish to ask my name?"

"Not particularly," Gale replied. But Chant was well versed in the difference between rudeness for rudeness's sake and rudeness born from an anxiety that was rapidly becoming unmanageable.

When the music shifted, he took Gale's elbow. "I could use some air. What do you say we go out to the terrace?"

Gale looked as though he might like to bash Chant over the head, but he was far too pale for the glare to be fully effective. Chant led him toward the French doors in back. Behind them, the band struck up a rousing tune, and revellers flocked to dance. By the time Chant drew Gale outside, they were nearly the only two on the terrace. He let go of Gale's elbow and watched carefully as Gale went to the balustrade and leaned with his forearms braced upon it. Bent slightly like this, it was apparent just how thin he was.

Chant quietly approached the rail and leaned on it as well. Gale's breathing had become more laboured, and he passed a hand over his mouth. "I don't know what is the matter with me," he said tersely.

"It is quite noisy in there," Chant replied. "And too stuffy."

Gale made no reply. When his lungs truly began to rattle, Chant stepped closer and placed a hand between his shoulder blades. He half expected Gale to buck him off, but all that happened was that the fellow tensed as though he had never been touched before in his life.

"Draw your breath in slowly," Chant advised.

"I do not require instruction on how to breathe."

"Of course not. But perhaps you could humour a new friend."

Gale gripped the balustrade and dragged in a breath through his nose.

"That's very good. Now let it out as slowly as you can manage."

Gale exhaled, his rigid shoulders softening a bit as he did.

"There, that's the way." Chant rubbed the back of Gale's coat. Gale still did not shrug him off, which Chant thought was something.

After a moment, Gale drew another uneven breath and muttered, "I do not like people. At all."

Chant smiled, though Gale wouldn't be able to see it. "Ah. I like nearly all people, it seems. Generally speaking."

Gale cast a glance at him, then stared out across the lawn once more. "I have no choice but to conclude there is something gravely wrong with you, sir."

"You are probably right. But it seems easier to like people than to dislike them. For me, anyway. Resentment takes such a lot of effort."

"I assure you it comes quite naturally to me." Gale attempted another breath, and Chant winced in sympathy at the wheeze in it.

He removed his hand from Gale's back and stood beside him in companionable silence. Then he began to talk as silence also seemed to him to take such a lot of effort. He commented on the roundness of the moon, and the light it cast on the branches of the Harringdons' sycamore tree. He spoke of his carriage ride here, and how the driver thought one of his horses had thrown a shoe. Once Gale's breathing steadied, he asked, "Do you wish to go back inside?"

"I have never wished anything less," Gale responded faintly.

Chant laughed. "I thought that might be the case. Will you allow me to see you safely home?"

Gale straightened abruptly. "I shall go to my private rooms tonight. I've no need for company."

"You are welcome to use my carriage if you do not wish to draw attention by taking your family's."

Gale's eyes flashed in the moonlight. "My sister. Good lord. Clarice, or Cadence, or Clarissa, whatever the hell her name is. I am supposed to be chaperoning her. My mother will flay me alive."

"Perhaps you could find someone to—"

"No. No, I've shirked this duty often enough, and I promised tonight..." The shiver that passed through Gale was impossible to miss. He reminded Chant, for a bittersweet instant, of Reid. The long lines of him. Shoulders stooped under the weight of the world.

"Lord Christmas," Chant said quietly, quirking his eyebrow at the half-wild glance Gale shot him. "I'll not keep you from your duty, but I feel it is *my* duty to remind you that I will be in there as well. Should you find yourself overwhelmed again, you may seek me out at any time for conversation or a trip to the terrace—"

"I was not overwhelmed!" The harshness was back in Gale's tone. "And I require no rescuer. I have attended dozens of these functions. I could chaperone Candace in my sleep."

Chant raised his hands slowly, more amused than insulted by Gale's prickliness. "Forgive me. I meant no offence."

Gale blew out a breath. Then, without another word, he turned and walked back inside.

"Well," Chant murmured to himself, "I'd say that went quite well."

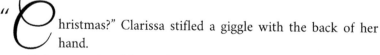

"*C*hristmas?" Clarissa stifled a giggle with the back of her hand.

Gale groaned and focused on the bumping of the carriage.

"Christmas!" insisted Anne-Marie, who was riding home with them. "Clarissa danced with a beau who—well, he found out she likes books, and he told her—about this book..." Anne-Marie collapsed back against the seat, giggling like mad.

"I cannot read."

"Don't be ridiculous," Clarissa said. "You read more than anyone I know. Except for me."

"You are a *bluestocking*," Anne-Marie giggled so hard she snorted into her gloved hands.

"Now there's the sort of ladylike sound that is sure to land you a spouse," Gale remarked.

"We cannot tell you about the book!" Anne-Marie doubled over, her laughter so intense it became silent, punctuated by a wheeze here and there.

Gale rolled his eyes up to the carriage ceiling and wished the horses would step a bit higher. "Is it *The Maiden Diaries*?"

Clarissa and Anne-Marie shrieked.

"Dear Lord." Gale placed his fingers at his temple. "I could use that sound to locate that drunkard's missing dog," he muttered, before raising his voice to be heard over his sisters' cackles. "You are too young to know about that book. If you say another word about it in my presence, I shall tell Mother."

It was useless. They didn't hear him.

"Christmas," Clarissa said after a moment. She pressed her lips together to stifle a last snicker. "Erm, we saw you dancing with Mr. Benjamin Chant."

"You never dance with *anyone*," Anne-Marie added.

He nobly held back a sigh. "And?"

"Did you *like* dancing with him?" Clarissa asked.

"Did he want to dance with you because you're famous?" Anne-Marie added.

"Maryanne—"

"My name is Anne-Marie."

"If you say so. I do not wish to talk about Mr. Benjamin Chant. I do not wish to talk about anything. Whoever stays silent the entire ride home gets whatever sweet they want from the bakery when I go out tomorrow."

His sisters both sat up straight and pressed their lips tightly together.

Gale exhaled his relief and leaned back. The next minute and a half was mercifully silent. Then Gale found himself opening his mouth. "Do you know much about Benjamin Chant?"

"You *talked*!" Anne-Marie cried, pointing at him.

"Well, yes, my own ability to remain silent is irrelevant. I can have whatever sweet I want anytime I want."

"But that is not fair because now we have to answer you!"

At the same time, Clarissa said, "Only that he is very kind. He helped Letitia find her shoe once when it came off on the Bellboroughs' footpath. And he is quite one of the most handsome gentlemen in all of London."

"Is that a fact?" he asked Clarissa.

Anne-Marie had tightened her lips again, though she looked as if she might burst if she did not get a chance to add to the conversation.

"Anne-Marie," he said. "You may have a sweet of your choice tomorrow if you tell me all you know about Benjamin Chant."

A little squeal made its way through her pursed lips, and then she puffed out air as though she had been holding her breath for some time. "He is handsome, and he is nice, and he lives in a house with very old stairs, and he has some half-brothers who are older, and they don't live in London, and he once had a sister, but she died, and there was a man named Reid, and everyone thought he and Reid would marry, but now Reid lives in France, and Mr. Chant's father was the old mad earl, but now he's dead too."

"Annie-M!" Clarissa cried, swatting her sister's side. "That's just rumour and speculation."

"But he *is* dead!"

"No, I mean that he was mad. Do not repeat such things."

"But Christmas said to tell him all I know of Mr. Chant!" Anne-Marie addressed Gale again. "Are you investigating him?"

"No."

"Is he a criminal?"

"No."

"Will you investigate him if he commits a crime?"

"I will buy you *two* sweets if you stop talking."

"What if he committed the crime *for you*?"

"A crime of passion," Clarissa added.

"That phrase does not mean what you think it means."

Clarissa huffed. "I should be pleased if—"

"Ah, look at that, we're home."

Anne-Marie shot him a look as the driver helped her from the carriage. "Mama asked me the other day if you still live here. You are always off in your private rooms."

"Do you even like us?" Clarissa pouted.

"You are my sisters," he said, for that was true enough. He stepped down from the carriage, helped them down, and bid them goodnight. A throbbing headache had come upon him. He thought briefly of Mr. Benjamin Chant's hand on his back. Gentle, steadying. He shrugged off the memory as though an invisible hand were still touching him. He was beyond exhausted.

When he arrived at his building in Russell Street, a figure waited in the near darkness. He frowned, hesitant to move closer. Mrs. Faulks, his landlady, must already be in bed, otherwise she would have chased this shadowy fellow off with all the fierceness of a guard dog. She liked Gale a great deal, and Gale slipped her a bit of extra money each month with the rent in exchange for keeping gawkers and news writers away from the place.

The figure was even taller than Gale, and stout. As Gale grew closer, his suspicions were confirmed.

He suppressed a sigh. "Darling."

George Darling straightened. "Gale. You're a hard man to track down."

"If only that were true. Is your business urgent? I'm rather tired."

"I wasn't sure if you'd seen the papers yet. The imposter who stole Lady Carstairs's brooch was found guilty, so I suppose congratulations are in order."

"Ah. So you came all the way out here, Darling, to tell me what I could have read in any news sheet?"

Darling ducked his head. Gale was vaguely aware that he was being unkind, but he could practically hear his bed calling to him. He knew what Darling truly wanted of him, and knew just as well that he would never be able to give it to him. Their recent collaboration on the matter of Lord Balfour seemed only to have bolstered the fellow's hopes, though.

Darling was a Bow Street Runner—below Gale's station, for a start—and Runners were bloody useless. Darling was better than most, but he still had an aversion to performing his job that Gale supposed he should have empathized with—except that Gale was a gentleman with nothing expected of him but idleness, while Darling was employed by the Bow Street Magistrate's office. The only reason it hadn't seemed like drawing teeth to get him to help collect evidence against Balfour was that the fellow would have done anything for a nod of approval from Gale. Gale didn't dislike him—at least no more than he disliked all of humanity as a rule—and he had, in his more desperate moments, imagined what it would be like to embark on an affair with the fellow. Yet he knew he could not. A man of his station could not make an honest man out of Darling, and for all his faults Darling deserved someone who could. Besides, more than any consideration to the fellow, Gale did not like what would happen if he allowed Darling to get close. There was something needy about Darling, something too eager to please that verged on obsequiousness, and Gale knew himself well enough to know that whatever feelings Darling fancied he held for Gale, Gale would poison them.

"I wanted to see how you were," Darling murmured.

"Tired," Gale repeated firmly. "And oughtn't you get some rest too? Who knows what tomorrow will bring for the brave constables of Bow Street."

Even in the dim light, Gale could see Darling make a face. "There's a fellow dead right now in Rotherhithe. Stabbed to death, they say."

"Then what on earth are you doing here?" Gale was genuinely appalled. "I don't investigate murders, you know. So you can't be seeking my help."

Darling waved that notion away. "Nothing to be done about it. Just a drunk killed outside a pub. The Belled Cat. Fellow who reported it says the dead man's out of Jacob's Island. Well, surely you won't be knowing that area."

"I know of it." Gale was intrigued despite himself. Jacob's Island, a name which would rarely crop up in polite conversation, and he'd heard it twice this evening.

"Wretched place—worse than what you're imagining, Lord Christmas."

"I see."

"The old sod probably said the wrong thing about the wrong fellow's mother, and it escalated. The office isn't sending anyone out."

Gale stared grimly through the darkness at Darling. "Some old drunk" out of Jacob's Island. A man living in poverty. A man not worth the magistrate's time.

Gale himself was no moral paragon, and he could hardly condemn the unfairness of Bow Street's attitude when he himself benefitted from his own position with every breath he took. When his position only existed because so many others had none at all. But it did infuriate him that the magistrate's office simultaneously lacked any nuanced understanding of *why* a person living in poverty might commit a crime and any inclination to seek justice for crimes committed against the poor.

"Thought about going out there just to have a look," Darling went on. "But without the magistrate's orders backing me up, I'd just be a fellow poking at a corpse in Fernside's cellar."

"Fernside took the body?"

"Oh, certainly." Darling's teeth caught what little light there was on the street as he grinned. "This one's Fernside's dream. The poor bastard had six fingers."

Gale stood so still that for a moment it seemed the whole street might merely be set dressing—a backdrop for the stage that Gale could lift of its hooks and shake out, leaving utter darkness in its place.

"Six fingers," Gale repeated.

And wasn't he wide awake now?

The dead man was Howe.

CHAPTER 2

Chant had just settled into bed and blown out the candle when a knock came at the front door.

Who on earth would be calling at this hour? The servants were abed, and he did not want any of them to have to rouse themselves for whatever oddity this was.

He got to his feet and made his way carefully down his home's very old stairs, feeling his way through the dark into the entry hall. When he opened the door, he was astounded to see Christmas Gale standing there, wearing an overcoat that looked as though it had been stolen off a costermonger, and a pinched expression that could only be his own.

"I am sorry," Gale said. "I do not usually apologise, as it always seems it is the world that should be apologising to me, but I am truly sorry to wake you. I—I did not know who else to consult. I thought Soulden at first, but, no, he is far too busy."

He trailed off, leaving Chant to stare and try to blink himself back to wakefulness. Chant recognised the name Soulden as a fellow from Bucknall's, but why Gale seemed less inclined to bother him with whatever the matter was than Chant remained a mystery.

"Come in." Chant opened the door fully and ushered Gale in. The man stood awkwardly in the entryway, his tall frame stooped as though he feared Chant's ceiling might not be high enough to accommodate him. Chant led him into the parlour and lit a lamp.

"My sisters tell me you are altruistic," Gale said without preamble. He did not immediately go on, so Chant wondered if he was supposed to confirm the statement.

"I... try to treat others well."

"Then you might be just the fellow I need."

The situation was growing stranger by the minute, but Chant confessed himself fascinated with Gale, and so he waited for his guest's story.

"A man has been killed."

Chant's eyes widened.

"His body was found outside a pub called The Belled Cat in Rotherhithe. A stabbing. The man is from Jacob's Island."

"Jacob's Island?"

"It's a wretched place, and I don't doubt that people are stabbed there with some frequency. But here's the rub. I know the fellow. Or rather, I met him. Earlier this evening."

"My God! Who is he?"

"A drunk by the name of Howe."

"How did you—"

"Listen. There's a man from the Bow Street Runners, George Darling. He told me about the murder, but his supervisor isn't sending anyone out to investigate. What's one more gin-soaked corpse in a city brimming with them? Yet earlier tonight Howe spoke to me affectionately of his young daughter. And there is no mother to speak of."

"That's terrible."

Gale stared at him.

"Did you tell this Darling fellow?" Chant tried.

"I did not."

Chant was confused, to put it mildly. "Perhaps you ought to have?"

"The Runners do not, as a rule, like me, and I do not like them. They consider me a meddlesome nuisance who only exists to make them look like bumbling fools, and I consider them, well, bumbling fools. Darling is tolerable, but…" Gale ran a hand through his hair. "He shares his colleagues' attitude toward the poor."

Again Chant waited, as that seemed to be more effective than attempting to make the correct interjections in a story he still did not understand.

"I would like to locate this girl and see what insight she can provide into her father's affiliations."

"You are going to take the case of this Howe fellow?"

"Please don't call it a case. And this is not a formal investigation. I only wish to have my curiosity satisfied. A fellow asking me about a missing dog and then turning up dead mere hours later—strange, is it not?"

"It is," Chant agreed.

Gale looked away from Chant, and after a moment, sighed, then spoke. "All right, if you must know"—Chant could not recall asking to know anything, but he did not point this out—"I find it hard to put the girl from my mind. I have sisters. Far too many. I am cursed. But however I feel about sisters, I… I know that objectively, morally, it would be wrong not to find this girl and… see that she is provided for."

And just like that, something in Chant's heart gave. Gale might fancy himself a misanthrope. He might use words as a porcupine used its quills, but he was not quite the cynic he pretended to be. And Chant thought, for a wild instant, that he should follow this man off the cliffs of Dover if Gale requested it—simply because he knew Gale would keep things lively and unpredictable right until the end. "I agree. What do you need from me?"

Gale hesitated. "I… do not know how to talk to children. I find them strange and horrifying. If we can locate Howe's house, and if we discover the girl there… could you speak to her in a way she will not find frightening?"

Chant opened his mouth slightly, unsure how to respond. "I suppose I can."

"Ah, wonderful. I knew from the moment I saw you that you would not frighten children. Come. Let us go."

"Where is it we are going?"

"I do not know the precise address, but it is in Jacob's Island, and we will find it."

For some unknown reason, Chant believed him. "Wait while I dress."

"Do not—" Gale wrinkled his nose and then folded his arms around himself like some anxious praying mantis. He was not, as Chant had noted earlier in the night, a conventionally attractive fellow, and yet he was compelling. His body was too thin, almost spindly, and his personality was equal parts sharp and sour, but for all of that Chant sensed a carefully guarded goodness about him, buried so deeply that he doubted most people even suspected it was there. And his eyes were mesmerising; they clearly held some sort of mystical power over Chant since he couldn't imagine why on earth he would be agreeing to step out in the middle of the night on this mad errand otherwise. "Do not wear your own coat. It may be best to borrow a servant's, unless you want to advertise the size of your purse to the denizens of Jacobs Island."

"Oh," said Chant. "I shall… I shall see what I can borrow off the servants, I suppose."

"Why do you live in such an unfashionable house?" Gale asked bluntly. "The whole of London knows your stairs creak. You *are* the third son of the deceased Earl of Farnleigh, are you not?"

"I am," Chant agreed, a knot forming suddenly in his stomach. Had Gale made inquiries about his family? About his father? And if so, what had he learned? Best not to fret about it. "Have you asked about me, sir?"

"I certainly have not," Gale said archly. He curled his lip. "I have simply read Debrett's *Peerage*."

"*All* of it?" Chant asked, astonished.

"Of course." A scowl furrowed Gale's forehead. "But you haven't answered my question."

If Gale had simply read Debrett's—well, "simply" was hardly the word for such a task—then perhaps Chant could relax. He didn't sense that this was a trap on Gale's part to get Chant to reveal family secrets. But if Gale *did* make inquiries… Well, one did not have to scratch too hard at the surface to learn what had become of Chant's family.

He steadied his voice. "If you must know, and clearly you must, from my bedroom I have the most enchanting view of the church-yard behind the house."

Gale narrowed his eyes, the faint light from the nearest gas lamp giving him an almost malevolent appearance. "You like it for the view?" he asked slowly, as though there was something about Chant's answer that he had entirely failed to comprehend.

"Yes," Chant said. He gestured toward the doorway. "Now, I shall wake the hall boy and see if he has an overcoat to lend me. Will you go and try to find a cab, or shall we stand here all night being quietly bewildered by one another?"

Gale's eyes narrowed farther until he was nearly squinting, and then, abruptly, he squared his narrow shoulders and began to stride towards the door on his long, thin legs.

And that, Chant supposed, answered that.

~

*G*ale brooded the entire way to Jacob's Island. He attempted to review what he knew about the drunkard Howe, but he kept getting distracted by Chant, who seemed to spend an awful lot of time watching him. As the cab bumped along, it occurred to Gale that he ought to share some of what he was thinking with Chant. The idea of conversation pained him, but if he wanted Chant's help in this endeavour, the man ought to know what they were up against.

"This man, Howe, worked at the dockyards at the Surrey Quays. That was near where I encountered him, in Rotherhithe. Though he lacks—lacked—education, he appeared to make up for that in brawn. He approached me earlier, wanting help to find his lost dog, but I declined to help him, and was rather short with him—"

"I can't possibly imagine," Chant murmured.

Gale ignored that. "And now he is dead." Was there a connection? Was he mad to think one existed? He told Chant all he recalled of his conversation with Howe.

"The dog skipped off a ship," Chant repeated. "Howe took the mutt home to his daughter. And then the dog ran away?"

"Those are the facts at present."

"And he just happened to find you. The one man in London famous for solving mysteries."

"They say Fate works in mysterious ways."

"What the devil were you doing in Rotherhithe? And right before the ball at the Harringdons'?"

"Visiting a molly house," Gale said bluntly.

Chant sat back, and Gale wondered if he'd offended him. Then wondered why he was wasting any time at all thinking about Benjamin Chant's feelings.

He changed the subject. "I think it's very likely the child has aunts and uncles and cousins, of course. Most people do. Entire infestations of relatives, like lice. This will most likely be a wasted trip."

"You're welcome," Chant said.

"What?"

"Oh, I thought that when you said it would most likely be a wasted trip, the apology for dragging me along and the gratitude for my compliance was implicit." Chant's mouth turned up in a smile. "Perhaps I was mistaken."

Gale ignored that too. "And yet he said the dog was a miracle, and that he and his daughter had been lonely." He tapped his gloved fingers on his knee. "No, not a wasted trip at all." He slanted a gaze at Chant. "Implicit apology retracted."

"Noted," Chant said amiably. He tilted his head. "For a man who affects coldness, I suspect you are kinder than you allow yourself to be perceived."

"Yes," Gale said dryly. "Not wanting a dead orphan on my conscience makes me a paragon of virtue, I'm sure."

He stared pointedly out the window of the cab, refusing to be drawn into further conversation.

He wasn't entirely sure why he'd sought out Chant for tonight's odd adventure, and he didn't want to dig too deeply to discover the reason because he suspected it would only serve to reveal his deficiencies. For a moment tonight, on the Harringdons' terrace, Gale had felt almost naked under Chant's gaze as though the man had the power to strip away all of Gale's prickly layers with nothing more than a glance. Yet Chant had not been teasing about Gale's obvious weakness, or cruel in any way, and while Gale didn't trust the other man's apparent good-naturedness, he was compelled by it all the same. Because there he was, sitting in a cab with him, hurtling over the bridge toward Jacob's Island. Of all the labyrinthine mysteries that Gale had ever uncovered—twisted lies wrapped around layers of barbed deceit and usually hidden behind honeyed words—the idea that basic human decency might exist in the world was somehow terrifying to him. Chant's touch had been solicitous, and Gale's stomach clenched just thinking about it. Good Lord. At least Teddy and the other fellows Gale knew in the same manner had the common decency to touch only to signal that they wanted to swive. What the blazes was Gale supposed to do with *concern*? Yet it was Chant he'd sought out.

Gale pressed his mouth into a thin line and scowled out the window of the cab.

When the cab left them, Gale took off at a quick pace, having no

wish to linger in any one spot. He could sense Chant's easy amusement turn to discomfort as they wended their way through the
shadows, rats skittering along the cobblestones to either side of
them. He was reconsidering the wisdom of passing through this
neighbourhood in the dead of night.

"Gale...what *is* this place?"

Gale didn't answer. He had no time for nonsense questions. To
their right, the moon glinted off the reeking water of a massive
ditch. The foulness of the smell was indescribable. He'd never
ventured so deep into a slum before; the seedier part of Rotherhithe had been his limit, and he couldn't tell whether it thrilled or
terrified him to find himself on such dangerous territory.

But they had come this far, and locating the girl was important
to the investigation. Not that this was an investigation.

He paid a drunk a halfpenny to give him directions to Howe's
house and then, a street or two later, he paid a molly a halfpenny
for directions that were less muddled.

His eyes were keen, but still he strained to make out anything in
the dimness. Were it not for a small fire a beggar had made nearby,
he might not have been able to discern Howe's building from any of
the others in the street, where they were packed in shoulder to
shoulder as tightly as headstones in a crowded graveyard. The
street was uneven, half the cobblestones sunk into filthy puddles,
and a narrow open drain cut down the middle of it. It stank of shit.
Gale counted down the ramshackle terrace houses as he passed
them, stopping at the fifth. The molly had said it was the one with
the green door; whether or not this house had a green door or not,
Gale couldn't tell in the darkness. The possibly-green door hung
from one hinge.

"Gale," Chant hissed.

"*What?*" Gale whispered irritably.

"I don't..."

Gale was about to snap at him to finish, but forced himself to
wait.

"I don't like this."

And Gale had thought Chant a man, not a shying horse who needed to be soothed, and he was an instant away from saying something to that effect. But there was real fear in Chant's voice, and Gale could hardly fault him for it. There was a fair chance they would both end up dead in an alley, like Howe. The memory of Chant's patience with him earlier that night was still strong. He took a breath.

"Nor do I. But we've reached our destination, Chant. If the child is not here, we won't pursue her any further. I will get you home. I promise."

He said no more, but stepped over a broken roof tile and climbed the steps. Chant stopped close to him, and Gale tried to ignore the soft sound of the other man's breathing. They stepped inside the dark passageway. A faint light flickered at the far end of the hall; a hanging lantern. It did little to light their way.

Gale approached the nearest door. The molly had said Howe lived on the ground floor, first on the left. He rapped lightly on the door, and when there was no answer, he tried the knob. The door creaked open, a sliver of moonlight growing wider across the floor-boards, casting shadow to the sides. He stepped inside, trying not to wince at the smell of mildew and unemptied chamber pots. The room was barely large enough to turn around in, and he unwittingly trod upon a straw mattress on the floor. He was now fully aware of what an idiotic idea this had been. All that would be accomplished here was that he or Chant would break an ankle. And yet as he brushed a hand over a rickety table, he felt crumbs not yet stale, and not yet carried away by vermin. The house was not empty.

"Elise," he called softly. "Elise, come out, wherever you are hiding. We know you're here."

"I have no wish to offend," Chant whispered. "But you sound rather like an axe-wielding madman indulging in a game of cat and mouse with his prey."

"What would you have me say?" Gale asked, annoyed.

"If she's here, she is probably very frightened. She does not know who we are or why we've come."

"And you think she'll be impressed if we announce our titles?"

It was too dark to see Chant roll his eyes, but Gale was certain that was what happened. "You said Howe told you she'd read the article about you? Let her know we're on the case—"

"Do *not* call it a c—"

He was interrupted by... he was not quite sure what. One moment he was standing in the darkness, arguing with Chant, the next, he was lying on his side on the filthy floor, his head throbbing.

"Gale! Are you all right?" Chant cried out above him.

Blearily, he felt around on the floor until his hand closed upon a small but heavy bit of rock. Footsteps pattered toward the open front door. "Stop her," Gale rasped.

"Elise!" Chant called out. "Elise, my name is Benjamin Chant. I'm here with Christmas Gale, the famous investigator—"

"Not an investigator." Gale's voice sounded as though he had swallowed chalk.

Chant ignored him. "He is here to help you find your missing dog."

"I most certainly am not," Gale objected, but the footsteps stopped. A moment later, a flimsy floorboard creaked, and a small face appeared above Gale, mostly shadow with a slip of silver across it from the moon.

"Christmas Gale?" piped a thin voice full of hope.

"Yes," said Chant and knelt beside them both. "Christmas and I have come to help you, Elise."

Gale pulled himself into a sitting position, trying not to groan.

"You're really Lord Christmas?" the girl asked again.

"Joy to the world," Gale muttered, rubbing the back of his head.

"D'you know where Flum is?"

"Flum, I presume, is the dog?"

"It's short for Flummery."

"Of course it is."

"I'm sorry I threw a rock at you. I thought you was burglars."

"Quite all right," Chant said. "We intruded in your home. It was very brave of you to defend yourself. And I must say, I'm quite impressed by your aim in the darkness."

Gale scowled, though the effect was rather lost in said darkness. "Oh, impressed are you?"

Chant stroked briefly down his arm and took his hand, pulling him to his feet. The gesture should not have made Gale's skin prickle the way it did.

Elise gazed up at them. "Pa ain't home yet. He might be playing cards. He said he'd help me look for Flum tonight."

Gale nudged Chant, hoping the man would take his cue and break the tragic news to the girl so they could move things along.

"Elise," Chant said carefully. "In order to help you, we must know if you have other family in the area. Any siblings... aunts or uncles... cousins?"

"It's just me and Pa."

Gale's stomach sank. Well, hopefully they'd be able to extract some useful information from her before turning her over to the parish.

"It might be best if we go somewhere we can have a proper conversation," Chant said gently. "Suppose we take a cab back to my home—"

Gale interrupted. "That—seems—not to be the best idea." In a low voice, he said to Chant, "We cannot just pluck a small girl from her house and cart her off to that creaky testament to bachelorhood you call a home."

"That is an excellent point. Your household is full of sisters and is probably far better suited than mine to provide Elise with a meal and some warm clothes."

"What are you doing, man?" Gale hissed.

Elise's voice cut through the shadows. "I got to start work at dawn."

"Where do you work, Elise?" Chant asked.

"The carpet fact'ry."

"All right. Well, Lord Christmas is going to send word to the foreman that you are assisting him in an important matter, and—"

Gale made a strangled sound, which did not deter Chant in the least.

"And we shall go to Gale's house for the time being."

"I don't think the foreman would like me missin' work to go look for Flum."

"Yes, ah, well, you see…" Here, Chant seemed at a loss.

It was too much—the throbbing in Gale's head, the smell of the house, this absurd idea of Chant's… If they didn't get to the heart of the matter, they'd lose valuable time investigating Howe's death. Not that they *were* investigating Howe's death. They had come here to see to Elise. That was the whole of it, so—Oh, dash it all! "Elise." His voice was louder than he'd intended. "Your father is dead, slain in a most brutal fashion. We require your help to find out who killed him."

There was a moment of perfect silence. Ah, Gale could have lived in that silence forever.

But it did not last.

Elise, instead of appreciating his forthrightness and his call for her assistance, dropped like a stone to the floor—as intractable as the one she'd lobbed unerringly at his head—and began to wail like a small, grubby banshee.

CHAPTER 3

"*D*amn you, Gale!" Chant exclaimed as he strode outside, his boots crunching on the dirt and rubble underfoot. If he hadn't had his arms full of a small, wailing girl, he rather thought he might have punched Christmas Gale.

Gale followed after him, a sour-faced praying mantis. He rubbed his temple. "Could you please tell her to be quiet before she attracts the attention of every criminal in a mile's radius?"

"You bloody fool," Chant snapped, not even sorry for his tone. "What on earth is wrong with you, man? Have you no decency?"

Elise continued to wail, and Chant rubbed her back.

"No." Gale looked away. "If by decency, you mean fellow feeling, then you'll find my lack of it is much remarked upon, both by my family and acquaintances, and by the news sheets."

Chant felt an odd stab of sympathy for the man, but it wasn't sharp enough to pierce his anger, not when Elise was weeping so violently that her small body shuddered in his arms. He strode up the street, wishing he'd thought to ask the cab to stay and wait for them. He had never heard of Jacob's Island before tonight, and why would he? He could think of no reason ever to come here—except to follow some heartless madman on a midnight quest, apparently.

The street was dark and narrow, and Chant imagined danger lurking in every inky shadow. But he was too angry to be frightened anymore of thieves and murderers. He walked rapidly in what he hoped was the direction they had come.

He didn't glance back to see if Gale was following him; he was certain he was.

Good Lord. He'd been almost enamoured with Gale earlier tonight on the terrace. He'd certainly been charmed enough by the cold, sharp exterior that he'd been so certain was hiding such vulnerability. Well, he'd been disabused of that notion, hadn't he? Gale was a pure misanthrope, just as everyone said.

The narrow street met a wider one, and Chant turned down it, heading for the river. He felt furious enough to march all the way to the Gale family home in St. James's Square, and yet his arms were already beginning to ache. Another few hundred feet brought him to a busier road still—the gin shop was doing a roaring trade despite the late hour, and Chant was both surprised and relieved to see a cabbie tending his horses at the side of the road.

The cabbie looked as startled to see a customer as Chant was to see him.

Chant gave him Gale's address, and climbed awkwardly into the cab with Elise. He thought about pulling the door shut in Gale's face but relented. Even Gale didn't deserve to be stranded alone in this neighbourhood after dark.

Gale folded his long limbs into the cab and stared at nothing as they got underway.

Elise's wails had subsided into quiet sobs as Chant rubbed her back.

"I don't know how to speak to children," Gale said at last, still staring straight ahead. "Or to adults."

If it was meant as self-deprecation, Chant wasn't amused.

"I play at it," Gale said, his voice softer. "My sisters believe it is an amusing affectation, or perhaps that's just what they tell themselves in consolation for having so cold a brother. It is a deficiency of character that I am more than aware of, sir. It's why I asked you to accompany me. At the Harringdons' ball, you seemed…" His brows tugged together, as though he was searching for the right word, although when he settled on one at last he didn't appear satisfied. "You seemed *kind*."

The word had a faint whiff of bewildered disapproval around it when Gale said it.

Chant's ribs felt tight. "You seemed as though you needed kindness. Now, Gale, I'll be honest, I'm not sure what exactly you need."

Gale looked at him sharply, and then looked away again.

They whole way back to Westminster, they sat in silence punctuated only by the girl's small, pathetic sobs.

~

*A*fter leaving a sniffling Elise and a stony-faced Gale at Gale's house in St. James's Square, and extracting a promise that Gale wouldn't simply stash the child in the coal cellar, Chant was too full of restless energy to sleep. He instructed the cabbie to take him to the Bucknall Club, which was never closed, and where he would at least be able to get a drink in company slightly better than his own.

Chant had only recently become a member of the club; he had a cousin who had sponsored his membership. Chant had thought it a ridiculous waste of money until he'd set foot inside and had been swept into a warm fire-lit sanctuary with good food, fine drinks, and a library that, although small, was rarefied. The Bucknall Club was a grand building in the Italian Renaissance style, its proud facade looking out onto Pall Mall. The brass sign above the door was discreet but unnecessary—everyone knew the Bucknall Club, and those who didn't were soon alerted to its purpose by the constant stream of cabs coming and going from the front.

The club was three floors of dining, reading, and gaming. The fourth-floor attic was where the footmen lived, and it was not the sort of club where one saw the servants' bedding, although Chant had noticed quite a few of the footmen were more than pleasingly fair—and several had a sparkle in their eyes that said they were very much aware of that fact. But the Bucknall Club was no brothel. It was barely scandalous at all. And, at this ungodly hour, it was almost empty.

"Good evening, sir," the doorman said, holding the door open. He had the good manners not to widen his eyes at Chant's borrowed overcoat.

Chant nodded at him and slipped inside, tugging off his gloves.

A boy scurried forward to take his gloves and overcoat, bright-eyed despite the late hour.

Chant headed for the stairs.

A low murmur of conversation came from the Blue Room, and Chant smelled the rich scent of cigar smoke and heard the clink of glasses as he passed the doorway. He had always favoured the Green Room over the Blue, for no particular reason at all, except, he supposed, that Christmas Gale and his friends—Hartwell, Soulden, Crauford, and Lightholder, amongst others—always sat in the Blue Room and, up until tonight, Chant had avoided them. They were the *haut* of the *haut ton*, and Chant had only just begun to feel his way back into Society. He wasn't ready to dive back into the thick of it quite yet.

He stepped into the Green Room. There was another man sitting in one of the wingback chairs. Chant had seen him around before. Stratford, he thought the fellow's name was. He seemed quiet and shy, and could usually be found reading or, as now, writing in the leather-bound journal open at the small table in front of him where the book jostled for space with what appeared to be a glass of claret. He looked up as Chant entered, a lock of dark hair falling over his unremarkable face.

"Good evening," Chant said.

Stratford mumbled the same and went back to his writing.

Chant took a seat on the other side of the room, and a footman appeared to take his drink order, and to offer him a selection of last evening's news sheets. Chant browsed the news sheets while he waited for his drink. He was completely uninterested in the goings-on of Parliament, or what the French or the Prussians were up to. He was even less interested in what the *ton* was up to, although there were plenty of pages devoted to that. Still, with little else to do, he turned back to the news from the Continent and read a few paragraphs. The Dutch were unhappy with the French over the murder at sea of Claude de Brouckère, brother of the Governor of Limburg. Meanwhile, the Prussians were unhappy with the Austrians, despite both of them being in the German Confederation, and everyone was unhappy that the Russian tsar was apparently getting a little too chummy with Metternich.

Chant sighed and set the news sheet aside.

He didn't care for politics, and he especially didn't care when thoughts of Christmas Gale swirled in his brain like the dregs of some bitter drink he'd been forced to swallow. He wanted to write Gale off. He *ought* to write Gale off. It had been foolish to think he cared for the fellow in the first place. Yet, in the cab, Gale had shown himself to be painfully aware of what he called his deficiency of character, and suddenly Chant had found himself caring again. Just as he had on the terrace at the ball earlier when Gale had seemed anxious to the point of distress.

He ought to be wary of caring too much—had he learned nothing from his courtship of Reid? But no, a man did himself a disservice when he feigned aloofness out of a misguided desire to protect his heart. He wondered if Gale could ever be convinced of that. His drink arrived, and Chant took a long sip, turning his thoughts from Reid and from the guilt that followed him as faithfully as a hound.

Speaking of hounds...

Ah, he should have liked to turn his thoughts away from Gale, and yet he could not help but wonder if Elise was sleeping now, well fed and warm in a proper bed. And if she would ever be reunited with her dog. She ought to at least have that comfort. Gale meant to ask the child about her father's associations. Did he intend to look for the killer? And would he also work to find Flum? Chant stared into his drink, then rapped lightly on the table, having made a decision. The prospect of returning to Jacob's Island alone was not a pleasant one, but surely in the light of day, the place would not seem quite so terrifying. He would travel there in the morning and look for Flum. A dog could nearly always find his way back home. If Flum wasn't back already, he would be soon. And Chant was quite fond of dogs.

He pushed his chair back. It would not be a terrible idea to go back to his "creaky testament to bachelorhood" and get some sleep. He smiled in spite of himself, remembering Gale's voice as he'd spoken of Chant's home—not so much derisive as matter-of-fact. Gale's mind seemed like one that was never still—speeding along through possibilities before good sense and common courtesy could catch up. It was not an admirable trait, yet Chant admired it anyway. That was, perhaps, his own deficiency of character: that he quite admired people, and the way they carried on through joy and grief and bitterness and hope, unable to be anyone but themselves. So much did he admire them that he fell in love more frequently than he ought—and with entirely the wrong sort of people.

CHAPTER 4

The Gale dining room, when Gale arrived early from Russell Street, was a scene straight out of a nightmare: Every single sister of Gale's, including at least one of whose existence he had not previously been aware, sat at the table, interrogating Elise about life in Jacob's Island. They all spoke over top of each other, their eggs and toast all but abandoned, and if Gale had been Elise, he'd have run screaming from the madhouse. But Elise seemed pleased by the attention, answering the questions with a sort of sly demureness that reminded Gale in some obscure way of her father.

In the light of day, he could see that she was a strange looking child. Her hair was an ashy blond and hung in tangles around a face that seemed wider than it was long. Her eyes were set rather far apart, and were a mix of dark blue and brown. Her smile showed tiny, peg-like teeth that made her look a bit like some mischievous fiend from a fairy tale. She'd been cleaned up, but her skin had faint grey and yellow tones, likely from exhaustion and malnourishment.

It had taken a long time to quiet her last night—a task Gale had left to his mother and Clarissa. But this morning, the child seemed in surprisingly good spirits. Howe had said she was seven years of age. Young enough, he hoped, to be possessed of the resiliency she would require on the path ahead. She shovelled eggs and bacon into her mouth as though she hadn't had a hot meal in weeks. And she probably hadn't. Good God, to imagine a child this small sent to work at a carpet factory... Gale was attempting to feel more charitably toward her as Chant's harsh words still weighed heavily on him. Although his first instinct was to continue to behave precisely as he liked in defiance of the fellow, there was something truly dreadful about being thought a "bloody fool"—and worse—by someone like Mr. Benjamin Chant.

"Enough!" Gale said as his sisters each fought to be the one who would lend Elise clothes for the afternoon. Only Eugenie's wardrobe would have even come close to fitting the girl, so he wasn't sure what they were all on about. "Let Elise eat. You're giving me a headache." In truth, he already had a headache—most likely the result of being nailed behind the ear with a rock. But his sisters were not helping.

"Remember, you promised to get me sweets today!" Anne-Marie cried over the din, giving him an imploring look.

"Listen to you!" Clarissa lectured. "Elise has just suffered a terrible tragedy, and you are talking of sweets!"

"Well, Christmas can get her some too! It will cheer her up."

"If you do not be quiet, there will be no sweets at all. In fact," Gale said, "if you all have quite finished—and it looks as if you have with the exception of Cordelia"—Cordelia looked up from filling her mouth with more seed cake—"I would request that you leave the room so I might talk with Elise."

He was unsure where his mother was. She usually took breakfast with at least a few of her daughters. It was rare for all of them to be in the dining room together, as Clarissa often took a breakfast tray in her room so that she might read, rather than listen to the others talk of gowns and routs, and Helene did the same in imitation of her oldest sister.

"Have you driven our mother from the room?" he inquired.

"She is talking to Cook about meals for the coming week," Eugenie replied, "if Elise is to stay with us."

"Who said anything about all week?" Gale tried to hide his alarm.

"Her father is dead!" Anne-Marie looked appalled by his insensitivity, which Gale felt was a bit rich for someone who had just suggested cakes might cure the grief one felt for a murdered father. "Where else is she going to go?"

He glanced at Elise to see if she was affected by this reminder of her father's untimely demise, but the girl was busy with her eggs.

Gale had not the heart to say she would go to the parish. "Mother did not seem upset by the idea of her staying?"

Anne-Marie shook her head vigorously, making her coppery ringlets fly. "No! She *wants* Elise to stay."

Elise beamed around the table, her little mouth glistening with bacon grease. "I like it here," she announced. "You got some fine furniture." She glanced at a lacquered end table with painted Grecian figures, a piece Gale particularly loathed.

He held back a sigh. "All of you, go. Clarissa, you may stay."

There came an immediate chorus of "Why Clarissa?", though the others did, thankfully, begin to push their chairs back and rise.

When the room was at last empty of all but himself, the girl, and Clarissa, Gale took a seat. Elise chewed a few more times, eyeing him, then swallowed and stared silently.

"Elise," he began. "I feel we may have started off on the wrong foot. It is entirely understandable that you are distraught over the loss of your father, and I was quite insensitive last night. Would you consider forgiving me?"

"Oh, Christmas," Clarissa whispered. "What did you say to her last night?"

"Clarissa, please." He kept his attention on the little girl. "I'm sorry, Elise."

He wished there was a way to tell Chant he had apologised to the child. He did not understand his own weakness in wanting

Chant's approval, but it would quell a certain amount of agitation within him to know Chant did not think him heartless.

Elise said nothing, but without taking her eyes from him, she slowly extended one arm and snatched another piece of bacon from the tray.

"All right," Gale continued. "Well—"

"Do you think it was the captain what killed Pa?" the girl asked before opening her mouth in a way that reminded Gale of a snake unhinging its jaw and stuffing the bacon in.

"Captain?"

"Yeah," Elise said around a mouthful. "I didn't like the look of 'im."

"Can you tell me more about this fellow?"

The girl chewed and swallowed. "It was two days past. I know, 'cause I spoke to him on my way to the fact'ry and it made me late. The foreman were—*was* furious." The girl's speech was an odd mix of her father's broad vowels and dropped *h*'s, and what seemed to be her own conscious efforts at elocution. "Did you send word like the other fellow said? Does the foreman know I'm helping you?"

"He does," Gale assured her. He had sent a note before the break of dawn. "Who was this captain, Elise?"

"A tall fellow. Taller 'n you, even. He was a giant. And he had horrible, pale, dry looking hair. Like twine. He's the captain of one of the ships at the docks."

"Do you know his name? Or perhaps the name of the ship?"

She shook her head. "He told me he was looking for a dog. Said his ship had rats, and he'd heard Pa and me had the best dog in town for catching rats. He's got himself a torn sail, so he's stuck 'ere for a bit, and says it's the perfect time to get rid of the rats. He wanted to buy Flum off us."

"Did you agree to that?"

Elise looked scandalised. "Course not! I told him I didn't have a dog, 'cause I didn't want him to get the idea of talking to Pa and offering him money. Pa prob'ly would've sold Flum to him. I don't think he believed me." She hunched slightly. "I told you, I didn't like his look."

"You did the right thing," Gale told her sincerely.

"Flum run off that day. Pa said he'd come back—dogs always come back to where there's food for 'em. But I was scared, 'cause we didn't have much food for Flum. Just bones what we got from the neighbours. So maybe that's why he won't come back."

"Flum ran off the day you spoke to the captain?"

Elise nodded and looked down at her plate. Gale saw that she'd set aside a small pile of fatty bacon scraps.

"Are you certain he ran away?" Clarissa asked.

Gale started to shoot her a glare, but as he had been about to ask the same question, he simply waited for Elise's response.

Elise swung her legs under the table and looked at Gale. "Flum don't catch rats, sir. So where would the captain have heard that? I told him Mrs. Carroll has a dog that's a good ratter, an' I even pointed the way to her house, but he didn't go the way I pointed."

"Elise, how do you know he ran off? Where did Flum stay when you and your father were at work? Did you keep him chained up? Shut in the house?"

"Pa built him a house outside. It weren't a very good house, but he liked it. We tied him to it with a rope. Mrs. Carroll said she saw him run through her yard that day—prob'ly chasing a cat, she said. She remembers 'cause she was sleeping, and Flum woke her with an awful racket, and it set her dog barking like the devil. She come outside to see what was the matter, and she saw Flum run by."

Gale rubbed a hand over his mouth. "All right, Elise, this detail is important. Was the rope on the doghouse—" Gale tried to think how to phrase this for her. "Did it look pulled apart like Flum snapped it himself? Or was it cut?"

Elise stared at him blankly.

Gale sighed. "Never mind. Did Mrs. Carroll say whether she saw anything unusual while she was outside? Anyone passing by?" *The captain, perhaps?*

"No, sir. She just saw Flum."

Clarissa said, "You're doing well, Elise."

Gale felt a flash of annoyance. He didn't see that Elise was doing anything particularly noteworthy in answering a few questions. But this was, after all, why he'd asked Clarissa to stay—to smooth things over in the event that he said the wrong thing to the child once again. The girl merely swung her legs and studied the table-cloth as though she hadn't heard Clarissa at all.

"How did you acquire Flum?" Gale asked.

"Pa brought him home. Said he found him running loose along the river. Thought he'd be good to watch over the house. And so he is. He wouldn't hurt a fly, mind. Prob'ly wouldn't even hurt a burglar. But 'e's big, and that scares people. He's got so much hair on him you can't tell which end is which." She laughed, but the joy of the sound quickly faded. She pushed her plate toward Gale. "Could we go to my house and leave bacon for Flum? Then maybe he'll come back."

Clarissa made a noise of sympathy, and Gale could feel both girls' eyes on him.

"I…" What Gale needed to do was go to the docks and locate this captain. But he thought of what Chant would say if he told Elise no. "I will go to Jacob's Island," he promised. "And I will do my best to find Flum while I'm there."

"Can I come?"

"I think it's best that you stay here. But I must ask, do you know of anyone who might have been angry at your father? You said he played cards. Did he owe anyone money, perhaps?"

Elise gave him that odd stare again. "We ain't debtors, sir."

"No," Gale agreed quickly. Those wide-set eyes were rather disconcerting, trained on him with such intensity. "But Elise, if you can think of any reason someone might have wanted your father dead, I need to know."

Something flashed in her eyes—it was there for less than an instant, a combination of surprise, fear, and anger—and Gale might have likened it to the child being caught with her hand in a cookie jar, except that seemed too frivolous a comparison to capture the depth of feeling he'd spied. "No," she said. "No one."

Gale rose, pushing in his chair. "All right, then. I'm off to Jacob's Island." He glanced at Clarissa, who nodded.

"Don't forget the bacon, Lord Christmas." Elise gathered the scraps in her tiny fist and held them out to Gale, who stood there awkwardly for a moment before extending his hand and taking the greasy scraps. He held them, unsure what to do, and then slipped them into the pocket of his buckskins. He was fairly sure he heard Clarissa stifle a snort.

Gale left the house with his pocket full of bacon, wondering why a small child had just lied to him.

~

*G*ale returned to the Howes' house—though to refer to the hovel as a house seemed a generous assessment—as it seemed likely the dog might have returned there too. There was a narrow enclosed space at the back of the house that didn't deserve to be called a garden. It was full of junk and refuse, and held not a single blade of grass. No fresh dog shit in sight either. He went to what he presumed was the doghouse—a lean-to constructed of wooden planks—and crouched before it. There was indeed a scrap of rope still tied to it, frayed in a manner consistent with it having been pulled to its breaking point. Gale rubbed his jaw. If Elise's captain had, say, located the Howe's residence and thought to make off with Flum, would he not have simply untied the rope or else cut it?

There were a few footprints in the mud—a man's boot, and smaller shoes that had to be Elise's. One that Gale couldn't quite identify—it looked a bit slimmer than the other boot prints, but the ground was such a mess, it was hard to say for sure.

He called for Flum several times, feeling quite foolish. He questioned a neighbour who was out feeding her chickens—the hens might once have been white, but were now a tarry black with filth. She glared at him suspiciously and said nothing particularly enlightening about the Howes or their dog. He asked where he might find a Mrs. Carroll, and she replied that Mrs. Carroll worked long nights and would be asleep. Gale decided it was not worth ruffling any further feathers in the neighbourhood to speak to Mrs. Carroll now, and chose to walk along the river toward the dock-yard where he would inquire after the captain.

He had just started off when he saw a flash of movement from underneath what appeared to be a pile of lumber. He paused, then approached the pile and knelt. Best not to think of the filth staining the knees of his buckskins. It would benefit his disguise, after all. He wore the same borrowed, shabby overcoat as yesterday, but he'd worried that his breeches—out of fashion but finely made—would prove conspicuous. His hat tumbled off as he craned to peer under the rotting boards. He spied twin glints in the dark: the eyes of what looked to be a rather enormous creature. By its panting, he could presume it was a dog.

He scarcely dared breathe himself. "Flum," he said carefully, almost warningly. "Here boy. That's a good fellow."

Slowly, he reached into his pocket and took out a piece of bacon. He could hear the beast lick its chops as he held it out. But the dog didn't come forward.

"Look at this, hmm? It's a gift from Elise. Wouldn't you like to see her again?"

He tossed the bacon a foot or so in front of him. At the movement, the dog flattened itself against the ground. Gale felt his patience wearing thin.

"Flum! Out with you!"

The dog cowered back. Gale sighed. He never had possessed that good-natured ease that allowed one to communicate with children and with animals.

"Come now." He tried to soften his voice again. "It can't be very comfortable down there."

The animal didn't budge.

"Flum!" he called sharply. "Here, boy!"

A soft whine, and the creature shifted. It was massive, he could see now. Its thick coat so matted with filth, Gale could hardly blame himself for not recognising it for a dog when he'd first checked under the lumber pile.

"Damn you, you wretched beast!" He tossed another piece of bacon, this time under the edge of the pile. The dog lunged forward, grabbed the bacon, and then retreated once more. Gale sucked in a breath through his teeth. He had not journeyed all the way to Jacob's Island and muddied the knees of his buckskins to leave without this dog. "Come! Sit!"

When the brute remained precisely where it was, Gale decided his morning couldn't really get worse, and started to crawl under the lumber pile. The dog emitted a soft growl, and, with a speed that surprised Gale given the animal's size and the narrow clearance of the pile, whirled and scrambled out the back way. The beast darted for the back fence, squeezing himself through a narrow gap and escaping. Gale fumbled, mud squelching between his fingers as he pushed himself upright, and then he raced for the fence. By the time he found a gate to push through, Flum was already halfway down the alley, cords of matted fur bouncing as he ran, and after another moment, he was lost from sight.

Gale gave a tremendous sigh and pressed a fist to his forehead. The scent of bacon grease combined with the stench coming off the nearby ditch was nearly enough to make his stomach heave. After a moment, he looked up at the grey sky. Well, at least they had proof the bugger was alive. He would simply have to bring Elise back here tomorrow so she could call the dog. Surely Flum would come to her. Breathing hard, and a bit embarrassed to find himself so winded after what was admittedly a very short sprint, he started toward the river.

And nearly ran into a man whose dress, underneath an unassuming brown overcoat, suggested he was closer to Gale's station than any of the inhabitants of this slum.

"Gale!" came the fellow's startled exclamation.

It was Chant.

So his morning could, in fact, get worse. And had. "Good day, sir," Gale said stiffly.

"What are you doing here? Well, I suppose that's a foolish question. You're looking for Elise's dog." Chant's gaze dropped to Gale's muddied knees and ruined stockings. "Rather committed to the task, I see."

Gale held himself as straight as possible. "She would not stop going on about him. So yes, I came here to look. What are *you* doing here?" The question was entirely unnecessary. "But of course, you've come to look for Flum too."

"I could not sleep for thinking about that girl. To have just lost her father and have not even her dog for comfort…"

Gale tried not to perceive the comment as a slight against his own character—though in all likelihood it was intended as such.

"I have seen the beast," he told Chant. "Not a moment ago, it was cowering beneath a lumber pile, but it would not come when I called. And when I approached, it fled."

"Which direction? Perhaps we might still find him."

Gale shook his head. "I have no more time to waste on the creature. Elise has informed me that she was stopped *en route* to work two days past by a fellow looking to buy her dog. He said he was a ship's captain and had rats on his ship. Said he'd heard her dog was a fine ratter. Yet Elise has informed me that Flummery is quite incapable of catching rats."

"But what of it?" Chant asked, confused.

Gale grimaced. "You see, this! This is why I do not like people! I have just laid out to you the facts of the matter, two points which are in absolute opposition, and you say, 'But what of it?' Whoever this captain is, he lied, do you see?"

"Yes," Chant said, "but perhaps this captain didn't know that Flummery was not—"

"No," Gale said, and jabbed him in the breast with a thin finger. "The dog disappeared later that day. Snapped its rope and ran off. A neighbour witnessed its flight. You tell me that's coincidence." Gale was aware that he was growing rather more agitated than the situation called for, but his mind was racing, and Chant's presence was a hindrance to putting his thoughts in order. "The captain tried to obtain the dog, the dog fled, and now Howe is dead. I don't know why, but the captain is looking for the dog, and so we must look for the captain. *I*!" He corrected abruptly, his face heating. "*I* must look for the captain."

"You must not!" Chant protested at once.

Gale furrowed his brow. "It is the most logical next step in this investigation."

"But what if this fellow is dangerous?"

"That is precisely what I hope to determine."

"You mean to traverse Jacob's Island alone, dressed as you are, and confront a man you suspect is connected to a murder?"

"Yes, I believe I have made that quite clear."

Chant's blue eyes had lost their usual good humour, and held instead a concern that Gale did not entirely understand. "I cannot let you do that, Gale."

Something in Gale blazed. "You are in no position to tell me what I may or may not do. Stand aside, sir, if you please." For Chant had widened his stance as though he intended to tackle Gale should Gale step forward.

"I'm coming with you."

"Nonsense."

"Wherever you go, I shall dog your steps." Chant paused. "The pun was not intended. Though it is apt, I suppose."

"You shall ruin my investigation with your presence."

"I most certainly shall not. I shall be quiet as a dormouse, unless this captain attempts to do you harm. In which case, I will kill him."

At some point during the exchange, Gale felt they had slipped into an odd sort of banter. They were not joking, precisely, but there was a speed and ease to their speech that suggested they had been bickering about such things for many years. It gave Gale a bit of a rush to trade words with the man. Odder still was that Gale did not doubt Chant meant his last statement sincerely. What an mix of feelings that knowledge brought—confusion, chagrin, and the smallest spot of warmth, lying in his stomach like a pebble. "I should think you would be glad to witness my demise at the hands of this potentially nefarious sea captain."

Chant looked aghast. "How can you say such a thing?"

"Based upon your statements last night, you do not think highly of me. I have no wish to trouble you further with my defective personality, which is why I ask that you return home, or visit Bucknall's, or indulge in whatever form of idleness best suits you." Perhaps it was a test. Perhaps some part of him hoped to prompt Chant into refuting him—*Of course I think highly of you, Gale. Your personality is far from defective. Trouble me all you like.* That part of him ought to be cut out with a carving knife and thrown to starving hounds.

"You fool." The fellow said it so simply—without rancour, but with complete authority, as though he found Gale more pitiable than vexing.

"How am I the fool in this equation? I have shown you your exit, and yet you insist on standing here, making conversation with me."

Chant's fingers curled at his sides. "I was angry last night, I'll admit. I am usually a fair judge of character, and I was drawn to you in a way I have not been drawn to another person in many years. I see what kindness you are capable of, and I do not understand why you choose to reject that side of yourself."

Why should that hurt? It did not; it did not hurt—Gale would not allow it to. He was about to point out the absurdity of having a conversation such as this in the small, mucky yard of a run-down house in a neighbourhood neither of them had any business visiting. But instead, he said, "You have misjudged my character, sir, if you think I am capable of kindness. I am sorry. Perhaps it smarts."

"I have not misjudged you," Chant insisted. "I do not wish for your demise. In fact, quite the opposite. Which is why I am going with you to locate this captain."

No. The word was on the tip of Gale's tongue, and yet he could not say it. Why—why on *earth* should Chant care what Gale did, or where he went, or to whom he spoke? *Drawn* to him; what did Chant mean by that? Balls! This was not where his focus should lie, not when he was meant to be investigating a murder.

Gale began walking down the alley, searching for a way back to the street. He could hear Chant's footsteps close behind him.

Damn it all, was the man serious?

Gale walked faster. So did Chant. Eventually, Chant matched his pace, and Gale had no desire to make a fool of himself by moving any faster, and so he was forced to walk side by side with Chant as they found their way again to the streets close to the river. Their strides were so long, it caused their arms to swing, and once, Chant's hand brushed Gale's, and Gale stumbled sideways as though Chant had shoved him.

When they at last reached the dockyard at Surrey Quays, Gale found his concentration had gone to hell. Who, pray tell, was he looking for? He could not remember. A ship's captain. Tall fellow. Hair like twine. Dash it, if Chant truly cared about the girl, he would not compromise Gale's investigation so.

He scanned the ships that bobbed upon the Thames. One in particular caught his eye: a square-rig merchant ship, her hull made of dark wood, her bow bearing a weathered figurehead in the shape of an eagle, wings outstretched.

The question he was most often asked by—the word made him sick—*admirers*, was how did you know? How did you put it all together? In truth, he didn't understand how his own mind worked. He rarely strategised consciously. More often than not, the moves he made during an investigation were based on feelings. Wretched things, feelings—though they were certainly preferable to sentiments. He looked at the ship, and the darkness he felt within himself upon looking at it matched the darkness he had felt last night, hearing Darling speak of a six-fingered corpse. And he knew, even before the wind lifted her sails, revealing a rip in one staysail like a jagged leer, that this ship belonged to Elise's captain.

He could not hope to stand and *think* for a moment with Chant breathing down his neck, so he strode purposefully up to a fellow who was manhandling a barrel of fish. Doing his best to ignore the stench, he informed the man that he was seeking a ship's captain, tall in stature, with hair like twine. The man looked Gale up and down with combined bemusement and disgust. "Hair like twine, you say? Wha', have you wrote me a poem about 'im?"

Gale forced a smile, disliking immensely the sensation of being mocked in front of Chant. "I'm afraid I got quite drunk the other night at The Belled Cat. Got to talking with the fellow I've just described. I can't remember his name, only that he was very tall and his hair was…"

"Like twine?"

"I suppose. Sort of… dry. And straw coloured. Anyway, I recall little of the evening, but I do remember him saying he could use a ratter on his ship. I've got a Parson terrier who's good for the job, if he's still looking to borrow a dog."

The worker eyed Gale again, his attention lingering on Gale's muddied buckskins. Then he gave Chant a once-over before returning his gaze to Gale. "What's a fellow like you doing drinking at The Belled Cat?" He laughed, revealing large teeth edged in brown. "You mean to tell me you come here dressed like that, and you ain't had your throat cut and your purse nabbed?"

Gale felt Chant tense beside him and took a breath. He wasn't used to making such errors in judgement. If only he could push Chant into the bloody river, *anything* to get the man out of his sight, perhaps he'd be able to salvage this conversation. "Let us say I prefer to indulge my vices where word will not get back to my family."

The man laughed again. "Oh, I've seen everything now, ain't I? Poor old Howe, not dead a day, and here comes Mr. Brummell himself, pretending he's ever set foot in The Belled Cat, asking about a captain with hair like twine." He looked Gale up and down, this time with open contempt. "What are you, sir? Out of Bow Street?" He snorted. "I warned Talbot not to go for the Runners. We take care of our own here. Have for a long time."

Intrigue outweighed humiliation in Gale's mind—though only just barely. "I'm not a Runner. I can promise you that. But I am interested in what happened to Mr. Howe. And I do wish to locate the captain of the ship with the torn sail."

The man sneered. "And why would you be interested in Howe?"

"We were acquainted. That is all the information I can give you."

The worker stared into his barrel of fish and seemed to be considering his next words. Finally he said, "I don't know any tall captain with hair like tw—"

"I know your man." Another fellow with a squint-eye and a ruddy, swollen nose came up behind the man with the fish and clapped him on the back while studying Gale. "It's de Cock you want." His mouth wavered so wildly that Gale thought at first he was about to weep. Then he burst out laughing. "Captain de Cock! That's his name!"

The fish man's eyes widened, and then he began to laugh too. "Captain de *Cock*? You're 'avin' a laugh!"

"God's honest truth! Oh, been here a few days, he has. And every time I says good day to him—Well, he never says it back, first of all. But every time I says 'Good day, Mr. de Cock', I make myself scowl" —he demonstrated—"so I won't fall down laughing." The red-nosed man turned back to Gale. "He ain't here now. Every morning he goes into town. Won't tell no one what he's doing, but he always comes back before midday, stinking of liquor, then boards his ship and don't nobody see him till nightfall."

Gale consulted his watch. The time was five minutes before ten o' clock.

"Aye." The man nodded at him. "You wait around here long enough, he'll show up."

"Thank you, Mister..."

"Lewis, sir."

"Mr. Lewis. Very good."

The first worker said to Lewis, "This gentleman was an acquaintance of Mr. Howe's."

Lewis looked Gale over, just as the first man had done. His red face was curiously blank. "Ah. Mr. Howe. Poor old bastard. Can't say I'm surprised, though. Put enough gin in him, and he'd fire off his mouth like a cannon. Insults to make a sailor blush. Or pull out a knife."

"Were either of you at The Belled Cat last night?" Gale inquired.

Lewis shook his head slowly, a small smile curving his lips for a mere instant, just long enough to send a chill down the back of Gale's neck. "No, sir. I was not. And if you've come here to make trouble, my advice to you is, don't."

CHAPTER 5

There was nowhere along the dock particularly suited to awaiting the return of a drunken ship's captain whom one wished to investigate for murder. Chant was fine to stand there, breathing in the morning air and thinking his thoughts—most of which centred on how to get them both home with their hides intact—but Gale seemed far less inclined toward patience.

First, the man shoved his hands into his pockets, then he flicked his gaze down to where Chant's hands were in *his* pockets and took his hands out of his own pockets. Then he rocked back and forth on his heels. Gave a weary sigh. Cast a disdainful look at a pigeon. Pushed his hat more firmly onto his head.

"Would you like to find a place to sit?" Chant asked mildly.

"I would like you to be quiet, as you promised."

Chant nodded. "Very well."

He gazed off across the river again, admiring the ships and trying not to recall Lewis's warning. There was a neat little sloop of the sort he and Reid had talked about learning to sail. Ah, and that towering dark ship with its ripped sail—the one Gale had fixed his gaze on at once—looked like something out of another century. It was rather battered and bruised to Chant's eye, though he knew nothing of ships. He sneaked a glance at his companion. Gale was a couple of inches taller than he, which was a nice change, really. Chant was quite tall himself, and he liked looking up at someone. Made him feel a bit cosy. He focused on the water again.

"Would you stop?" Gale pinched the bridge of his nose.

"Stop what, my friend?" Chant deduced the answer was *existing*, though he doubted even Gale would put it so bluntly. He bit back a smile. Was it not hard work to be so surly all the time? It seemed like hard work to Chant.

"Just… please."

"I'm afraid I cannot comply unless I know what I am supposed to stop doing."

"Standing so… so near to me. I cannot think."

Chant took two steps away from him. "Is this better?"

"It is better, though still far from ideal."

Chant's nod was agreeable. "Ideal would be if I stepped off the dock and drowned?"

"I did not say that!" The force of the words seemed to surprise Gale as much as Chant.

Chant lifted his brows, but said nothing.

Another few minutes passed, and then Gale barked, "Say it, man!"

"I thought I was not supposed to say anything?"

"Yes, but I can feel you yearning to remind me that you were not in favour of what seemed a dangerous plan. And now I have made a hash of questioning the dockyard workers, and we have received an ominous warning, so I'm sure you feel quite smug."

"I do not feel smug," Chant said truthfully.

"Most of my past investigations have concerned peers. In truth, I do not spend much time in the less savoury areas of the city."

"Except when you visit molly houses?"

Gale's temper flared. "If that does not sit well with you, then I promise my other vices will not either."

"I meant no judgment. It was merely a question." In fact, it was quite a relief to Chant to hear that Gale sought molly houses. It saved Chant the trouble of having to ask if Gale were inclined toward men. Gale had danced with him last night, yes, but that did not necessarily mean what Chant would like it to.

After a few more moments studying the boats, Chant spoke: "You see that little slip of a thing over there? The one bouncing with each gust like she can't wait to get back out to sea?" Gale did not answer, and Chant did not mind. "A companion of mine wanted to sail one like that. All the way to America, he said. Oh, we'd have capsized and drowned before we were off the Thames, to be sure. But we did love to tell one another stories of our future adventures at sea."

Still no response. When Chant turned to Gale, the fellow looked quite lost.

Finally, Gale said, "I had a mind to go to The Belled Cat to see what we can find out about the events of last night. But it is early in the day, and we are not dressed to blend in." He glanced down at himself. "In fact, looking at my disguise now, I see that this wretched overcoat in combination with my usual day dress perhaps draws excessive attention to my person."

Chant inspected his own ensemble. "The same could be said of me." He looked Gale over once more, secretly pleased that Gale's effort at disguise was no better than his own. "I should think an investigator would have a whole wardrobe full of costumes, for any occasion."

"Perhaps an investigator would. But I am not an investigator."

"Ah. Right."

"We could visit Fernside and ask to see the corpse, but Fernside does not like his work interrupted any more than I do. We should send a note first."

Chant did not know who Fernside was, and he felt it best not to point out Gale's repeated use of *we*. But inwardly, he grinned.

Gale's hands clenched at his sides, and he hissed air from between his teeth. "Oh, I cannot *think*."

"I know you do not want my opinion, but I shall still give it. You are hungry."

Gale's brows knitted in the way Chant was coming to like. "Hungry?"

"Yes. Your colour is not good, and your hands shake."

Gale looked down at his balled hands, then up again, and Chant was once again struck by the softness of his eyes—such a contrast to the rest of him.

"I went to breakfast before coming here."

"Did you *eat* breakfast, or did you merely *go* to breakfast?" Chant asked gently.

"I…"

"Perhaps you chatted with Elise during her breakfast and forgot to have any of your own?"

Gale turned his head and inhaled, rolling his eyes heavenward, but when he let the breath out, his lips twitched. "Perhaps I should leave this investigation in your hands. Your power of inference is not altogether terrible."

A smile spread across Chant's face. "So I am correct?"

"I shall neither confirm nor deny."

"We could walk a while and perhaps find pastries. Walking would keep us warm, at least." He shivered theatrically.

Gale's gaze lingered on Chant for a surprisingly long time, and it was impossible for Chant to feel the morning's chill with those eyes on him. The fellow looked almost pained, and Chant wondered what that was about. "If you are cold," Gale said with no hint of his earlier snappishness, "then you should go home." His tone was low and unexpectedly soft, and there was a trace of rueful humour in his eyes that Chant would have called out of character, except that it looked so purely Gale, so absolutely suited to the man. "Leave the matter of the captain to me."

Chant's lips parted, though he did not speak right away. He felt a pull—toward Gale? Toward memories of Reid? He could not say. There was something bright and soft inside him, and he wanted to let it be for a moment. "I am more worried about you. Your borrowed coat is not so fine as mine."

"My coat is perfectly suited to its task."

"I cannot leave you here cold and hungry. It is against my nature."

"Yes." Gale's eyes narrowed shrewdly. "I do believe it is."

It was perhaps not quite a compliment but neither was it said with disdain, and Chant laughed. "I cannot help myself."

"We shall stick out anywhere we go. What with your hall boy's fine overcoat."

"Do not blame my hall boy's coat. It is your regal bearing that marks us as outsiders."

Gale snorted. "Very well, then. You must give your overcoat a good dunking in that fish barrel, and I must slouch."

"Or, we could stick close together. Watch out for one another." Chant said it teasingly enough, but he hoped, privately, that Gale would not mock the idea.

"All right. Let us hurry, then, before I starve to death."

Ah, Chant could not have held back his smile if he tried. The water lapped softly against the docks, the rhythm filling Chant with pleasure. And with the weak sun sneaking through the clouds, and the cry of gulls around them, the breeze lifting Gale's hair so the light caught the red in it, the sorrows of the world did not seem insurmountable.

～

*R*otherhithe was a busy, muddy place that stank of the worst of the Thames. Still, Gale had to allow that the pie cart Chant located sold passable wares. Passable enough that he bought a second pie after the first, and inhaled it as much as ate it. He couldn't remember the last time he'd eaten, and it vexed him that Chant had guessed much of his irritability had stemmed from the hunger he hadn't even felt until he'd begun to assuage it. He often forgot to eat and to sleep because he was usually doing more important things, and in the middle of them, his narrowed focus didn't allow for such considerations.

He wiped his pie-stained fingers heedlessly on his overcoat as he and Chant headed back to the riverside, to where they could see the ships and the men coming and going from them.

"I confess, I wish I knew more about this mysterious captain," he said in an undertone.

"Oh," said Chant. "You are interested in de Cock?"

"Of course," Gale said before he caught the way Chant's mouth twitched. Embarrassment swelled up in him, along with indignation. "Good God, man, is this Surrey Quays or Vauxhall Gardens? This is neither the time nor the place for cheap bawdry."

Chant's faint smile faded. "I apologise."

"You apologise, but you are not sorry." Gale's tone was grim.

Chant merely shrugged good-naturedly, his hands deep in his pockets. Despite his assertion that his hall boy's overcoat was a quality article, Gale worried that Chant was cold. *Wondered if*—not *worried that*. Chant was a grown man; obviously Gale was not inclined to worry about him. If Chant was cold, it was his own fault for coming here—and staying, in defiance of Gale's protests.

He was still hungry, even after two pies, and so Gale reached into his pocket and pulled out a scrap of bacon, nibbling it as they walked. He felt Chant's gaze on him. "My God man," Chant said. "What are you doing?"

"We didn't even need pies, Chant. I forgot I brought bacon." He pulled out another piece. Offered it to Chant.

Chant stopped, and so did Gale. "Why do you have bacon in your pocket?"

Gale shrugged, twisting his mouth to one side to keep any trace of amusement from his face. "It was for the dog." He ate the second piece of bacon slowly, eyes locked with Chant's.

Chant burst out laughing, and at that, Gale had to fight a smile.

"Look at you!" Chant declared. "You are trying to make me laugh."

"Nonsense."

"Yes, you are."

Was he? Gale supposed there was something rather intoxicating about the sound of Benjamin Chant's laughter. It was loud and open and unabashed, and it trailed off into a series of helpless chuffs in a way that some might consider charming. "Perhaps I am merely trying to persuade you that I am poor company to keep so you will go home."

Chant's grin only broadened, which was terribly annoying. Gale had nearly forgotten, for a moment, what a burden Chant was; how he had no place in this investigation, yet had wriggled his way into it and refused to leave. Gale had the strangest urge to touch Chant's face, red from the wind. And then maybe smudge that smile off with his thumb as though it were a trace of pie stuck at the corner of the fellow's mouth. It was not that Gale hated the smile. It was that he suddenly wanted to see what that face looked like with something darker in it. The mirth in those blue eyes replaced by hunger, those lips no longer curving up, but parted in anticipation.

No. Oh, for Christ's sake, no. What was the *matter* with him?

Gale was saved from a dreadful moment of introspection by a strange sight. "Look there," he said at once. Just a few yards away was an ale house—a working class establishment with high class aspirations. Ever since the dockyards had opened along the Surrey Quays, bringing jobs aplenty to Rotherhithe, every low-rate business within a mile of the river suddenly fancied itself Clarenden's. And at a table outside the ale house, seemingly oblivious to the cold, sat the tallest fellow Gale had ever seen—taller than Gale himself. A man with alarmingly pale skin, eyes a shade of blue so light Gale could note the colour even from this distance... and a mop of yellow-white hair as dry and dishevelled looking as a haystack. His shirt was open, and his dark velvet coat was old and in need of a wash—its brass buttons had probably gleamed at one time, but now had a patina on them. He had his arms folded on the table as he stared at rows of playing cards, an empty glass at his elbow.

"My God," Chant whispered. "Is that de Cock?"

"I think it is de Cock." Gale felt his lips trying to curve up once more. Something about this situation was making him nearly giddy —not a word that could, under any usual circumstance, be applied to him. The whole mess was horrible, yes. A young child's father was dead, Gale was having his investigation impeded by a fellow of incessant good cheer—Gale's least favourite kind of cheer—and a perfectly fine morning that could have been spent at Bucknall's had been wasted along this stinking river. And yet, Gale's chest had a strangely fizzy feeling to it, and he was fighting the urge to laugh.

Chant whispered, "Certainly larger than I expected."

"Stop it!" Gale hissed.

"I am sorry. But his reputation must be fearsome indeed if it has survived having that name attached to it."

"It is Flemish."

"It is something, all right."

A chuckle escaped Gale, and, horrified, he tried to turn it into a cough.

"Are you going to speak to him?"

"Yes, if you'll stop talking."

Chant gave an exaggerated gesture for Gale to lead the way.

Gale squared his narrow shoulders. Lovely. Now he had to find a way to approach a man who looked as if he dined on kittens for breakfast and crushed children's toys under his boots for fun. His boots. His boots were new. The rest of his garb was outdated and in poor condition, but those Hessians gleamed smooth and bright as the eyes of a hare.

He strode forward, feigning a confidence he did not feel. De Cock was engrossed in his game of Patience. He was also drunk— all around his unnaturally pale irises was a rather uniform shade of red, and his hand trembled as he laid a card down.

At the precise moment that de Cock looked up and his eyes, the colour of ice on the Thames, met Gale's, there came a commotion from the docks. Men shouted, and footsteps pounded over wooden planks. A splash.

Gale turned, straining to see what was happening at the dock. He began to pick out individual voices from amid the ruckus:

"Is he drowned?"

"Someone 'elp me pull 'im out!"

"What on earth?" Chant murmured.

"He's dead!" someone shouted.

"Good God," Gale said, his focus narrowing to the two large men crouched and straining at the water's edge. "They're pulling a body out of the river."

CHAPTER 6

*U*p to this point, Chant had more or less been content to let Gale lead the way on the morning's adventure. But now he felt himself drawn as if by some spell toward the water's edge, where a crowd had gathered around a prone form.

"Chant!" Gale quickly caught up to him and took his arm as though to draw him back. Then he let go.

"We must help him!" Chant insisted, panic rising in him. He could become shaken quite easily in the presence of sickness or death, and while he did not know this fellow, he could not stand to see his corpse crowded by gawkers. He hurried on, Gale's footsteps close behind.

When they reached the crowd, Chant discovered it was not a corpse at all. The fellow on the ground had begun to cough, sending up a spray of water and mucus that landed on his grey, swollen face.

"Good Lord." Gale sounded irritated. "He's not even dead. Chant, our captain has slunk away. We must follow. We do not have time to waste on a fellow who has not the decency to be a corpse."

"They are crowding him! The poor man probably feels as

though he still cannot breathe." Chant moved closer. "Everyone, move back, please. Move back, I say. Give him some room!"

At first the crowd ignored Chant, still chattering excitedly at each other and at the half-drowned man. Chant sharpened his voice and shouted, "I'm a doctor!"

He wasn't, of course. Fainted at the sight of blood, in fact. But he was dressed well underneath his borrowed coat, and several bystanders seemed to note that fact and let him through.

"A shark's been at his leg!" someone called.

"There are no sharks in the Thames," Gale said, sounding bored. "There was once, quite famously, a polar bear, but the wounds do not match that either."

Chant made the mistake of looking at the fellow's leg. The large gash in his left thigh was not ragged enough to be a shark bite. The slash in the trousers and the blanched edges of the wound itself suggested a blade. Through the torn fabric, Chant could see swollen flesh—black, grey, and pink. He swallowed down bile and turned away; his claim to medical knowledge would be proven a lie within seconds if he vomited.

The crowd quieted slightly as Chant knelt beside the spluttering fellow. If anyone was confused as to why a well-to-do doctor just happened to be walking along the dock at the precise moment a drowning man had been pulled from the Thames, they had the decency not to wonder aloud.

"Can you speak?" Chant asked the man.

The man wheezed, choked again, then nodded—although he did not actually speak.

"He were floating on that piece of wood!" an onlooker announced, gesturing to a broken plank bobbing in the water. "But his face were in the water, so I figured he was dead."

Chant helped the man sit up, not minding that the man's sopping clothes dampened his own. "There now." He tried to clap the man's back with some authority. "That's a good chap. Get it all out."

The man coughed up more water. The skin of his fingertips was wrinkled as though he'd been floating for some time.

"How did you come to be bobbing in the river?" Chant asked gently.

The man gasped, which caused him to choke again. When the fit ended, he looked first at Chant and then at Gale in frank desperation. "I was aboard the *Condor*, sir. First mate. I—I don't know what happened. I was up there, trying to patch the sail, and—" He wheezed. His voice was high and hoarse. Chant initially thought his accent French, then realised it was Dutch. His English was good, but the strain in his voice meant Chant had to bend close to hear him.

Gale was suddenly beside Chant. "Yes?"

The man nodded and whimpered. "Along came a great gust, and I fell from the rigging!" His wheezing was painful to hear.

Chant called to the crowd, "Someone get this fellow food and fresh water. Blankets, if there are any to spare."

"The *Condor*," Gale said, leaning down. "It wouldn't happen to be within sight, would it?"

The fellow's jaw trembled, and he looked around at the ships docked nearby. "It—" He swallowed audibly. "There it is. Far away, there."

Chant and Gale both turned. Chant was not at all surprised to see that the fellow pointed to the dark ship with the bird of prey figurehead.

"And your captain would be de Cock."

The man gasped again, then seemed to collect himself. "Yes, sir."

"When did this happen?"

Someone offered a flask of water—at least, Chant hoped it was water—and Chant helped the fellow drink. Then he took off his hall boy's overcoat and draped it over the man's shoulders, for he was now shivering fiercely. "C-c-couldn't say, sir. I must have hit my head going over. I was barely conscious, sir. I found a plank and I held on to it for dear life. I was going in and out of sleep…"

"Did you hit your leg too?" Gale asked dryly.

The man raised his head to glimpse his gruesome injury, then whimpered, letting his head fall back against Chant.

"Where was de Cock?"

The man closed his eyes. His breath rasped in and out in a manner that made Chant think he was buying time before answering. "I don't know, sir."

Chant looked at Gale, and Gale's gaze met his.

"De Cock's out drinking!" someone called. It was Lewis, the man who had warned Chant and Gale about causing trouble. "Done nothing else since he docked four days past. You've got a surgeon on your ship, don't you?"

The man shook his head. "The surgeon was only ever coming as far as London with us. His contract's up. He's off somewhere in the city now." He exhaled through clenched jaws. "The captain will have my head."

"Why?" Gale asked sharply. "For falling overboard?"

"He… he doesn't like incompetence, sir." Now the man's eyes darted fearfully.

Gale spoke, low enough that only Chant could hear. "He is lying through his teeth. We must get him away from the crowd."

Chant nodded and looked round at the spectators.

"This man needs tending to by a doctor," he announced. And then he remembered his own lie. "Which is why I will tend to him. Now." He glanced desperately at Gale.

Gale stepped in smoothly. "But that will require instruments, which my friend the good doctor does not have on his person. So we shall take him into our custody."

Chant scarcely had time to offer Gale a grateful look before he was helping Gale hoist the man to his feet. They half dragged, half carried the fellow, who could scarcely put weight on the injured leg. Chant had no idea where they were going, but Gale seemed to have a plan.

"What is your name, man?" Gale asked their charge. Chant had not even thought to obtain that critical information.

"Visser, sir." The man panted.

"Visser. While the doctor tends to you, I will ask you a number of questions—all of which I need answered in a truthful manner. Am I understood?"

Visser muttered an affirmation.

Just when Chant was beginning to grit his teeth with the effort of hauling Visser up and down side streets, they arrived at a narrow terrace house where a man met them outside. He was short and a bit on the stout side with a round, honest face that looked disconcertingly young for someone in his profession. He had wispy, ash-brown hair that stuck in all directions, and his mouth was the sort of tiny bow Chant could only ever recall seeing on dolls.

Gale started visibly as the man approached. "Fernside!" he called.

"Hello!" the man called.

"This is the Fernside you mentioned earlier?" Chant asked Gale in a low voice.

"I could count on two fingers the number of times I've seen him outside his home. He is the consummate hermit. A surgeon by trade, but I suppose he also doles out medicines to the locals if they need them. He also studies corpses in his cellar. Pays for them off the street."

Chant felt queasy enough that he nearly lost his hold on Visser.

Visser, who had heard their exchange, began to twist between them. "*Corpses?*"

Fernside reached them. "This is the fellow they've just found in the water?" he asked as though Visser's sodden clothes did not make that clear.

"News travels fast," Gale said. "I've a few questions for our patient, Mr. Visser here, if you don't object to my presence as you tend to him."

"Not at all."

"We will be speaking on a matter that is not yet of public record. I would ask for your discretion, Mr. Fernside."

Fernside readily agreed.

They entered the surgeon's home—a narrow, austere house, poorly furnished but well-lit—and helped Fernside deposit Visser on a cot near the tiny kitchen. Chant shivered, wondering where the corpses were. The cellar, Gale had said. Chant's general modus operandi was to shake his head in gentle amusement at life and all of its oddities, but he did find it difficult to be gently amused by corpses. Visser apparently agreed; his eyes darted as though the room might be occupied by a restless spirit escaped from the cellar. Gale urged him brusquely to lie down. The surgeon immediately set to boiling water, and Gale set to questioning Visser.

As Chant watched, he could not help but be impressed. This was what had made Lord Christmas Gale famous: the ability to ask the right questions, to shroud his true intentions in more palatable inquiries that invited more honest answers. Gale asked Visser about the *Condor* and its crew—where they'd started their journey, what they were transporting, where they'd stopped. When Visser became reticent on certain subjects, Gale circled back calmly and approached from another angle. He'd have made a fair solicitor, Chant thought.

Fernside finished examining Visser's head and, with barely a second's hesitation, stripped off Visser's torn and blood-stained trousers and whistled at the leg wound. Chant tried very hard not to look.

Gale asked, "What happened to the *Condor*'s sail?"

"A storm," Visser said. "Delayed us two days."

"That must have been rather frustrating."

Visser snorted. "We were at each other like dogs. Everyone was in a foul mood."

Visser began to breathe more rapidly as Fernside approached with a bottle of brandy. He laughed, the sound high and nervous.

"Like dogs," Gale mused.

At that point, there was a great deal of screaming as Dr. Fernside cleaned the leg wound. Chant had to turn away.

"Tell me about the dog," Gale said as though the screaming had not taken place. "The one on board your ship."

Chant started. They had no confirmation of a dog on board the *Condor*. Was Gale referring to Flum?

It was several moments before Visser's breathing steadied enough for him to reply, and Chant began to understand the tactic at work. Visser was so focused on the pain, he didn't appear to consider why Gale was asking about a dog. "A funny thing he was—so big and hairy. Like a sheep. He came aboard in Rotterdam. He was not... um, how is it—he was not a good rat-catcher? But we all grew very affectionate toward him anyway. Shared our rations with him—and I assure you, sir, there wasn't much to share."

"What became of the dog?"

"He escaped when we docked." Visser gritted his teeth for a moment. "Agh. I'm sorry, sir. This is—Oh, it does hurt."

"Take your time," Gale said.

Visser nodded, hissing.

"Did he come back?" Gale asked eventually.

"No, sir. I imagine he's got more to eat on the streets here than he did with us."

"Was the captain sorry to see him go?"

Visser's eyebrows lifted, and his face contorted. Chant thought at first it was pain, since Fernside had begun, silently and efficiently, to stitch his leg. But then Chant saw it: fear, more than pain, in the man's eyes. "I don't think so. He did not like the dog."

"Ah. I've heard from a couple of people that de Cock has been searching town for a ratter. But you said that wasn't your mutt's specialty."

"Well, I suppose... I suppose having him on board put the idea in the captain's head that maybe keeping a dog is good. A dog that is better at killing rats, yes?"

"Yes." Gale nodded amiably as though this might well be the case. "Do you know, I saw a great hairy dog just this morning. In an alley behind The Anchor, wasn't it, Chant?" He didn't wait for Chant's reply. "Feasting on scraps from the ale house. I wonder if it was your mutt."

Visser's lips parted, but he said nothing. Chant watched Gale watching every movement of the man's face. "Perhaps," Visser whispered at last. Then his brow furrowed, and Chant could fairly see gears turning in his head. "Sir? May I ask... what are you?"

"What am I?"

"Are you a"—he appeared to search for the word—"constable?"

Gale snorted. "Hardly. I'm merely a fellow who likes to make sense of things."

There was a tension about Visser's eyes and mouth that suggested a growing wariness. His gaze cut to Chant. "He said he was a doctor."

Gale did not answer.

Fernside finished the stitches in what seemed to Chant record time, then went to clean his hands.

Gale spoke again. "The good news, Mr. Visser, is that you do not appear to have a head wound. Isn't that right, Fernside?"

"No head wound," Fernside confirmed, almost cheerfully.

"So the damage is confined to this leg wound, which appears to have been made by a blade, not a shark or a polar bear. And which is not fresh. Is it fresh, Fernside?"

"No, it's not fresh," Fernside agreed. "Perhaps two days old? Three?"

Gale nodded. "I do wonder, Mr. Visser, what your captain was doing sending you up to fix a torn sail when you had so recently been stabbed in the leg. The blade used appears to have been triangular, and so it opened the flesh in a most devastating way. Do you see why I find this befuddling?"

Visser was starting to sweat, and Chant did not think it was entirely from pain. The Dutchman's eyes darted, and he swallowed hard.

"And since there is no head wound," Gale continued, "perhaps, now that your initial trauma is over, you are able to recall how long ago you went overboard? And whether you were truly fixing a torn sail when it happened? And even, if you're feeling especially ambitious, how you got stabbed in the leg."

Visser licked his lips. Chant found his heart was pounding as though he himself were the one who had walked into Gale's trap. But Visser looked Gale directly in the eye, and said steadily, "I was up on the rigging. Fixing the sail. A gust of wind pushed me off."

"Very well," Gale said, much to Chant's surprise. He stood. Stretched. Glanced down and then frowned slightly. Chant couldn't say for sure, but there was something theatrical about the gesture, as though Gale were pretending to notice something he had in fact noticed long ago. He reached down and took Visser's arm, pulling up the sleeve of his shirt.

Raw, pink marks wrapped around the man's wrist, and Chant had only to glance at the man's other arm to spy a matching injury.

"I've seen vicious rope burns before," Gale said conversationally. "On sailors' palms or inner arms. I can't say I've ever seen them go all the way around like this." Visser looked too stunned to pull away. Gale met his eyes for a moment. "Strong winds."

He let go of Visser's arm and turned to Fernside. "Fernside, old fellow, I hear you have a corpse I might be interested in."

Fernside confirmed that he did, in fact, have a fellow in his cellar, and before Chant knew it, Gale was giving him a nod and saying he'd be back in no time at all. And then he followed Fernside through a door and down a set of stone stairs.

Chant was not sure whether to talk to Visser or not. He didn't have the confidence to continue Gale's line of inquiry, but he desperately wanted the Dutchman to explain how he'd acquired the leg wound.

Visser glanced at him but didn't speak. He lifted his gaze to the ceiling, and Chant made a point of studying the aging furniture.

True to his word, Gale and Fernside were back in a few minutes. "Fernside, I am leaving a small sum with you. When you are assured that Mr. Visser's condition is stable, I would like you to have him transported somewhere private to recuperate."

Fernside agreed, his eyes widening hungrily at the coins Gale pulled from his purse.

"Mr. Visser," Gale said. "Though it may be a while before you walk again, please do not go anywhere without leaving word for me as to your destination. I may have more questions for you."

"Yes sir." Visser was shivering again, and to Chant's unpractised eye, looked rather unfocused. "Of course, sir."

Fernside walked them to the door, and as they stepped out, Gale said quietly to the surgeon, "Be careful. I don't know whether he is dangerous, but he has an associate who concerns me."

Fernside nodded, and they left.

They stayed clear of the docks, winding their way through the foul smell of Surrey Quays, heading westward. Chant wanted to speak, but sensed Gale needed this time to think. At last, Gale stopped and turned to him. "I wish to go somewhere private and discuss what we have learned today."

"Oh? Am I a partner in this investigation now?" Chant tried to tease, though the afternoon had taken much of his energy and had left him unsettled.

"Hardly. But it would help to talk things over with someone, and you are my only prospect."

Such a polite fellow. "Well, my home is at our disposal if that would suit."

Gale seemed to consider this. "I suppose it will do. I have rooms in Russell Street, but they are extremely small."

"Very well. Would you object to my calling a hack?"

Gale shook his head.

They eventually found a cab, and once they were both inside,

Chant took in Gale's pensive scowl. He risked speaking. "Gale. Visser was… well, he was lying about nearly everything, wasn't he?"

"Yes," Gale said, though he did not look at Chant. He was still, clearly, lost in his own mind. "I believe that if we hadn't seen the *Condor* with our own eyes, he would have told us it was a bright purple sailboat with wings on its sides. Everyone is lying to me today, Chant—save perhaps you. And I'm quite tired of it."

CHAPTER 7

*U*pon second study, Chant's home was not so barren as Gale had initially thought. True, the decoration was sparse, but there was something comforting in the clean lines of the place. The furniture in the sitting room was all dark wood, bearing none of the carved curlicues and fleur-de-lis that adorned everything in the Gale family home. There were cosy touches throughout: a bookcase tucked in a corner, its leather-bound tomes leaning untidily against one another. Stubby candles on nearly every surface, the wax puddles at their bases looking rather like icebergs floating on a mahogany sea.

The settee was old and out of fashion, but Gale sat on it at Chant's invitation and found it incredibly comfortable. He had not realised how weary he was until he sank onto the plush cushions. He loosened his cravat slightly, aware his breathing was rough.

"Tea?" Chant asked. "Or do you require something stronger?"

"A stiff belt of whisky would not go amiss. But I shall limit myself to tea. Thank you." He continued his study of Chant's home in the light of day. There was warmth in it—most likely because Chant was there, and Chant was a warm person. But it did not escape Gale that this was a house of sadness. That, although its rooms were small, they did in certain moments seem cavernous and empty. This was what grief could do to a place, Gale supposed, thinking of what Anne-Marie had said about Chant's dead sister, and the old mad earl, and the former beau who was now in France.

There were elements of the decor that were not purely Chant. Not that Gale knew the man well. But the gold mantle clock with its base of swirls and splashes, like molten lava hurled up from the earth—Gale could not see Chant choosing that for himself. Though its colour matched Chant's hair quite nicely. Not that this was in any way relevant.

Two hideously gaudy vases painted in the Oriental style—no doubt by some piss-poor English artist who thought the fashion exotic but had never been farther east than Dartford—sat in opposite corners of the room. The vases were not Chant either. The bookcase was Chant's doing, as were the melted candles, and the simple writing desk with its chair of faded red upholstery.

Chant sat, not on that faded chair, as Gale would have thought appropriate, but at the other end of the settee. Gale stiffened, not sure what to make of their sudden proximity.

Surely there was nothing to make of it. He had sat this close to Hartwell numerous times. Closer than this to other fellows at salons and gaming hells, at Bucknall's. Why did it feel so... improper to be this close to Chant?

Chant did not appear to share Gale's awkwardness, though he was rather quiet for Chant. He offered a small, tired smile, one elbow braced on the back of the sofa, his chin resting in his hand.

"So what are your thoughts on the case?" he asked at the same time Gale blurted, "Your companion who wished to sail. Does he often call here?"

Chant's lips parted.

"I'm sorry. I should not have asked." Gale paused. "I do mean that sincerely. I'm told I have a tone of voice that makes me sound sardonic even when I do not intend to be."

"It is all right that you asked," Chant said too slowly for him to mean the words entirely.

"No. You are not a suspect for me to interrogate." Gale shifted on the settee. "I have grown used to these little escapades I find myself involved in. I have also grown used to treating everyone as a source of information rather than a... a companion."

"I am a companion now?" The amusement was back in Chant's eyes. "I rather thought I was a nuisance who had impeded your investigation."

"You are far from a nuisance." Gale uttered the words as unexpectedly as he had blurted the question about Chant's former consort. Consort was not the right term. The fellow had been more than that or else Chant's eyes would not have filled with such shock and remembered sadness when Gale had asked. The consort, Gale guessed, was the Mr. Reid whom Clarissa had mentioned on the way home from the Harringdon ball.

Now Chant's eyes filled with a softer surprise. "You do not have to lie to me, Lord Christmas. I know you did not wish me there today. But it is in my nature to worry about people. And I did genuinely worry for your safety."

"I would not be here now if I wanted to be rid of you," Gale answered truthfully.

Chant smiled, and Gale's face heated in response.

Fortunately, a servant brought in the tea tray then, and Gale occupied himself with spooning sugar into a cup of strong Ceylon.

He did not miss how Chant had neatly avoided answering his question, and Gale thought it best to let the matter drop.

But Chant took a long sip of tea, then stared into his cup. He looked up again, his gaze finding Gale's with a disarming frankness. "He does not call here at all anymore. He is no longer a part of my life."

"Ah. I would not have asked, but the clock did not look like something you would choose."

Chant barked a laugh and looked towards the mantle. "That was my sister's doing, actually, not Reid's. Reid was responsible for the vases, which I saw you looking at with unrestrained contempt earlier." His eyes returned to Gale, and they sparkled with amusement. "But no, the clock was a find of Jenny's. She does so love shiny things. *Did*," he said in surprise, shaking his head as if he could not quite believe himself. "It has been so long since I've done that."

"I had heard that your sister was deceased. I am so very sorry to have touched upon a painful subject."

"It is quite all right. She is deceased. To refuse to speak of it does not change the fact. She loved God, and she is with Him now."

There was something in Chant's tone that prompted Gale to ask his next question, despite logic dictating that he should change the subject entirely. "Does it comfort you, to think of her with God?"

Chant hesitated a long while. "I am undecided on the matter of God. I am sorry if that shocks or disturbs you. It comforts me that her last thoughts were perhaps joyful ones—excitement over the prospect of her journey to a place she believed in with all her heart. While there may well be a higher power who takes an inordinate interest in our little lives, I rather think it is wise to make the most of our time on earth. Just in case there is not so much beyond that as we think."

"That does not shock me," Gale said quietly. "Rather, it quite aligns with my own beliefs. Except that I seem incapable of making the most of my time on earth."

A tilt of Chant's head. "Why do you say that?"

"I presume that by 'make the most' of our time here, you mean finding love. Spending time in the company of fine friends. Starting families. Doing good deeds. Smelling the roses, watching the birds. Cooing at infants. All right, I do not know what you meant. But I do none of those things. I bristle when another soul comes near me. I manage very few acts of kindness. I think flowers are given far too much credit, and that birds are annoying. Do not even get me started on infants."

Chant laughed—the sound was, as always, clear, loud, and

genuine, and seemed to melt something bitter and sharp in Gale, softening the scowl he felt on his face into what was very nearly a smile. Chant took a last sip of tea, then set his cup aside. "You have helped a good many people find answers to questions that plagued them. Your skills have brought them peace. This is kindness."

"I solve mysteries that I do not even mean to solve. And I do it to entertain myself, not to please anyone else."

"I have my doubts on that front." Chant placed his hands on his knees. "But I'll allow you to believe it if you must."

"You think well of everyone. I assure you, you are under no obligation to think well of me."

"I am under no obligation. And yet I do."

"I wish you would not."

"I rather think that what you tell me of Lord Christmas Gale is comprised mostly of stories you have told yourself, not the truth of you."

"A romantic notion."

"I also think you are a bit disingenuous. Surely a man as perceptive as yourself has noticed that when I look upon you, what is in my eyes is not merely platonic affection. I am also certain you have gleaned by now that my Reid was not merely a companion. I wonder that you would ask if he is still a presence in my life when I have invited *you* here. What do you take me for, my lord?"

It took Gale a moment to realise Chant was teasing him. And another moment to comprehend what Chant had just confessed. He cleared his throat, glowering. "I took you for a proper gentleman, who was inviting me here out of the goodness of his heart because I needed a place to rest—not because he was thinking indecorous thoughts."

Gale's teasing did not show itself for what it was as easily as Chant's did. He had trouble calling forth a light tone of voice. And so he was quite relieved when Chant tipped back his head and laughed again. "I did invite you here out of the goodness of my heart. But my heart has a few dark corners as well."

"I somehow doubt that."

"Then you do not understand the full extent of the indecorousness that plagues my thoughts when I am in your presence."

"You are forward, sir."

"If it makes you uncomfortable, I hope that you will tell me so. For I do not wish to offend."

"I am not offended. I merely wonder what madness you suffer if you feel such desire for me."

Chant's expression was so patently dismayed that at first Gale thought it part of the joke. But the play of sentiments across the fellow's face was genuine. Gale could not fathom why this comment, of all the reckless, insensitive comments he had made thus far, had upset Chant so.

Gale quickly apologised. "To each his own taste. I am rather flattered that you think of me in such a way. You are not exactly ugly yourself."

Chant smiled tightly, and Gale knew it was time to redirect the conversation to something that would take Chant's mind off his pain. "Howe's corpse had a grotesque chest wound that looked to be made with the same triangular blade that injured Visser."

Oddly, this did not seem to lift Chant's spirits.

"So you see, this supports our suspicion. Well, my suspicion—I don't know if you share it—that de Cock killed Howe and wounded Visser."

"That's good, I suppose." Chant did not seem as focused as Gale would like. "Well, not *good*. But good that we are getting some answers."

"Based on the wounds, I would say the blade used is a ballock dagger. So named for its distinct handle, which has twin globes at the hilt"—he sketched out the shape in the air—"that resemble a pair of kidneys, or perhaps a set of..." He trailed off.

"Balls?" Chant supplied.

"Yes."

"So de Cock's sword..."

"Well, dagger."

"Has a set of—"

"Balls, yes."

They sat there for a moment in contemplation.

"He really embraces it, doesn't he?" Chant remarked.

"You almost have to admire him."

"I wouldn't go that far."

"No, of course not.

Another moment of silence.

Gale cleared his throat. "But I cannot figure out why Visser would feed us that ludicrous story about fixing the sail. Is he protecting de Cock? Afraid of de Cock? Probably the latter."

"The marks on his wrist…"

"Yes?"

"I don't know," Chant said. "What do you make of them?"

Gale stared absently at the ugly vases. "It looks as though Visser was bound. Somewhat recently."

"By de Cock?"

"I don't know yet. Suppose there was trouble between Visser and de Cock. De Cock imprisoned him. Stabbed him, at some point. Perhaps realised that keeping Visser captive indefinitely was not feasible and threw him overboard?"

"But why throw him overboard at a busy port?"

"The *Condor* is docked far enough out that I imagine unsavoury tasks could be carried out without anyone noticing. But you're right, throwing him overboard doesn't make sense—the body would naturally wash up somewhere along the yard."

"I would kill Visser first and weigh the body down before throwing it over."

"Well, listen to you, Mr. Chant. Dark corners in your heart indeed."

That won Gale a smile. "I don't know anything about crime, really. I just… Well, suppose Visser escaped and jumped overboard?"

Gale nodded, feeling oddly proud of Chant. "That was my thought."

"Are you only saying that because you don't want to admit I had the thought first?"

"Don't flatter yourself, sir. It is a possibility I've been turning over in my mind for some time. But I'm pleased to see you arrived at that hypothesis as well."

"How does Elise's father fit into all this?"

Gale sighed. "That, I have not yet figured out. I asked Elise this morning if anyone had a reason to want her father dead. She said no, but there was something in her eyes..."

"You asked a child of seven years if anyone wanted her father dead?"

"She is old enough to understand the question. And more than old enough to know the answer. And certainly old enough to lie about it."

"Why would she lie?"

"I suppose for the same reason Visser lied. She's afraid of someone. Of something."

"Is this all to do with the dog, somehow?"

Gale slumped forward, suddenly exhausted. Placed his face in his palms and then dragged both hands down his cheeks to steeple beneath his chin. "It must be, but I can't for the life of me see how it fits together. I saw the beast this morning. He hardly looks to be some valuable breed. Maybe he's canine Dutch royalty. Maybe he shits golden turds. I don't know, Chant. But if de Cock is looking for the dog, and he knew Howe had the dog, and then Howe was killed..."

"The dog is the key."

Gale raised his head again, hands covering his mouth to contain his frustration. "Part of me wants nothing to do with any of this. But then I think of Elise without her father. She is an urchin, yes, but she could be one of my sisters. Not *actually* one of my sisters—I just mean that she is a child, same as they are. Or as some of them are. Some of them might be upwards of forty, for all I know. But if one of them were left alone in the world… I cannot bear to think of it."

"I know precisely what you mean."

Gale cast him a mild glare. "So are you satisfied now? You were right about me. I am by no means a good man, but I am not completely heartless."

"I knew that when you roused me at midnight to go find the girl in question and take her to safety. I knew that when I found you this morning searching for her dog in Jacob's Island. And I rather think I knew it as soon as I met you."

"Yes, well, any decent man could reasonably be assumed to care about a child's wellbeing."

"Precisely."

"You think you have tricked me into calling myself decent when in fact I meant you only assumed that decency because you would assume it in anyone. Not because you could see at once that I was soft-hearted as a lamb."

Chant said nothing. Merely placed a hand on Gale's back as he had the previous night when they'd stood on the Harringdons' terrace. Gale resisted the urge to pull away. It did not feel entirely terrible, the way Chant rubbed between his shoulders. In fact, if he allowed himself to relax, it was quite pleasurable—a realisation that immediately made him tense again. To mitigate the awkwardness he felt, he leaned back against the settee, tilting his chin toward the ceiling. He expected Chant to pull his hand out from where it was now wedged between Gale and the upholstery. But he simply moved it to Gale's shoulder. His thumb passed along the seam of Gale's coat, and despite himself, Gale breathed out some of his tension. He turned his head toward Chant.

"I have never been involved in something so serious. This is murder, Chant."

"Perhaps we have reached a point where it is best to let the magistrate's office take over."

Gale shook his head. "They are useless."

Chant's brows drew together. "Do you really think so?"

"Darling said Howe was just a drunk."

"Didn't you also tell me Howe was just a drunk?"

"I said he was *a* drunk. I didn't say he was *just* a drunk. The Runners don't care what happens to a man from Jacob's Island. What do I do? Go to Darling and say I believe a dog is the key to the murder of a drunk? Never mind trying to explain Visser. The only reason Visser was talking to me at all is that on some level he believed me when I said I was not a constable. Drag Darling in to question him, and I guarantee Visser won't say another word."

"You really want to solve this—I won't say case. This puzzle. Don't you?"

"I feel I owe something to Elise. She… thinks highly of me. Or she did before I… said what I said."

"You have already done her service. It is enough that you have taken her in during her time of need. Concentrate on finding her dog. I do not presume to speak for Howe, but that would be the outcome I would want, were she my daughter. Far more than justice for myself. Let the Runners handle de Cock."

Gale grimaced, trying not to smile.

"Oh, come now, I did not mean it as—"

"You do not think I can handle de Cock, Mr. Chant?"

"I rather think it depends which cock."

Gale lifted his brows. "There's really only one I'm interested in handling at the moment."

Chant inhaled sharply, then licked his lips. Gale wondered if he had gone too far. Conflict was evident in the other man's eyes. Gale shifted closer and saw hunger flare in Chant's gaze. Not since Teddy at the salon had Gale so much as offered himself for any carnal act that was not with a molly. He leaned closer, placing a hand on Chant's thigh, and there it was, that sweet, soft longing he'd imagined on Chant's face. That *need*. Chant let out an unsteady breath and leaned forward a fraction of an inch, his lips parting…

And then he drew back.

The small room suddenly had that cavernous, empty feeling, and Gale knew at once that Chant's thoughts were somewhere in the past. Gale's first instinct was to be mortified. But there was enough desire and regret in the other fellow's gaze that he knew Chant's hesitation was not a reflection on him.

And so Gale smiled softly, even though his heart pounded and the back of his neck felt hot as a brand. "No," he whispered, almost to himself. "The time is not right." He brushed Chant's thigh reassuringly with his thumb, then removed his hand and straightened.

"I am sorry." Chant exhaled.

"Nothing to apologise for," Gale said briskly, picking up his tea cup and putting it to his lips, though nothing but dregs remained in it.

"I find you so very attractive. I do not even understand my own hesitation."

"Your Reid's memory is quite alive in here. Let there be no self-recrimination, my good man."

Chant sighed. "I have cooled the heat of the moment, have I not? Ah, what a fool I am. Should you have the patience for me, Gale, I assure you I am… I will be… willing. At some point."

"Sir, you have already been endlessly patient with me. Think no more of it."

"Oh, I shall think of it every waking moment and probably even when I sleep." Chant scrubbed his fists over his eyes then let his hands drop to his knees.

"Well, the more time you spend thinking of it, perhaps the sweeter it will be should the day come when you feel ready."

Gale meant the words sincerely. Yet he could not help but think of Teddy. How close they had been to stripping off each other's clothes and enjoying whatever the night had to offer. How unexpectedly thrilling it had been to brush Teddy's tight curls back from his forehead and imagine kissing those soft lips… and then how Teddy had turned from him and gone off to tup that French artist.

Men seemed to enjoy gazing deeply into Gale's eyes, but eventually they all saw something there that made them recoil.

No, he admonished himself. That was not what had happened here. Chant had not rejected him. The fellow was merely fighting the ghosts of his past. He was clearly a man who felt deeply and therefore hurt deeply. There was actually something quite pleasing in how obviously he wanted Gale but how a part of him remained loyal to this Reid.

Chant was studying him with an expression Gale couldn't quite sort out. "Do not ever tell me you are not a decent man," Chant said seriously.

Gale swallowed. As he had just proposed an act of grave indecency with a fellow to whom he was not married, it seemed rather shortsighted of Chant to call him decent merely for withdrawing that proposal.

"If it will not make you think me horribly inconstant," Chant continued, "might we sit nearer? If you do not like my hand on you, you need only say, but I do rather enjoy the contact."

Gale shifted closer, until their thighs met. The front of his breeches was still a bit tight.

Chant put an arm around Gale's shoulders as comfortably as though they were the oldest and dearest of friends. They sat in silence for a moment. Then Chant's hand drifted up, his fingers threading through Gale's hair. Gale stiffened. Forced himself to take measured breaths. What on earth... ? Chant carded the strands gently, and Gale felt a strange but not unpleasant prickle go up his spine. Chant's fingers brushed the hair at Gale's temple, and then his nails dragged very lightly to the back of Gale's scalp where they dug in just a little. This time, Gale's whole body seemed to jump like a candle flame.

He swallowed hard. "What... what are you doing?"

"Shall I stop?"

"No. I—I just don't understand what..." He trailed off.

"Have you truly never known the pleasure of having your hair stroked?" There was a smile in Chant's voice, but a sadness in his tone that made Gale at once defensive.

"I… I'm sure I…" But he could think of no instance where anyone had run their fingers through his hair this way. The room grew completely still, until there was nothing but Chant's gentle touch, and Gale's awkward pattern of tensing, then letting go, and then tensing again as he tried to acclimatise himself to the sensations. "No," he muttered finally as though conceding a great defeat.

"Do you dislike it?"

"The only thing I dislike about it is that I am perpetually dreading the moment you'll cease," Gale snapped.

"Well, then I shall never cease."

Gale snorted in spite of himself.

"If you will indulge me, I'll arrange you so that it is easier for both of us."

"Chant…"

Chant seemed to be waiting for the rest of whatever Gale had to say. But Gale did not have more to say. He inhaled and then released his breath, trying to slacken his body but to little avail. "All right," he whispered.

Chant huffed in amusement. "I shall not eat you alive, poor fellow." He took Gale's shoulders and eased him down so Gale's head rested on Chant's thighs. This did nothing for the strain at the front of Gale's breeches, and Gale did not see how this position made things any easier for him. Perhaps for Chant, who now had greater access to Gale's hair, and was—oh God—making full use of that access while Gale lay rigid with his legs folded awkwardly on the settee. It was as though pure warmth were cascading slowly down his spine, over and over again. His scalp tingled pleasantly, and with each new path Chant's fingers traced, Gale found it harder to stay still. He squirmed a little. Then attempted, quite involuntarily, to press into Chant's touch. Chant gripped a lock of Gale's hair by the roots and tugged lazily.

Gale gave a most undignified sigh, a ragged sound that nearly turned into a plea on its way out. He swallowed. "Do you think Howe knew the dog was de Cock's when he took it?"

"I think you must stop thinking about the case for the day and let yourself rest."

"Do not call it a case."

Chant ran the tips of his fingers over Gale's nape, and Gale groaned.

"All right. You may call it whatever you wish if you'll only do that again."

Chant obliged.

"Oh God," Gale whispered. He turned so that his face was partially pressed against Chant's thigh. The back of his head nestled against the hardness in Chant's breeches, and Gale rather thought that what they were doing right now was far more intimate than anything they might have accomplished with their matching cock-stands. He was truly at a loss to think of a time when he had known more pleasure. What a pathetic thing to admit, and yet it was true. He allowed himself a few breaths to regain his composure, then turned his face outward again. "And where is de Cock now?"

It seemed a credit to Chant's inherent decency that he did not reply *in my breeches* or any such thing.

Chant did not answer at once. He stroked Gale's hair with a feather-light touch, then tugged again at the roots—a gentle, back and forth tug that seemed to convey mild chastisement and a great deal of affection. Neither of which Gale knew what to make of. "If you will not let the Runners handle this, Gale... then what is the next step? To find the captain?"

Gale frowned, thinking again of the captain's pale eyes. Visser's absurd story. He imagined a group of sailors offering up scraps of their scant rations as Flummery bounded among the men. He thought of Elise, alone in the world.

"The next step, Chant," he said slowly, "is to find that damned dog."

CHAPTER 8

*C*hant, like all of England, had read of Christmas Gale's exploits in the news sheets, but he'd never given much thought as to the man's methods. When Gale had said their next step was to find Flummery the dog—a ludicrous detail the news sheets would no doubt adore—Chant had thought that they would return at once to Jacob's Island, possibly laden with a string of sausages to lure the beast out. Instead, he found himself, much to his surprise, accompanying Gale to Bucknall's where Gale folded his long limbs, encased in clothing borrowed from Chant's wardrobe, into a comfortable seat and ordered a late luncheon.

Then, as Chant watched with increasing confusion, Gale emptied his purse and stacked up a pile of silver threepenny pieces. Then he gestured one of the footmen over and murmured something to him. The footman nodded, then vanished. Moments later, a boy entered the room. He was about twelve or thirteen, if Chant had to guess, with a freckled face and otherwise unremarkable features. Gale spoke to him in an undertone and then swept the stack of threepenny bits off the table and into the boy's cupped hands.

"The hall boys here are the most remarkably useful little

fellows," he remarked to Chant. "They are terribly resourceful. By tomorrow, we shall have such a parade of hairy dogs from Jacob's Island that you will hardly believe your eyes." He quirked the corner of his mouth up briefly and then said lazily, "I gave him your address, of course. My mother would be horrified were I to set a parade of boys and dogs upon her."

Chant narrowed his eyes. "Did you not tell me you had rooms of your own in Russell Street?"

"Oh, I'm afraid that slipped my mind for the moment."

"The devil it did." But Chant laughed and enjoyed what he suspected was a flicker of surprise in Gale's eyes at his reaction. Had Gale thought he would be annoyed? For all that Gale had said that he would wait for Chant to be ready, Gale was nothing if not a contradiction. He reeled Chant in with one hand while he pushed him away with the other.

The footman appeared again with drinks. "Lord Soulden is here, my lord."

"Ah!" Gale exclaimed. "Please ask him to join us."

The footman bowed and slipped away.

Soulden. Chant knew the fellow as one of Gale's friends. He was handsome and rich, and said to be quite the fop. He cared more for the state of the buttons on his gloves than he did for the state of the world and all its tangled mysteries, and Chant was curious as to what Gale, who was currently sitting in front of him in a flat cravat with a stain on it—his own, not one of Chant's—could ever have in common with the fellow.

Soulden entered the room shortly thereafter. He was tall and well made, the very pinnacle of manhood, with an easy smile and a wide gaze.

"Christmas!" he exclaimed and sat down at their table. "How are you, my dear fellow?"

"I have told you that if you call me Christmas, I shall call you Pip," Gale said, narrow-eyed and prickly. He waved a hand at Chant. "This is Chant."

Soulden smiled. "Have we met? I'm terrible with names, and I do apologise."

"It is a pleasure," Chant said and shook his hand.

"Chant and I have rather got mixed up in a mess," Gale said. "With a merchant ship's captain called de Cock."

Soulden's expression sharpened suddenly, and he cast a curious glance at Chant. Then he leaned back in his chair and tapped his fingers against the knee of his pantaloons. When he spoke at last, he sounded mildly bored. "Have you?"

Gale sounded just as bored. "What do you know of de Cock?"

"Why, my dear fellow," Soulden said, "I'm *quite* the expert."

"Soulden," Gale drawled.

Soulden's mouth twitched. "Very well. What do I know of de Cock? Very little, I fear, but more than you if you think he's the captain of a merchant ship."

Gale's brow furrowed. "Is he not?"

"He's a privateer, Gale."

Chant reeled back a little in shock.

Soulden continued. "And I have heard whispers."

Gale seemed singularly unsurprised by Soulden's revelation about de Cock. "What kind of whispers?"

"Whispers that perhaps de Cock does not think himself bound to his letter of marque."

"And whose toes might I step on if I take this any further?"

"I'm sure if anyone was in danger of having their toes trodden on, they would most certainly let you know," Soulden said blandly.

"Yes," Gale said. "Thank you, Pip."

Soulden snorted and rose to his feet. "It was a pleasure, as always, Christmas." And then he fixed his smile on his face and strode away.

Chant watched him go. "What was that about?"

"I'm sure it was exactly what you imagine, sir," Gale replied softly.

"And you will tell me no more than that, of course," Chant said, though he felt a flush of warm pleasure not only that Gale thought he was smart enough to make a startling inference about Philip Winthrop, Viscount Soulden, but also that he had not shut Chant out of the cryptic conversation to begin with. If what he suspected about Soulden was true, it was a demonstration of great trust on Gale's part. Chant felt honoured.

"Of course," Gale replied, ducking his head to hide a quick smile.

"You really are the most astonishing fellow," Chant said, and there wasn't even a hint of flattery in the words. It was the simple truth.

Gale sighed and gazed at the bookcases that lined the room.

"Have you read all of them?" Chant asked curiously.

"Yes," Gale said. "I have read nearly everything, I dare say."

"If any other man told me such, I should think he was bragging."

Gale hummed and tapped his long, thin fingers on his knee. "I find bragging to be a singular waste of time and energy."

Of course he did. Chant couldn't help his smile. Gale had to be contrary in every way, didn't he? Even pride was petty to a man with his curious and extraordinary mind.

Presently, the footman brought them spring soup and bread, and Chant fell upon it gratefully. The food at Bucknall's had been one of his main reasons for joining the club; he was hardly a social creature at all nowadays, but to be able to come to a place and be fed hot, hearty food at any time of day or night gave him the impetus to leave the house once in a while.

Gale ate a little of his soup but not his bread, and Chant again studied the thinness of his limbs and the pallor of his skin and did not like the conclusions he drew. His mind was no analytical marvel like Gale's, but even he could see Gale was so deeply in thought he had almost entirely forgotten to eat.

"You are an example of vitalism, you know," he said, knowing that would get Gale's attention.

Gale looked at him, his eyes bright. "Oh?"

"Yes," Chant said. "Your thoughts and consciousness are completely separate from all the other urges of your body." He caught Gale's faint smirk. "By which I mean hunger, of course, not any other appetites."

"Of course," Gale agreed. "So you think Mr. Abernethy should drag me into the Royal College of Surgeons as evidence against Mr. Lawrence's controversial lectures on materialism, do you? Because if you think that would solve the debate, sir, then I am not sure if you have quite grasped the intricacies of it to begin with."

"I am sure I have not," Chant agreed. He shoved the plate of bread closer to Gale's elbow. "Eat."

Gale tore off a piece of bread, ignoring the knife and fork completely. "So, vitalism. Do you think my consciousness is God-given, sir, or are you an atheist? You seemed unsure when last we broached the subject."

"I'm sorry I brought it up now. I suspect I thought I was being clever, but of course I was not. I know very little about materialism and vitalism and whatever it is the Royal College of Surgeons likes to argue about. But I think you are quite unique, Gale, whether it is God or nature that has made you so."

"I cannot decide if you are a flatterer or not."

Chant shrugged. "I find flattery to be a singular waste of time and energy."

That won him a laugh, the sound faint and tinged with surprise. "And yet you are dodging the question, sir. Atheist or no?"

Chant considered that for a moment, his old melancholy colouring his thoughts on the subject as it always did. "I think that I am rather an atheist," he said, "and my unwillingness to admit it comes from the fact that I wish I was not."

The shadow of Gale's smile faded. "Yes," he said. "It would be easier, would it not, to believe in justice delivered and wrongs righted beyond this world?"

"Oh, I am not so high-minded as that, even," Chant said. "And my motives are not as altruistic as yours. I have lost people I loved, and I should like to think of them as peaceful and happy and not just gone. That is all."

Gale held his gaze for a long moment, and then he said, at last, "I think you are not as selfish as you believe, sir."

A warmth filled Chant, and he wasn't sure it was entirely due to the soup. They finished their meal in companionable silence.

Once outside Bucknall's, standing on the pavement, Gale shuffled awkwardly. That calculated boredom he'd displayed in the club seemed to have deserted him. And then he said something entirely surprising: "Would you consider joining my family for dinner, Chant?"

And there was that warmth again, spreading through Chant quick as his own blood. He ought to be careful—he faced a greater danger standing here in front of Gale with all this heat and confusion and *want* inside him than he did hunting down a murderous privateer. Perhaps it was only the alcohol that had made Gale extend the invitation, but Chant was not one to look a gift horse in the mouth. "I would be delighted."

"It will be loud," Gale cautioned him. "I have sisters. At least four, and possibly as many as seven."

"What a treat it will be to meet them."

"You think that now."

Chant grinned. "If I do not enjoy myself this evening, I shall hold you personally responsible and will resent you all my life."

"Well, if that resentment dampens your willingness to accompany me on what is proving to be a rather dangerous investigation, then perhaps I shall pay my sisters in confections to sabotage the evening."

Chant took his arm gently, ignoring the way Gale's expression flashed from surprise to alarm to irritation in a single second. "It is your safety I am most worried about. I realise you do not need or want my assistance. But I promise to keep my presence as insignificant as possible throughout the investigation if you will promise not to make any moves on your own."

Gale stared at him. "I cannot promise that."

"I have nothing to offer to secure your word, except a sincere plea. I... I do not know if my wishes mean anything to you, but I appeal to that decency that you so wish to deny. Please, Gale. Do not endanger your life."

"I may well have to. But I shall not endanger yours along with my own."

"Any attempt to locate lost dogs or sinister captains will be safer with two of us," Chant insisted, gripping Gale's elbow a bit tighter.

Gale continued to hold his gaze, which surprised Chant. The fellow's typical reaction to outbursts of feeling was to turn away, but he didn't, not this time. He seemed to reach some decision, one which softened his expression for a fleeting moment. He pried Chant's hand gently from his elbow. "I will try. That is all I can promise."

"All right." Chant sighed. While Gale's answer was not what he had hoped, he noticed that Gale still held his hand, and it was suddenly quite difficult to recall how to breathe.

Gale ran his thumb over Chant's knuckles, then let go. "I am sorry I cannot offer more."

Chant was not sure what to say. He understood that his unofficial position as Gale's assistant was tenuous. But Gale had said *we*, over and over throughout the day. He had come to Chant's home specifically to discuss the investigation with him. If they were indeed a *we* now, then Chant ought to have some say in how they proceeded. The trouble was, he had little idea what this investigation would require—of himself, of Gale, of the two of them together.

He nodded.

Gale's lips parted slightly, and then there was a small inhale and a furrowing of the man's dark brow. "I will see you for dinner at seven. And while you are there... might you ask Elise if she will accompany us to your home tomorrow to identify that cursed mutt?"

"You could ask her yourself, couldn't you?"

Now Gale did turn away. "I suppose." His gaze flicked back to Chant. "But... couldn't you do it?"

"Are you afraid of a very small child?"

"Not afraid! But she will respond better to you." He paused, and Chant saw him struggle to make his next admission. "I fear saying the wrong thing."

One corner of Chant's mouth curved up, and there was, in his chest, a rather disconcerting mix of tenderness, exasperation, and a sort of pleasant fizz as though he'd just sipped champagne. "I see. Very well, Lord Christmas. That shall be my collateral. I will speak to the very small child for you if you promise to invite me on all errands pertaining to the investigation."

"That is hardly fair."

"Do not be petulant."

"I am not petulant."

"You are a bit petulant."

"I am leaving now."

"And I shall see you soon."

Chant caught the hint of a smile on Gale's angular face. He felt a moment's melancholy, soft and faded by time, as he recalled how he used to draw Reid out of sour moods. A small smile, just like Gale's, had always been the first sign that his efforts were yielding results. Reid would spend another few seconds feigning dourness, and then a laugh would spill out of him, bubbly as a young girl's, and he'd come willingly into Chant's arms. Chant missed the feel of him— the weight of Reid against his chest, the softness of his hair. That voice, always a bit breathy, higher than most men's, but so lovely to listen to.

That memory carried him into another, in which he tried to cheer another man the same way. A man who sat in the same chair, day after day, staring at the same wall. A man who had lost his daughter—the joy and light of his life. Chant was a poor substitute for Jenny, but he'd tried. Tried until he could not try any longer.

His heart pounded. If Gale thought him a good man, he was sorely mistaken.

"Are you quite all right?" Gale asked.

"Yes. Just thinking about... de Cock." It was all Chant could come up with.

Gale's eyebrows lifted, and he nodded. "I assure you, I am too."

Chant snorted. "Will the joke ever grow stale, do you think?"

"Not any time in the near future," Gale assured him. He gave Chant's shoulder a light squeeze, and there went a flame through Chant's core—hotter and more persistent than the warmth he'd felt earlier. "See you tonight, sir."

And then he was gone, his long legs carrying him back toward St. James's Square.

~

*W*hen Gale reached his home, he had to stand outside for a moment to compose himself. The ease he'd come to experience in Chant's presence had fled, and his stomach knotted up. How long had it been since he'd had dinner with his family? For weeks, he'd spent his evenings in Russell Street, or at his salons, or in bed with some moll. He rather felt he should be commended for attending the Harringdon ball with Clarissa, but knowing his mother, that wouldn't count for much.

Upon entering, he had only just had his overcoat taken off him when he was accosted by Anne-Marie.

"Have you found out who murdered Elise's father?"

"It was a drunken fight that got out of hand. Mr. Howe is not considered a man of consequence. Kindly forget the whole thing."

"You always say everyone is of equal consequence."

"No, I always say everyone is equally inconsequential. Human beings are a blight on this planet, but that does not mean that the rich should be served justice while the poor are not. Pay attention, Annalise."

"Anne-Marie."

"That's what I said."

"Will you just *tell* me?"

"Tell you what?"

"If you found the murderer!"

"That area is full of murderers, I'm afraid. It's rather like looking for one murderous needle in a murderous haystack."

She blew a raspberry. Then straightened as though something had just occurred to her. "There's been a letter for you."

"Where is it?" Gale asked at once.

"I shall give it to you if you promise to tell me its contents, should it concern the murder."

"There will be a murder in this very room if you do not tread carefully."

"Ugh! You're horrible."

"I'm told I'm rather a decent fellow, actually."

She snorted. "Who has told you that? They may need their head examined."

"The Honourable Benjamin Chant. He'll be dining with us this evening."

Anne-Marie squealed. "You two are in love!"

"We are mild acquaintances at best, and we tolerate each other just barely." Gale tried not to recall placing his head in Chant's lap. The wretched indignity of experiencing such pleasure over so small a thing as Chant's fingers passing gently through his hair.

"Then why have you invited him?"

"To give you and the others something to gossip about."

"Oh! Oh, this is so exciting."

"I do aim to please."

"Did you get me a pastry?"

Gale sighed, cursing himself inwardly. "No. I forgot. I am sorry, truly."

"It's all right. You were busy investigating a murder."

"I was not!"

"Christmas, stop fighting with your sister." Their mother glided into the drawing room, wearing a gown of pale green with rose lacework crossing the bodice. Her gauzy shawl matched the gown, and its beading caught the lamplight as she moved.

Their mother was tall and slender with large, dark eyes and glossy brown hair that she wore in intricate curls pinned tightly atop her head. Gale didn't think he'd ever seen a woman of her age more beautiful—if a fellow could think that about his own mother without it being indicative of some sort of Oedipal malady. She was also the most imposing figure Gale had ever known. "Anne-Marie, go elsewhere. I need to speak to your brother alone."

It was all Gale could do not to gulp as though he were a young boy once more, and his tutor had just told his mother that he was "rebellious in spirit, if not in action." His mother had enjoyed a good laugh about that, actually—after she had lectured Gale to within an inch of his life about giving the man grief.

Anne-Marie stuck her tongue out at Gale and crossed her eyes, then hurried from the room.

"Well," his mother said as soon as she was gone, "what is this about a dinner guest?"

"I hope you don't mind. I've invited Mr. Benjamin Chant to dine with us."

"Anne-Marie!" his mother suddenly bellowed.

"What?" came Anne-Marie's distant voice.

"Tell Cook we will have an extra guest!" She returned her attention to Gale.

"We have a bell, Mother, so you may speak directly to the servants without shouting."

"Ah, but it feels so good to shout once in a while."

"Far be it from me to criticise the way you run your household."

"Don't be clever."

"I cannot help it."

She held out a small envelope. "A letter arrived for you."

"So Anne-Marie said." He took it from her, intending to open it, though the sender had been rather over-enthusiastic with the sealing wax. "Do tell me it's a document from our solicitor, legally emancipating me from this family."

"We see you so scarcely, I dare say you are already emancipated."

He leaned against the wall near the mantle, sliding the letter into his pocket. It was likely some old fool writing to him about their daughter's nephew's haunted sheep farm, but just in case it was Fernside with news of Visser, he ought to read it as soon as his mother finished with him. "I went to the Harringdons' last night, did I not?"

"I don't know. I wasn't there. I hate balls."

"Well, I was there, protecting my sisters' virtues the whole night."

"In that case, let me see if I might have a statue of you commissioned to stand in our courtyard titled *Loyalty Itself*."

"You're too kind."

"Mr. Benjamin Chant, you say?"

"Yes."

His mother's eyes narrowed. "Clarissa said you danced with him last night."

"I did."

His mother took a seat on a baroque chair that Gale imagined even Louis XIV himself would have thought gauche. The woman successfully walked the fine line between high-class and gaudy, but her taste in decor fell firmly into the latter category. "Clarissa has had a proposal."

"Really?" Gale was genuinely startled. "From whom?"

"Lady Alice Faber."

"Good Lord. That family is money all over."

His mother sighed. "Yes. Clarissa wishes to think on it. She likes Lady Alice well enough, but marriage is a big decision."

"Of course."

"Anne-Marie was paid considerable attention last night as well."

"That's... good?" Gale ventured. In truth, he did not much like the idea of anyone paying his sisters attention. He supposed they all had to marry eventually, and at least marriage would get them out of his hair, but it put him off-kilter to picture them all grown up and moved away.

"Society has turned its eye upon our family in a way it has not before. And that is thanks to you."

Gale was not sure whether it was a compliment or an accusation. Coming from his mother, it could be either.

"Seven children," she said.

"Yes," he agreed, unsure where this was going.

"That is a lot of children. And children are expensive."

"Rather shortsighted on your part, wasn't it?"

"I blame your father."

"Always a safe bet."

His mother's lips twitched. "It would behoove us to get the girls married as quickly as possible. And with the attention you have garnered, we might be well on our way. Should Clarissa accept Lady Alice's proposal, or any other in the next few weeks, she'll be wed at nineteen. Anne-Marie is now turning heads at eighteen. If the Lord is merciful, they'll both be matched by the end of the Season."

"He is not merciful. Nor is He real."

"Christmas Gale, don't you dare bring your atheism into this house."

"On close personal terms with God, are you? Name literally anyone from the Bible, Mother."

"Goliath. Oh, we should have had you thrashed regularly when you were young. But you were so appealing in a bony, Gothic-orphan sort of way."

"I shall consider myself fortunate that my bleak, traumatised countenance called forth some trickle of pity from the stone of your heart."

His mother smiled fondly. "I did love how mournful and haunted you seemed. As though you had witnessed far more of the world before you were out of leading strings than I had in my whole life. Now that I am older, I see that men like to appear world-weary, as though they are shouldering a great burden by laying claim to all the power they have placed at their own fingertips. When they are, in fact, no more worthy of that power than a group of chimpanzees would be. Still, the brooding is a nice effect."

"Flatter me any further, Mother, and I shall start to get an inflated impression of myself."

"No, my flattery stops here. But speaking of bony, traumatised orphans…"

"Ah, yes. How is the one I left in your care?"

His mother grew serious. "She wept all morning."

"Well, it is understandable that she—"

"She kept asking when you would return."

"*Me?*"

"Oh, your sisters eventually got her involved in some games, and then she was quite content. But she missed you."

"Well, I was busy… you know…"

"Trying to determine who killed her father? Did you find anything of interest?"

"I discovered much, but I cannot say anything for certain at the moment."

His mother nodded.

"I do not wish to take her to the parish just yet." Gale tried for brusqueness but did not quite succeed.

"No," his mother agreed.

A silence.

"I think she would like to speak to you."

Gale swallowed hard. "I must get ready for supper."

"We've put her in the blue bedroom. With Eugenie."

"Well, I will… I will try to speak with her." It was an impossibly daunting prospect. He would rather wait for Chant to do the speaking for him.

"All right, Christmas. I look forward to meeting your friend."

"Friend?" Gale was momentarily confused.

"Mr. Benjamin Chant."

"Right. Yes, of course."

She flashed him a knowing smile. "It's been such a long time since you've invited anyone to dinner."

"I had Darling here not two weeks ago."

"Oh, Christmas. Darling isn't a *friend*. You know exactly what I mean."

"I'm not sure I do." And yet, he did.

"It's been a long time since you've joined us for dinner."

That was most certainly an accusation. "I have been busy."

"You have been over-interested in yourself."

That ought to be something he wore as a badge of pride. But the thought of disappointing his mother was somehow every bit as mortifying now as it had been when he was a boy. "I get quite nervous in... company." He did not know why he finally felt able to admit this to her after twenty-odd years. It was not as if she didn't know of his anxieties—she could read every shift in his expression the same way he read the face of a suspect under interrogation. But he had never before said the words out loud. If forced to guess, he would say Chant was responsible for this unpremeditated confession. Chant, who did not consider Gale's aversion to socialising a horrible flaw in his character.

"We are your family."

"I know. I'm sorry."

"Christmas. Look at me. I feel as though I have not made a proper study of you in days."

He glanced up, meeting his mother's gaze with a shrug that was equal parts guilt and apology. How far he now felt from the Lord Christmas Gale who had sat in Bucknall's not two hours earlier, casually orchestrating a search party for a dog as though the answer to the entire matter was only a stack of threepenny pieces away. His mother saw through all of it. Not just the carefully culti-vated misanthropy and the chronic sarcasm, but the way he used the solving of outward problems as a shield against having to know anyone too deeply. Finding a missing heirloom couldn't put a broken family back together. Uncovering an imposter did not get at the heart of why people lied about who they were. He knew that. It was just so much easier to focus on missing heirlooms than on the missing pieces of people's hearts.

His mother assessed him for another moment. "You are too thin."

"You've been saying that since I was five years old."

"And it's always true. Get something for yourself when you go to buy pastries for your sisters."

"I do."

She glared at him sceptically. Then softened. Her eyes, which normally glinted like the edges of blades, sparked instead with tenderness. "It was a good thing, what you did for Hartwell."

He lifted his brows. His mother could change subjects as the wind changed directions, trusting always that he would follow. And, if he were honest with himself, he usually did. "Hartwell? What does he have to do with anything?"

"Do not feign ignorance with me. You worked yourself to the bone to expose that repugnant Balfour for what he was so Hartwell and the Warrington boy could marry."

"I exposed nothing. Lord Balfour was overtaken by a sudden desire to travel." A lie through and through, but he'd repeat that well-rehearsed line all the way to his grave.

Her mouth twisted wryly to one side. "What sort of fool do you take me for?"

"I do not take you for a fool. But if I uncovered anything damning about Balfour, I assure you it was to challenge myself, not to aid Hartwell in marrying that dullard."

"Very well. I will let the subject drop. I only want to say, my dear, that although I do not know what is between you and Mr. Benjamin Chant, if he is kind to you... would you consider accepting it?"

"Accepting it? What on earth do you mean?"

"Do not try to convince him that what he sees in you is not the truth. Allow yourself a bit of the happiness you wanted for Hartwell."

How did she *know*? "Chant and I are acquaintances, that is all. I don't imagine he has spent much time reflecting on my character."

Lies, lies, lies. He told them so casually these days. Chant did think him decent. Had calmed him at the Harringdon ball, had forgiven him his rudeness this afternoon and last night. Gale deserved none of that kindness. He would do well to distance himself from it and put it down to Chant's own foolishness. For if he let himself believe the good things Chant thought about him, then would he not be obligated to behave accordingly? That seemed an awfully difficult task.

His mother said nothing, simply studied him, drawing her own private conclusions.

"I cannot be who you wish me to be," he said sharply. "I think I've made that quite clear over the course of many years."

She stood and came toward him. He took a step back, startled. She put her arms out slightly from her sides, her expression questioning. "Would it be all right?"

He swallowed hard on a rush of gratitude. She had understood from his earliest years that his aversion to being touched was not obstinacy or temper, but rather as much a part of him as his long legs or brown eyes. And she had always asked permission. "Not right now," he said softly. "I'm sorry." Much as he cared for her, an embrace from anyone at this moment would give him the sensation of his skin crawling.

"I've told you, you must never apologise for saying no."

He nodded, looking at the mantle rather than at her. He slowly put out his hand until she took it, and he squeezed gently. That was the best he could do.

She squeezed back, then murmured something about needing to make sure the girls were presentable. She left, and he sagged against the wall. Why should he now feel as though an embrace would scrape his nerves raw? Had Chant not touched him this afternoon without Gale's skin crawling in the least? What small, vulnerable hollow had Benjamin Chant exposed that left Gale feeling as though everyone could suddenly see inside him, and that the best defence against this exposure would be to barricade himself in his room and never come out again?

His head throbbed thinking about Chant, so he decided to trade one headache for another, and go dress for a dinner that was sure to render itself indistinguishable from a circus.

CHAPTER 9

Chant arrived at Gale's house just before seven. He was immediately ushered inside to meet his hostess for the evening, Lady Gale, in a bright, well-appointed sitting room. Lady Gale rose to meet him. She was nearly as tall as her son and just as imposing, and Chant thought within seconds of taking her hand that her son's prodigious intellect was no accident at all because the same light shone in Lady Gale's eyes, though perhaps not quite as sharply. But then who was the intellectual equal to Christmas Gale? Chant doubted such a person existed.

"How nice of you to join us," Lady Gale said. "And how unexpected for Christmas to bring home a friend!"

As though he and Gale were scab-kneed tousle-headed boys who'd met playing in the park.

"It's a pleasure to be here, Lady Gale."

"It's a sign of the apocalypse is what it is," a young lady announced, sweeping into the room in a whirl of ribbons and curls and a cloud of sweet perfume. "Christmas made a friend!"

"Oh, Clarissa," Lady Gale said, but her tone was equal parts amused and exasperated, and Chant knew immediately that this was not the sort of household where anyone stood much on formality or on any polite foundation of manners at all. Of course a spirit like Gale's could never have been formed except by an extraordinary upbringing, and he wondered if all the Gales, like their name, were prone to wildness.

"Lord Gale is still away," Lady Gale said, waving her hand as though *away* might encompass anything from here to the Cape of Good Hope. "He and Edward have been travelling on the Continent. It is a most inopportune time for travel, but when one is at the beck and call of the crown, what can one do?" Her eyes sparkled, and Chant had no doubt that not a single person in their entire extraordinary family was under anyone's beck and call, nor had ever been.

Lord Christmas Gale might have been a favourite of the news sheets, but his father and brother were just as famous. Richard Gale, Marquess of Shorsbury, had chaired numerous committees for the House of Lords, and Edward Gale, Christmas's older brother, was a hero of Waterloo. Whatever they were doing on the Continent, Chant was sure it was not a pleasure trip.

"This is Clarissa," Lady Gale said. "Clarissa, Mr. Chant."

Chant bowed.

Another girl poked her head around the corner of the sitting room. This one was younger. "Is this Christmas's friend?"

"This is Mr. Chant, yes," Lady Gale said, and clapped her hands together. "Come, we shall all go to the dining room. I haven't the patience to introduce everyone piecemeal. Eugenie, go and find your brother and drag him out of whichever book he's lost himself in. Tell him Mr. Chant is here, and if he doesn't show his face immediately, it will be too late, and we will have poisoned Mr. Chant against him for all time by sharing all his embarrassing boyhood stories."

The younger girl laughed and hurried away.

Lady Gale hooked her arm through Chant's and led him down the hall and into the dining room. "You must think us terribly ill-mannered, I am sure."

"No," Chant replied honestly. "Having met your son, Lady Gale, should I have expected a conventional family?"

Lady Gale laughed. "Oh, one should expect nothing when it comes to Christmas, and I suppose that includes the rest of us as well."

They were joined in the dining room by yet another two sisters and little Elise.

"Mr. Benjamin!" Elise exclaimed. "Christmas said you were coming! Did you find Flummery yet?"

She was wearing a dress that seemed a little too large for her skinny frame, but it was clean. As were her cheeks, which had been scrubbed and possibly rouged by the same enthusiastic but unpractised hand that had also curled her hair.

"Not yet, I am afraid, Elise," he said. "But we have the best people looking."

He looked up to see Gale standing in the doorway with a pinched, narrow expression on his pinched, narrow face. His auburn hair was in disarray, and his cravat was crooked, the pin drooping sadly from the layers of muslin like a wilting flower. There was a blot of what appeared to be ink on the front of his waistcoat. Chant felt a smile spreading across his face at the same time warmth filled his chest. It had been a long time since a man had captivated him in the way Christmas Gale did.

"You're here," Gale said in a flat, disinterested tone that Chant barely believed.

"I'm here," he agreed. "You invited me."

Gale gazed right through him as his sisters tittered.

"Christmas never brings friends to dinner!" one of the girls exclaimed.

"Christmas doesn't have friends," said another.

"Oh, stop," Clarissa told her sisters. "He brought Mr. Darling to dinner, remember? Such a handsome man."

Chant ignored the sudden sting of that, and turned his attention back to Elise. "Tomorrow, Elise, I would like you to visit my house.

Some boys will be bringing by some dogs, and it is my dearest hope that one of those dogs is Flummery, and that we can restore him to you."

Elise gasped sharply, her eyes wide. "Thank you, Mr. Benjamin!"

"It was Lord Christmas's idea," Chant said, only to realise his mistake when Elise turned and flung herself against Gale like a tiny whirlwind, gripping him tightly. Gale looked highly uncomfortable to have a child clinging to him, but he tentatively patted Elise a few times on the head as he attempted to extricate himself. And Chant found himself for a moment ridiculously jealous of a small girl.

"Come now, Elise," Lady Gale said, slapping her hands together sharply. "It is time to eat. You can attempt to scale Christmas again later."

The sisters tugged Elise off Gale and escorted her to the table.

There were, as Gale had said earlier, a lot of sisters. Five, by Chant's count, but they were so loud and lively that, like a cage of fast, fluttering birds, it was quite difficult to be certain of their number at a quick glance. Chant wondered if Gale was mordant and biting simply because his sisters were so sweet and cheerful, and he felt the need to distinguish himself from them in some way. Or perhaps he would have been just as caustic had he been an only child.

Dinner was served shortly after they had taken their seats. A pair of footmen brought in trays of mutton, roast beef, and vegetables and a tureen of white soup. Chant, sitting with Lady Gale on one side and Gale on the other, at first listened to the sisters chatter about the *ton*, and who was wearing what, or invited where, or courting whom, but he gave up attempting to follow along when it appeared the topic of greatest interest this season, apart from Lord Hartwell's hastily arranged marriage, was which young gentleman wore the most stunning hats—Mr. Morgan Notley or Mr. Loftus Rivingdon.

"Tiresome, isn't it?" Gale sighed over his roast beef.

Chant considered for a moment. "I think perhaps I am a little out of practise when it comes to Society."

That won him a quirk of the mouth too brief to be called an actual smile. "And I think perhaps I never learned."

"Oh, it was not for lack of trying, darling," Lady Gale said fondly, and leaned over and rested her hand on Gale's for a moment. "On our part, at least. We did try to beat some manners into you, but it never took."

Gale snorted. "You never raised a hand to me, Mother."

Her eyes sparkled. "Perhaps that was where we went wrong."

"Earlier today she said I looked too bony and pitiful as a child to thrash." Gale raised his eyebrows.

"You were," Lady Gale said. "But you could still outrun or outwit all your tutors. I can still recall seeing that fellow—what was his name? Marsh! Yes, your father and I watched for hours as Marsh waited for you underneath the oak tree, slapping a switch in his hand, but you outlasted him, remember? Eventually he fell asleep, and you climbed down past him and crept back inside. You slept in the attic for days to avoid him until he finally gave up and resigned his post." She took a sip of wine. "That poor man. I think you quite destroyed his spirit."

"One can only hope," Gale said dryly, but Chant caught something in his eyes—some flicker of an old bit of uncertainty or sadness that was there and then gone.

Chant forced a smile despite the ache in his chest. The Gales were an eccentric family, but they were close. There was a fierce protectiveness in Lady Gale that was impossible to miss, even though she wore a carefully constructed mask of carelessness. Chant could not be sure whether he had ever had this closeness with his own family. When he thought of Jenny, feeling preceded memory. He did not even see her face in his mind's eye; there was only warmth, settling over him like the rays of the sun on a summer afternoon. He could close his eyes and bask in that warmth, but only for a moment—then a cloud passed over, and a chill hit his skin. The sensation that followed was of an emptiness so vast he could no longer be sure he was anchored to the earth.

And when he thought of his father... a wrenching despair. The sense of reaching for someone in a dream, only to find the person's face quite changed; they were now someone else altogether.

He was snapped back into the present by a crack of laughter—from Gale, of all people. Chant did not know what had been said to make him laugh so, but Gale was now grinning down at his plate, shaking his head. And Lady Gale wore a smirk as she took another sip of wine, suggesting she had been the source of her son's amusement.

"If Elise's dog is found," said one of the younger sisters—Eugenie, Chant was fairly sure— "can he come and stay with us?"

"If he does, I shall move out," Lady Gale replied. Then, seeming to remember that Elise was present, she gave the girl a sympathetic glance. "Though I'm sure he's lovely. If one enjoys dogs."

"Mama! You like Lady Notley's dog!"

"*Like* is such a strong word. I find it amusing that it can be carried in a reticule is all."

Elise seemed unfazed by her hostess's slight to Flummery. "You said the boys would bring *some* dogs," she said to Chant. "What happens with all the dogs that ain't Flum?"

"Well..." Chant glanced at Gale, who lifted his dark brows as if in reminder that communicating with small children was strictly Chant's purview. "They shall each be given a butcher's bone and taken back to where they were found."

Elise eyed him sceptically. "What if where they was found was somewhere cold? Or full of mean people?"

"Mr. Benjamin is a very kind man," Gale said smoothly, reaching for another roll. "I'm sure he would never turn one of God's creatures out in the cold."

"So you'll keep them all at your house?" Elise asked.

"I..." Chant could suddenly see where a sound thrashing might once have done Lord Christmas Gale some good. It was clearly too late now.

"Can we go and visit them?" cried Anne-Marie.

"Every day?" added Cordelia.

"Girls," Lady Gale warned, though she was fighting another smile.

They were silent for all of ten seconds before Anne-Marie blurted, "Mr. Chant, is it true you were to marry Mr. Reid before he disappeared to France?"

It was as though Chant had been thumped in the gut.

"Anne-Marie!" Lady Gale's tone was sharp this time, and she turned to Chant, her expression aghast for a moment before it settled back into its usual coolness. "Please excuse my daughter."

"I only wanted to know!" the girl protested. "It seems a very romantic and tragic story."

"I will turn your life into a tragic story if you do not shut up," Gale snapped, all amusement gone from his face. "Really, Anne-Marie, have you no shame?"

Anne-Marie mumbled an apology and returned to her dinner.

"Why did he disappear to France?" Eugenie piped up.

Lady Gale put her fork down loudly. "That is *enough*. We may not stand on ceremony in this house, but I still expect my children to show common courtesy to our guests."

"It's quite all right," Chant said, hearing the thinness of his own voice. He looked at Anne-Marie, who was still staring, red-faced, at her plate. "Mr. Reid and I were not well suited for each other, in the end. I am not sure why he left the country, as he said nothing to me of his plan to do so. I suppose he did what he thought best for himself."

"I'm sorry," Anne-Marie said softly, and Chant at first thought she was apologising again for bringing up the subject. But then she went on. "I wish you knew where he was, so you could at least write to him and say goodbye."

"Or tell him what a scoundrel he is," Clarissa said. "If he was a scoundrel."

"Enough," Lady Gale repeated, a thread of steel in her voice. "Mr. Chant, I do apologise."

"It's quite all right," Chant said again, his heart thumping so loudly he could barely hear himself speak. He wasn't certain if he'd whispered his response or shouted it. Even now, years later, he still felt the sting of Reid's... betrayal? He didn't know if he could call it that or not. He didn't know *what* to call it. He supposed that people fell out of love as often as they fell into it, and perhaps he might have come to terms with that had Reid spoken to him. But the silence... the silence still felt black and cold around his heart.

"It's not." Gale's voice was low. "I violated Mr. Chant's privacy with a similar line of inquiry this afternoon. Anyone would be hard pressed to be as rude as I was. See to it that none of you rises to the challenge." He looked at each of his sisters in turn.

Elise stared around the table, her lips parted and her spoon held loosely in her hand. Then she went back to shovelling food into her small mouth.

Chant wished desperately to change the subject, and so he did, to the progression of Cordelia's pianoforte lessons, which had been mentioned earlier. The conversation never quite reached its previous levels of liveliness, but the pain of memory soon faded, and Chant thought again that this was the sort of family he'd longed for as a boy—large, loud, teasing each other endlessly. How fiercely he had loved Jenny and her strangeness—though it was the sort of strangeness that well-bred parents attempted to keep out of the public eye. Jenny had languished in their small, quiet childhood home, her every outing carefully monitored lest she embarrass herself, and, by extension, the family. Their father had attempted to make up for her near-captivity by doting on her. And when she died, their quiet house became a silent one—the old mad earl dwindling in both body and spirit until he was no more substantial than a ghost, his wife disappearing one day as Reid had done, unable, Chant thought, to bear the silence.

Chant had discovered, at seventeen, that nothing could bring ghosts back to the realm of the living. Not battering walls nor battering other people at Gentleman Jackson's. Not shouting, and not being silent and agreeable to a fault. So he'd learned to care for the shell of his father, chattering softly and good-naturedly about mundane things without the anticipation of a response. And he'd learned to tend to his sister's memory like a garden, raking over the images of her bizarre outbursts and terrifying fugues, cultivating his recollections of the two of them chasing each other about the yard as children, playing games of chess in the drawing room, their frowning concentration growing so intense that eventually one of them broke and snickered, and then they both dissolved into laughter. And he planted recollections of a life that never was— birthdays they would have celebrated, operas they would have attended, each of them crying at the other's wedding...

He finished his pudding, declaring that he couldn't recall when he'd had so enjoyable an evening.

"You flatter us," Lady Gale said with a tight smile.

"Not at all. I should return the favour of a dinner invitation if I had room enough at my table for all of you."

Once he'd made his goodbyes and assured Elise once more that even the dogs who were not Flum would be treated as guests of honour in his home tomorrow, Gale volunteered to walk him out. They lingered outside the Gale home, Chant quite suddenly wishing he did not have to leave.

"They are appalling," Gale said tersely. "As am I, I know, but it is perhaps worse to be set upon by all of them at once."

"I was not set upon. They were merely curious."

"You don't have to do that, you know."

"Do what?"

"I cannot believe I'm saying this, as I normally think of sentiments as disgusting things, rather like garden slugs that I should like to pour salt on and watch burn away. But..." Here he glanced at Chant in the darkness. "You don't need to pretend the world is some unending, amusing diversion, and every hurt in it is to be regarded with a bit of wry head shaking. It is all right to be angry—with my sisters, with me, with Mr. Reid. I have seen you angry. I have seen you angry with me. You are a man who feels what he feels with good reason. I shall not think less of you for any expression of those feelings."

Chant stood very still. A memory of his fist making contact with the wall of his bedroom. Of pressing abraded knuckles to his lips and sucking at the bleeding spots, hoping that this time his father would rise from his chair, would thunder his name and ask him what the hell he was doing. No sound but the pulse of blood in his head.

He shook it off, and let Gale's words sink into him. Yes, Gale had said that sentiments were like slugs that should be burned to nothing. But the part after that had really been quite kind for Lord Christmas Gale.

"I also think," Gale hurried on, "if you'll permit one more reference to a subject that I promise shall be forever more off-limits, that Reid was a fool to leave you. He may have had good qualities—in fact, I'm sure he did, for you are too intelligent to have fallen in love with somebody who had nothing to recommend him—but in this particular regard, he sounds an absolute cod's head."

Chant did not know what to say. Gale shifted his weight beside him.

"I have spoken out of turn again," Gale said at last.

"No. No, I appreciate all you've said. Just..." He sighed. "I do wish to know how he is. Reid. I know he is living the life he longed for, and that life does not include me. I must learn to let him go."

"Ah." Gale said nothing more.

"And I shall," Chant assured him quickly—though he was not certain Gale sought such an assurance. "I already have. Mostly."

"I am sorry my family and I have made it more difficult for you to move forward."

"You have not." They were standing so close that Chant might have moved his arm under some innocent pretence and brushed his hand against Gale's. The mere thought of it produced a shiver. "I suppose I must return to Mayfair and make my home ready to host a pack of dogs."

"I imagine dogs are not picky houseguests."

"No, but I promised a butcher's bone for each, didn't I?"

"You did." There was amusement in Gale's tone. "Or rather, I did. On your behalf."

Chant gazed at him with a fondness that was in danger of turning into something wickeder if he looked into those dark eyes much longer. "Thank you for having me tonight. Despite what you may think, I did sincerely enjoy myself."

"It was good of you to come." Without much light to see Gale's face by, the man's voice took on a rather pleasing array of notes all at once—it was soft and deep with just the slightest rasp, and the formality that Gale had perhaps intended was undercut by an undeniable sincerity.

Chant could imagine that voice saying other, filthier things. Could imagine Gale's tone losing any trace of formality as Chant slid his hand down the front of the man's breeches. Oh, Gale's voice would become ragged then, capable of nothing but pleas and encouragements as Chant tumbled him into bed...

He ought to have taken Gale up on the offer when he'd had the chance. What if Gale did not offer again?

"Chant?" Gale inquired. "Dogs? Butcher's bones?"

"Right," Chant said, still hesitating. *May I kiss you* was on his tongue. But how ludicrous a notion. Dark as it was, they were still on a public street, and perhaps Gale had changed his mind about wanting anything of a physical nature from Chant, and perhaps...

Good Lord, Chant realised suddenly. If anything were to happen to this man, he would not be able to bear it. If Gale disappeared without a word. If he were harmed or killed in the pursuit of a murderer. If he let his disgust for humanity drive him to the bottle and slowly drank himself to death over many years... It didn't matter what sort of harm was done, or how far in the future it happened, Chant simply couldn't bear the idea of it. He had a sudden sensation of dread deep in his gut, a fear that if he left now, the world might wield one of its many terrible weapons against Gale in the night, and Chant would never see him again.

A childish fear, and yet he could not seem to break its grip.

He had no right to feel this strongly about a man he'd only just met, especially when he could not be certain of Gale's feelings toward him.

He reached to put a hand on the man's shoulder, for that seemed a familiar enough gesture now to both of them. Gale jerked back as though Chant's palm were a red-hot poker.

"I'm sorry," Chant said, startled by the intensity of Gale's reaction.

Gale cleared his throat. "I am tired. I think I shall retire early. Goodnight, Chant." He turned to go back into the house, leaving Chant feeling as though the whole golden flame of the evening had been blown out like a candle.

CHAPTER 10

*W*hen had Gale's life become such an absurdity? He shook his head as he stared at Chant's sitting room, which was currently occupied by himself, Mr. Benjamin Chant, two grubby, spindly boys, young Elise in another oversized dress, and six panting dogs.

To be fair, Chant was perhaps the one who should consider his life an absurdity just now, and yet the man looked positively delighted.

Elise was kneeling on the floor, attempting to pat all the dogs at once. None of them were Flummery, but one of the boys had promised that a third boy was on his way with yet another dog captured early this morning, and so Elise had not yet lost her optimism. Gale tugged his coat straight. He'd woken later than he'd intended, after a troubled night spent dreaming in fragments about murderers, dogs, and hands grabbing at him. He'd been unable to stand the thought of even his valet's impersonal touch, and so he'd dressed himself, which he'd realised as he'd strode toward Mayfair —Elise in tow—had meant he'd pulled on the same coat from yesterday afternoon. On the way, he'd stopped at a stationer's to scrawl off a note for one of the dog wranglers to give to Soulden.

This had prompted a series of questions from Elise, most of which he'd successfully ignored.

Between one thing and another, he and Elise had arrived at Chant's home to find it already full of dogs and urchins. He cleared his throat. "I said hairy, boys—and large. This one looks like a squirrel who's been pecked half to death by rooks." He nodded at a small, crooked-lipped dog who might have been hairy at some point in his miserable life, but now had hideous bald patches covering most of his body. This deterred Elise not the slightest from kissing his pathetic head and assuring him he was the finest dog in the world, excepting Flum.

"Sorry," the boys said in unison. One continued, "We was just bein' thorough."

"That's right," said the second. "Maybe he were hairy before but lost all his hair yesterday."

Gale was glad that Chant and Elise both seemed magnets for these beasts, for their ready affection kept the animals away from Gale. He looked for an opportunity to slip his note to one of the boys. He didn't want to do it while Chant was watching, in case Chant had as many questions about the intended recipient as Elise. The request he was making of Soulden might not yield any results, but Gale had decided it was worth a try.

A tall dog with some of the Afghan variety in it—long silky hair and a curling, whip-like tail—ambled over to Chant and put its head in his lap, gazing up at him with soulful eyes. Chant murmured to it in a way that made Gale's stomach tighten with an unexpected bolt of... envy? Surely not. He was not jealous of a dog.

Chant had been a bit frosty upon Gale's arrival, which Gale supposed he deserved after his terse parting from Chant last night. But were his actions not justified? Chant had stood on the Gale doorstep for rather a long time, looking like a baffled spectre, and then his hand had come out of nowhere in the dark, and Gale had neither the inclination nor obligation to explain to Chant that a grown man of five-and-twenty, who uncovered dastardly crimes as a hobby, was at times inexplicably terrified by the sensation of physical contact with another human being. That this terror could come on suddenly and without warning, even mere hours after he'd lain his head in Chant's lap and fantasised about them swiving.

The crow-pecked dog slunk over to Gale, who sat as far back in his chair as possible, hoping the creature would go away. He heard Chant's soft, amused snort from the sofa. "You might rub behind his ears, Lord Christmas. He's quite sweet."

"I would rather not," Gale said brusquely. Chant gave him a small smile, more in the eyes than about the mouth. It seemed to hold secret knowledge of Gale, and that realisation made Gale's stomach all the tighter. So Chant was not angry with him, then? Gale supposed that was good. Not that he cared either way what went on in Chant's head. Or rather, he did, just not to any notable extent.

Well, no, he'd cared last night that Chant might have been hurt by the conversation about Reid. But that was...

And he'd cared enough to pen his message to Soulden this morning, which, while Chant was busy gazing into the Afghan's eyes as though the creature were a treasured lover, Gale handed to the nearest boy with a whispered instruction. The boy nodded in response.

As Gale slipped his hand back into the pocket from which he'd withdrawn the note, he came upon another square of paper. Great Scott, yes, the letter his mother had given him last evening. He'd forgotten he'd put it in his coat before changing for dinner. He was irrationally angry with himself and now irrationally angry with Chant, for it had been Chant who'd distracted him from reading the note yesterday. First his mother's talk of Chant, then Chant's presence...

It really did not suit him to have a partner in this investigation. Truly, Chant's involvement dulled his mind and made him sloppy. He tore the seal from the note and unfolded it.

Damnation!

It could not be. But it was, and if Gale had seen this news last night, he would fucking well have done something about it.

Instead he'd spent the evening with his cursed family, gazing moonily at Chant from across the table like a young boy dangling after a schoolyard playmate.

A thousand curses. He stumbled around the tangle of dogs to the door.

"Where are you going?" Chant asked. "Gale?"

"I must go," Gale said tightly. "Stay here with Elise and see if the last dog is Flum."

"But where—"

Gale had his greatcoat and was out the door before Chant could finish the question.

He reached Rotherhithe in what had to be record time, and was out of the hack before the vehicle had fully stopped. The smell of the dockyard assaulted him, but he ignored it and made his way to Fernside's townhouse. He knocked rather harder than was necessary.

Fernside answered at once, stepped back to let him in, and then closed the door quickly behind him. "I know you'll be wanting my hide for this, but truly, I had my assistant watching over him day and night. Here's the fellow now if you wish to speak to him. Fitzgibbon, this is Lord Christmas Gale. You'll have heard of him. Gale, this is Fitz, my assistant."

Fitzgibbon—Fitz—was a short, thin fellow with very short dark hair, whose body seemed to possess the same boneless, drape-able quality as a cat's. He rubbed Gale the wrong way at once, though Gale could not say why. "Neither one of us heard Mr. Visser leave the house. It seems almost impossible that he could have done so without our hearing. It happened in broad daylight."

Gale turned to the assistant. "So what is it? You fell asleep at your post? No, not asleep. There's a stain on your shirt cuff—gravy, by the look of it. You got up to get something to eat. And in your absence, your patient managed to slip away."

Fitz glanced at his cuff, frowning. "No, sir. This stain is blood from helping Mr. Fernside with the patient. And anyway, it happened yesterday afternoon—the disappearance, I mean. I've changed my shirt since then."

Gale could have struck himself upside the head. What a fool he was making of himself. Damn Chant! The man had addled Gale's brain to such an extent that he could not even tell blood from gravy, nor could he keep track of a simple sequence of events. It was a good thing Gale intended to cut Chant out of this investigation just as soon as he was done here. "Yes, of course," he said as smoothly as he could manage. "I regret that there was a delay in my receiving your news. I only got the note this morning and arrived as soon as I could. I'm afraid I'm a bit... disoriented."

Fitz went on. "I must have fallen asleep, Lord Christmas. Though I do not recall feeling tired. As far as I can recall, I blinked, and the fellow was gone."

"Well, you must have done more than blink," Gale said shortly. "What time did you wake?"

"It was half five. Mr. Fernside had been working in the cellar, and I figured he must have taken the patient downstairs with him for some reason. But I found him down there alone. I'm a light sleeper. I cannot fathom how the patient could have got out of bed without waking me. With his injury, he would not have been graceful in his movements, and it would have been difficult to keep quiet about the pain."

"Please do not insult my intelligence by making out that the real mystery here is how he could have slipped past you. You fell asleep on the job, plain and simple, and in doing so you have lost me my best chance of catching a murderer."

Fernside stepped closer to his assistant, looking a bit protective. "There is little to be done now except to figure out where the fellow has gone. Or been taken."

Gale pressed the tip of his tongue to the point of one tooth. "You think he may have been kidnapped?"

"It seems possible from what you have told me of the situation."

"So your light sleeper here"— Gale gestured to Fitz—"would have had to sleep through an unfashionably tall captain breaking into your house in daylight, stealing your injured patient who struggles to walk on his own, and exiting the house?"

Fernside's jaw grew tight. "I told you, Gale, I do not know how it happened. I should have heard footsteps above me while I was working. But I myself fell into a trance for part of the afternoon, and recall little of how I passed the hours."

Gale forced himself to look about the room. Once again, he could not *think*! He closed his eyes, and he saw a flash of gold hair. The pale skin of Chant's cheek with its natural flush. He opened his eyes, half expecting to find himself in Chant's humble home, not in Fernside's practise.

There were blood stains on the sheets of Visser's cot. *Or were they gravy stains* he thought sarcastically. The covers were thrown back, but not twisted so violently as to make Gale suspect a struggle. No blood on the floor that he could see. Nothing knocked over. He went to examine the front door. Neither door nor lock appeared damaged.

He wondered briefly about the surgeon and his assistant. He knew Fernside from a few odd nights spent looking at corpses together and from gossip. Hardly well enough to know what lay in the man's heart. Perhaps the fellow had sold Visser out to de Cock. Though Fitzgibbon seemed the more likely culprit for that sort of betrayal. Looking at the fellow, Gale should have liked to draw from him an admission that it was his own folly that had lost them Visser. None of this *but it couldn't have happened that way* when it clearly had happened that way. Or perhaps Fernside had seen in Visser an opportunity—had slipped him something to ease his passing and taken him to his cellar for study.

Fitz suddenly turned quite pale under Gale's gaze. His body trembled slightly, his throat worked, and he whirled, swinging his head desperately back and forth for a couple of seconds, and then vomited into the basin where Fernside cleaned his tools.

Fernside and Gale both stared. Fitz turned back to them, shame-faced, the back of his wrist pressed to his lips. "I am sorry," he murmured. "I don't know what has come over me."

"A guilty conscience, perhaps," Gale said with icy pleasantness. He caught a strange smell in the air, something mixed with the acrid stench of bodily expulsion. Gale walked over to the basin and studied Fitz's vomit dispassionately. He sniffed.

"Opium," he said, almost to himself.

"Opium," the surgeon repeated.

"Did you give Visser laudanum?" Gale asked.

"I did."

Gale looked at Fitz, who had regained some of his colour. Though he still appeared shaken. "Do you make a habit of sneaking a few drops yourself?"

"I would never, sir!" the assistant said sharply. Gale well knew the difference between genuine outrage at a false accusation, and outrage that was just a bit too effusive to be real. This was the former.

"I trust Fitz with my life," Fernside said.

"My apologies," Gale assured them both. He had just needed to see how Fitz would react. To Fernside, he said, "Did you have any visitors yesterday?"

"A fellow named Kemp brought us some fish he'd caught as he often does when we have our hands full with either a corpse or a patient. Fitz and I made a late luncheon of it."

"Did Visser eat the fish?"

"He did. Only a few bites, but he did."

"Is there any left that I might examine?"

"No, Lord Christmas. We ate it all, but for the bones and heads, which we tossed out to the cats."

Gale sighed. "Well, I must assume both you and your assistant were dosed with laudanum. And quite a bit of it, if I was able to smell it in Fitz's vomit." He relished the flame in the assistant's cheeks. "Either by Visser himself if he made an escape, or, to indulge your kidnapping theory, perhaps the fish was dosed before it was brought to you. If Visser ate only a little, perhaps he knew it to be contaminated and was avoiding it. Or it may be mere coincidence, and he was found rather more conscious than his kidnapper would have liked. How much do you trust this Kemp?"

"He's never given us reason not to trust him," Fitz said hotly, as though Gale were slandering his own mother.

"All right, then. I should like to talk to him. And any neighbours that were likely to have been home at the time of Visser's disappearance." He got information about Kemp's whereabouts and the names of a few neighbours and left.

He paused once he stepped outside the house. His head felt quite fuzzy all of a sudden, and he could not decide whether it would be better to seek out Kemp immediately or to speak to Fernside's neighbours to see if anybody had witnessed anything suspicious yesterday evening. In the weeks since Gale's unexpected rise to fame, interrogations had become more difficult. People craved fame by proxy and would spin falsehoods without a second thought in what Gale supposed was a misguided attempt to impress him.

He would rather gain a better idea of whether Visser had escaped or been taken before he put himself at the mercy of the surgeon's neighbours. There was almost no reason to believe Visser had been kidnapped. The fact that the lock on the front door was undamaged suggested that Visser had let himself out. Likely Visser had got hold of Fernside's laudanum, incorporated it into the fish eaten by the surgeon and his assistant, waited until the house was quiet, and then made his escape. But how could he have walked? That leg wound had been bad. It had taken both Gale and Chant to drag him to Fernside's residence. If Visser had escaped, his progress would have been slow and would have drawn attention.

If he could speculate as to which direction Visser might have gone, perhaps he could look for clues. A spot of blood on a cobble-stone. A patch where a useless limb had been dragged through pebbles or horse manure. But if he attempted to follow Visser's trail, then what about Kemp?

The dockyard loomed around him, shrouded in grey. A fog seemed to hang above the river, and the faint sun was too weak to pierce it. He spotted a small path that wound among several derelict homes. Easy enough to take that path and shield oneself from the main streets. But what about prying eyes at the windows of these houses? The inhabitants had been away at the dockyards and factories, he supposed. He began to walk along the path, a sense of unease growing within him. His insides felt all at once like a stagnant marsh, attracting all sorts of buzzing insects. The dwelling beside him was dark and had one jagged broken window. He would not be surprised to learn it had been unoccupied for a long time. He glanced inside, his lungs tight. He was not sure what he hoped—or feared—to see. Visser's sallow face, staring out at him? Flummery, curled among soot and broken glass on the floorboards?

And suddenly, he was facing the water again, gazing into the fog draped like a shroud over the Thames. The mast of the *Condor* penetrated the gloom like a spear. Her sails rippled in the breeze. He was still hidden from sight of the dockyard. Could de Cock have come here to this very spot and stood watching Fernside's home, waiting for his chance to take Visser? Could Visser be hiding in one of these buildings? What did the first mate stand to gain by escaping? He had not been Fernside's prisoner.

The obvious answer was that he had not wanted Gale to know he'd left or where he was going. Fernside would have sent word to Gale immediately if the patient had insisted on departing before he was healed. Now Visser was beyond any protection Fernside or Gale could offer.

The dog.

It all came back to the dog somehow. He and Chant needed to

find the dog before Visser or de Cock. No, not he and Chant—he alone.

He walked on and was too surprised to even cry out when his arm was grabbed, and he was swung around easily as though he were a partner in a dance and pulled through a narrow doorway into one of the derelict buildings.

A large, shiny black boot kicked the door shut and planted itself between Gale and the only visible exit. Its twin stepped inward to join it.

Gale had the sudden, hazy realization that the print he'd seen in Howe's yard—the narrower one—must have been made by one of the boots he was studying right now. His gaze travelled up the tall boots, over stained breeches long out of style, up the panels of a velvet coat with tarnished buttons, to a cravat, yellowed by sweat and hanging nearly untied—until at last he met the pale, terrible eyes of Captain de Cock.

he seventh dog, much to Elise's obvious disappointment, had not been Flummery. She wore her disappointment well, though, with a determined set to her jaw and an unyielding faith that Lord Christmas Gale would solve the case. The news sheets said there was nothing Gale and his extraordinary brain could not do, and Elise seemed to think that, just as the sun would rise tomorrow, Flum's return was imminent. Chant didn't have the heart to poke holes in that faith; he simply agreed when the boys finally left with their pack of dogs that next time they would return with Flummery.

He returned Elise to Gale's house, hoping Gale was there, but he was not. Chant left Elise in the care of Anne-Marie and took a cab to Russell Street.

The day was grey and bleak, and Chant couldn't shake his unease. Where was Gale? He'd fled from Chant's house as though he had the devil at his heels without a word of where he was going. The damnable, frustrating fool! Had he not agreed to make no moves on his own?

Chant groaned and pressed his gloved fists to his eyes, digging his knuckles in hard enough that dark shapes bloomed in his vision.

No, he had not agreed, had he? He had said, *"I will try. That is all I can promise."*

The man had no regard for his own safety, and it was becoming increasingly clear he had no regard for Chant either. Perhaps Chant did make a rather useless assistant, but, good Lord, if Gale was in danger, at least he could hope to be of some help. Gale was impossible. He was the most vexing man Chant had ever met, and Chant could not understand how he had not been murdered before now. And not just because he skulked around the docks looking to unravel mysteries concerning sinister privateers. No, Chant couldn't understand how nobody had stabbed him at a supper party yet.

At Russell Street, Chant instructed the driver to wait and then enquired of a woman selling apples where he might find Gale's address. She pointed him to the correct house—a large and imposing building with a cream-coloured facade. Chant approached it and had scarcely reached the front steps when a small, grey-haired woman came rushing out and shooed Chant away as though he were a pigeon. She gave him no chance to explain who he was seeking or why, but she shouted, "He's not in!" as though she knew exactly whom he sought, and he thought it best to leave before she grew more agitated.

He returned to the street, his concern rising, and told the cab driver to take him to Bucknall's. Where the devil was Gale?

He gave his hat and gloves and walking stick to the boy on duty in the foyer of the Bucknall Club and climbed the stairs. He checked every room, searching for a glimpse of Gale's auburn hair and not finding one. He looked for Gale's mysterious friend Soulden too, but there was no sign of him. Stratford, the shy young man, was seated in his usual chair, scribbling away in his leather-bound journal. Chant didn't see anyone else he recognised until a man turned away from the bookshelves in the Blue Room, holding a book out to his companion and asking, "This one?"

The younger man was sitting at a table with several volumes already spread out around him. He clicked his tongue. "No, not that one. The one next to it."

Instead of appearing annoyed, William Hartwell, Marquess of Danbury, looked smitten.

Chant, having once been the subject of sharp whispers by even sharper tongues, did not follow gossip, but the scandal of William Hartwell and Joseph Warrington had been impossible to avoid. And it was very fresh too. A loaf of bread baked on the morning the news had broken that Warrington had been undone wouldn't have gone mouldy yet. Hartwell and Warrington must have only been days married, and yet they had an ease about them that suggested their new nuptials were underpinned by years of familiarity.

Chant had no wish to intrude upon them, but Hartwell looked up and saw him standing there.

"Good day," he said. "It's Chant, isn't it?"

"Yes," Chant said, stepping forward and holding out his hand.

They shook.

"Hartwell," Hartwell said. "And Warry, my husband."

Chant felt a tinge of jealousy at Hartwell's broad smile. "Congratulations, both of you."

"He comes here to read, can you believe it?" Hartwell asked fondly.

"Well," Warry replied, not even raising his eyes from whatever book he was perusing, "some of us *can*, you know."

Hartwell's smile grew broader. "Will you join me in a drink, sir? And perhaps a round of cards?"

Chant's first thought was to refuse—he needed to locate Gale—but he'd already checked Gale's house, and his rooms in Russell Street, and the club, and where else was there to look? "Perhaps a drink."

He and Hartwell sat, and a footman came to enquire what

Chant wanted to drink. Hartwell appeared to be drinking port, although the hour was not yet late, while a silver coffee pot sat at Warry's elbow.

"A port," he said firmly to the footman. He didn't want to end up in his cups, but at the same time, after the day he'd had, he needed something stronger than coffee to settle his nerves. He said to Hartwell, "You are a friend of Gale's, are you not?"

Hartwell made a noncommittal sound. "I do not think Gale *has* friends. But, if he allowed such a thing, I flatter myself I would be counted one."

"He is… very peculiar," Chant said. "And most vexing."

"Most vexing," Hartwell agreed. His expression sharpened. "And what of you, sir? Do you consider yourself a friend of Gale's?"

"I do not know what I am to him," Chant said, shrugging helplessly. "The more time I spend with him, it seems the less I know of him at all."

"Yes, well…" Hartwell shot a glance at Warry, who did not look up from his book, though his eyebrows lifted. "We had the pleasure of running into Gale's oldest sister today. Clarissa. She was out for a walk with Lady Alice—Faber, is it, darling?"

"Faber," Warry agreed.

Hartwell smiled at Gale. "Lovely woman. Has a nose like a horse, Warry's mother thinks, but it works for her."

"You don't mean Clarissa?" Warry frowned.

"No, of course not. Lady Alice. You were there when your mother made the comment about her nose."

"My mother comments on many noses." Warry scanned the page before him.

"Does she like *my* nose?" Hartwell asked as though the thought had come upon him suddenly.

"Mmm." Warry made a noncommittal sound.

"She does not like my nose? What's wrong with it? It is very fine, I'm told."

"Who told you that? Your own mother?"

"Do *you* not like my nose?"

"Clarissa Gale and Lady Alice were walking…" Chant prompted.

Hartwell straightened. "Ah, yes. Anyway, Clarissa said you'd been to dine at Gale House last night. As Gale's guest, no less."

"That is true." Chant let the bittersweet memory of the previous evening wash over him.

"She said it's the first time Gale has invited anyone for supper in the whole of her lifetime."

Chant accepted a port gratefully from the footman, and had to keep himself from sucking it down in great gulps. He sipped once, twice, then set the glass down. What was he to make of this information? What good did it do him? So oughtn't that mean that Gale should *like* him well enough not to flee from him twice over?

"Untrue," he said, affecting a casual tone. "I was told last night that a Mr. Darling has dined with him previously."

"Darling?" Hartwell's brow creased. "Oh, the *Runner*." He snorted. "No, I do not think he counts."

Chant leaned back, sliding one leg out in front of him and staring at his glass. He was unsure whether or not to trust the rush of relief he felt at Hartwell's assertion. "I had a good time," he said honestly. "Though it would be hard to say from his behaviour whether he enjoyed my company."

Hartwell laughed raucously. Even Warry snickered and finally tore his gaze from his book, saying, "I have never seen that man enjoy anything."

"Yes," Hartwell agreed. "I do not think we can use Gale's behaviour as a gauge for what he enjoys. But the news sheets certainly enjoyed the fact that you dined there."

"I'm sorry?"

Hartwell waved a hand. "It was in some rag or the other. 'Lord Christmas and his mysterious new partner are investigating…' something."

"A murder," Warry supplied, his attention back on his book.

"Yes, that was it." Hartwell's eyes widened suddenly. "Are you really? A *murder*?"

"It is complicated," Chant said, his heart beating faster. Gale had warned him of the potential for publicity once they were seen together. He had thought himself at peace with that, and yet... "The papers. Do they think we're..."

"Oh! So far, no. Last Season Gale was seen in the company of Lady Carstairs. It was regarding a fake diamond brooch and a fellow posing as a parson's son, or a parson posing as some fellow's son, but anyway, Gale and Lady Carstairs whispered for so long together that the gossipmongers went wild with the story, and now most of Society is convinced Gale is inclined toward women, when he is inclined at all."

Chant nodded. He didn't mind if the news sheets thought he and Gale were courting. Indeed, he wished *Gale* thought they were courting. But if the gossips simply believed him to be Gale's investigative partner, perhaps they would dredge up less of his background than they would if they believed him Gale's beau.

"Is there any use in..." Chant tipped his glass toward himself and rolled its base in a circle on the table. "In attempting to bond with a man like that?"

"Well," Hartwell said thoughtfully, "I should say Gale has his uses, if you need a mystery solved or someone to commiserate with you on how dull the quadrille is. But as far as bonding..."

Warry finally shut his book. "I do not believe he is as much a misanthrope as people think. Or as he thinks himself."

"Oh?" Hartwell gazed at Warry as though the young man had just relayed the most fascinating piece of news in all the world.

Warry looked at Chant. "He is simply afraid."

"He never seems afraid of anything." Chant was not sure he wanted more of his port, which suddenly tasted too sweet. "Except... well, he is made nervous by crowds, I have gathered, but he is not *afraid*."

A shrug from Warry. "I do not know him well, I suppose."

Hartwell leaned forward, gaze locked with Chant's. "When you say *bond with…*" He *oofed* as his husband elbowed him. "I was only asking!"

Warry shook his head and made to open his book again. Hartwell scooted closer to him and lowered his head, speaking in a sort of croon in Warry's ear. "The light in here is growing too dim to read by. You'll ruin your eyes."

Warry pushed his shoulder briefly against Hartwell's. "You didn't think twice about ruining *me*, yet you worry about my eyes?"

Hartwell's brows lifted. "Is it not rather too soon to joke about that? Anyway, it is rude to read when we are talking to Mr. Chant." Hartwell's gaze met Chant's again. "What do you say to a game of cards to pass the time, Chant? If we wait here long enough, Gale is sure to turn up."

~

Gale's head spun as he staggered away from whatever gaming hell he had just wreaked havoc upon. He could not recall its name—only that far too many of its inhabitants had shouted his when he'd entered. But soon he'd been so foxed, he hadn't cared. He was by the river now. How pleasant. He'd been heading in the direction of Bucknall's, but then he'd seen the water and couldn't resist. The sky was dark, so he'd passed some hours at the faro table. His purse was considerably lighter than it had been when he'd entered. Perhaps that was a good thing. There was an art to gambling, depending on the game, but mostly it was chance. Gale was tired of solving puzzles. How strangely reassuring it had been, to know his fate at the card table was but the luck of the draw.

He'd only left because it had got so bloody crowded. People had jostled him, he'd been caught in clouds of reeking breath, words thrust into his ears like blades. Ah, even now—look at his hands! They were shaking. From drink, he hoped, rather than from the weakness in his mind. The weakness Chant had seen two nights past at the Harringdon ball. It was one thing to disdain all of humanity but quite another to let it render you a quaking mouse. Leave the quaking to Hartwell's little dullard, Warry. Since when was Hartwell the marrying type? It made no sense. Hartwell! It might be a lark to see Hartwell now. Hartwell was good for a laugh, much as Gale disliked laughter as a general rule. But Hartwell was probably at home, in bed with little Warry. Gale made a face at the pavement, which, in turn, spun under his feet. Most unkind.

He touched the side of his neck, dug his nail under the small scab there, and was pleased to feel a bead of fresh blood form.

"Most unkind!" he declared to the night sky.

He jolted when a voice said, "Lord Christmas?"

He thought for a second it might be Chant's voice, but what a foolish thought. Chant's voice was much softer and warmer than this... bray.

Teddy stepped into the pool of light from the nearby street lamp.

Gale's stomach seemed to detach from whatever held it in place within him.

Teddy from the salon. Teddy, who had turned away from Gale and gone to fuck the French artist. Gale's last encounter with him had involved a fair amount of alcohol too.

"What are you doing out here?" Teddy asked.

"I am walking by the river," Gale said. At least, that's what he hoped he said. His tongue felt thick and rather useless.

"Are you all right?"

"Where is Hartwell?" Gale blurted. That was not what he'd meant to ask.

"I don't... You mean Lord William Hartwell? Your friend?"

"He is not my friend. I have no friends." Gale rubbed the back of his head. Where was his hat? Had he come here with a hat? "Chant is not my friend." It seemed very important that Teddy know this.

"Gale, shall I call you a cab?" Teddy squinted through the lamp-light. "You're bleeding." He stepped forward.

Gale stumbled back. "Don't!"

A voice, thin and higher than he'd expected. The accent more English than Dutch. Pale eyes, boring into his. *Do I need to tell you what will happen, should you continue to pry into matters that don't concern you?*

Gale hurried along, ignoring Teddy's voice behind him. He needed to clear his head, but how? If he sobered up, he might remember too much of his afternoon. But if he stayed as he was... he could not see, could not think. He was exposed out here. He doubled over suddenly, his hands on his knees. He could not draw breath. There were... He did not know how to describe it, even to himself. There were things that belonged *inside*. Inside himself. His thoughts, his feelings, the occasional hours he spent in the dimly lit rooms of molly houses. The days he spent in Russell Street, in his rooms, where no one could reach him. He had only ever wanted a life lived inside, protected, private. And now so much of him was being forced out into the open. By the papers, by Society, by Benjamin Chant... Chant was the worst of all. With Chant, he could not stay within himself, not entirely.

And it was not fair.

He made his way toward the pier, hunched and stumbling. There was no one there, not at that precise spot. There was just black water glittering under the light of the moon. The moon that Chant had spoken of on the Harringdon terrace. A breeze hit him full in the face and seemed to clear some of the fog from his mind. He could breathe again, though it took some effort. He leaned over and stared into the water.

De Cock had bent to remove his boot. *"I must have a stone in my boot. It's been bothering me all afternoon."*

He heard the creak of boards and turned his head to discover Teddy was standing next to him, his handsome mouth illuminated by moonlight but his eyes hidden in the shadow cast by his hat.

"I think there is a metaphor in that somewhere," Gale muttered, and glared for a moment at the small, hazy moon as though it were its fault.

"A metaphor, sir?" Teddy asked.

Gale grunted and waved his hand at Teddy. He'd had rather too much to drink to explain neatly why the fact he could see Teddy's mouth but not his eyes summed up their entire relationship. What had it been, after all, but a series of transactions? Gale had paid—if not coin and not directly—for that mouth, but he had never been terribly interested in the man behind it. He wondered if Teddy's artist was kinder than he had been.

"How is what's her name?" Gale asked.

Teddy's mouth curled into a smile. "Do not pretend you don't know her name, sir. I know there isn't a single fact you have ever overheard that you have then forgotten."

Gale grunted. He'd thought so too, once, before *Chant*. Then last night he'd been so distracted by Chant's presence at dinner that he'd failed to remember the letter in his pocket. It was unaccountable and most certainly unprecedented. Now Visser had either fled or been captured right from under Gale's nose. And there was something about the surgeon and his assistant that Gale could not put his finger on. Something about that house, and yet, whatever it was, Gale just couldn't *see* it.

Even now, staring at Teddy's pretty visage and remembering all the things Teddy could do to make Gale's blood turn hot in his icy veins, it was *Chant* he was thinking about. Chant with his captivating eyes, that little crease that appeared between his elegant brows whenever he regarded Gale—as though Gale confounded *him*, ha!—and that golden hair he wore too long. Gale wanted to tug that ribbon free and comb his fingers through Chant's hair. More than that, he wanted Chant to do the same to him. He wanted to feel the scrape of Chant's nails against his scalp, the slight pressure, the strange thrill of the touch that had lit him up from the inside.

He had never petted Teddy's hair or wanted Teddy to pet his.

Chant made no sense. *Nothing* made sense, Gale's own mind least of all. And of everything in the world, Gale had always been certain of his own mind. Now he felt adrift, unanchored and uncertain, and it wasn't just his drunkenness. Was this how other people felt all the time? People like Hartwell or Warry or even Soulden, who experienced their lives as a series of random events occurring at the whim of a capricious universe and did not see the pattern to it all? The order? How horrifying.

He shivered as he stared into the black water.

Chant had ruined him. He had lured Gale in with his odd, unasked for compassion toward him, and he had ruined him.

He glanced at Teddy again and wondered if he ought to invite him back to his rooms in Russell Street. He and Teddy had enjoyed a few assignations there. Except, no. Not even the memory of Teddy's pert and inviting arse could get a stand out of Gale. Not even a damned twitch.

Ruined.

And all because of—

"Gale!"

Gale spun around on wobbly legs to see Chant hastening toward him. "What the devil are you doing here? How did you even find me? Have you belled me like a cat, sir?"

The Belled Cat. Howe had died in the pub's back alley. Stabbed by the same blade that had been pressed to Gale's throat hours ago.

Chant pulled up short, and the men behind him almost barrelled into him. Gale squinted at them. Hartwell? Hartwell and Warry?

"You asked for Hartwell," Teddy murmured. "I sent a boy to Bucknall's to ask for him there."

Good Lord. How had Gale not realised that? A child would have realised that.

"I have lost my mind because of you!" Gale said, pointing an accusing finger toward Chant. "I have lost all my mental faculties, and now I am a gibbering idiot like Hartwell!"

"Do I gibber?" Hartwell asked. "Warry, do I gibber? Am I a gibberer?"

"Hush," Warry said. "Gale, are you drunk?"

"I am drunk," Gale said. "But there is much I understand."

For a moment, he saw two Hartwells, both beckoning him. "Come on off the pier now," the Hartwells said.

"That is not what I wish to do." Gale walked out farther, and the rest of the world fell away as he approached the edge.

Behind him, he heard Chant say, "You all may go. I'll handle this."

Handle this? Gale did not need to be handled. Not a one of them realised what Gale himself had handled today.

De Cock's breath had reeked of fish and gin as he'd touched the point of his dagger to Gale's throat. Gale had remained calm. Disturbingly calm. He would have expected the prospect of death to be terrifying, but the moments he'd thought would be his last had seemed somehow as ordinary as all the moments that had come before.

Later, he had gone to the hell with his cravat fastened high around his neck to cover the spot where the dagger had drawn blood.

"Are you sure?" he heard Hartwell ask Chant. "He was of service to me recently when I was in my cups. I should be glad to return the favour."

"You were a gibbering idiot that night," Warry put in.

"I need no favours!" Gale called back.

The water was filthy. The moonlight outlined every bit of rubbish that bobbed in the river. Gale should not have minded throwing himself in with all of it. It would be better than letting Chant *handle* him.

The water lapped the dock, and a scrap of metal collided with what looked like a burlap sack. How cold would the water be? He heard low voices. Footsteps retreating.

"Gale."

He made no answer.

Chant did not come closer. Gale didn't know whether he was relieved or disappointed.

"I do not like you so close to the water," Chant said.

"I do not like you having opinions on my proximity to the water."

All at once, an icy and horrible feeling rose in Gale. Was this the terror he ought to have felt earlier in that ramshackle room with de Cock? He did not want to face Chant. Not until things made sense again.

"Will you not come to me?" Chant asked gently.

Gale closed his eyes. It seemed he still saw the pattern of moonlight on water against the back of his eyelids. He wondered idly if this was how Flummery had felt, cowering under the lumber pile in Jacob's Island as Gale cursed and commanded him. No wonder Gale could not get even a dog to like him. If, in this moment, Chant were to shout at him as he had shouted at Flum, he would jump into the river.

"No." If he said it enough times, Chant would give up and leave him in peace. It was a strategy that worked on everyone except Gale's mother.

His gut felt as if it were being wrung like a rag. He needed to get to Russell Street. Needed to shut himself in his room and stay there.

"I wish to go home. But I am not coming off this pier until you are out of the way. Stand aside, sir."

"And just what is it you fear I mean to do?"

"*Fear?* I think you mean to embrace me and fret over me and whisper reassurances as you would a babe. And I have not the stomach for that." The stomach in question suddenly felt hollowed out by longing—though for what, he could not be sure. Perhaps for precisely what he had just accused Chant of wanting to do.

"Then we are at an impasse. For I cannot let you walk off this pier without taking you in my arms and determining for myself whether you are too cold, or too hungry, or too unsteady on your feet to be left alone."

"Then I shall stay here forever."

"All right," Chant agreed. A moment passed. "What if we compromised? You come off the pier, I embrace you, but I promise to whisper no reassurances. It shall be a silent embrace."

That longing pulled at the core of him again. Perhaps it would not be so terrible to be in Chant's arms, just briefly. "You may whisper one phrase of your choosing. It need not be a reassurance."

"Very well. Are you coming here, or shall I go to you?"

"I am…" Gale did not know. "I am coming. In just a moment."

"All right. I shall use this interlude to think of my one phrase."

Gale stared at the water and sighed. He had given Chant every opportunity to leave, and the fellow was still there. So could Gale be blamed for… for accepting whatever Chant was offering?

"I must have a stone in my boot..." And Gale had made no sound, no movement, even as De Cock overturned the boot he'd removed, and a small item fell out, landing with a soft *thwick* on the dirty floorboards.

He began to shake as he left the pier behind. He did not want Chant to see him in this state. Had Chant not seen enough of this sort of feebleness at the ball the other night? Perhaps he would put it down to the cold.

Even with strange shadows cast over and about him, Chant's form was familiar. The gold of his hair gleamed where a bar of lamplight caught it, and he stood as relaxed as though he were simply taking in the night air.

Gale walked right up to him, difficult as it was, and stopped, unable to meet Chant's gaze.

Chant's arms came around him, and while he made an irritatingly sympathetic noise at Gale's shivering, he did not speak right away. He pulled Gale closer to him, and, unsteady as Gale was, he ended up leaning against the other man for balance.

There was the darkness and quiet he craved, and Gale sank into it. He lowered his head. With his face pressed to Chant's shoulder, he could shut out the rest of the world. With Chant's arms around him, he did not feel nearly so exposed.

"You old fool," Chant whispered in his ear.

He made it *sound* like a reassurance, which was a talent Gale could almost admire.

Gale inhaled, but there was no hope of letting the breath go smoothly. Chant rubbed his back as the air shuddered from his lungs.

He was not sure how much time passed after that.

"What did you mean," Chant asked softly, "going off on your own like that? Getting in such a state?"

Gale bit his tongue as what started as annoyance turned to something else entirely—a warmth, rather like embarrassment but lacking the sharper bite of shame or resentment. It was, in some odd, obscure way an almost pleasurable sensation. He flushed quite helplessly with it, and was glad Chant could not see his face.

"Your whispered reassurances need some work," Gale muttered.

"These are not reassurances. These are chidings. You are being chidden."

Gale felt that flood of warmth again. Was he really so foxed that his very blood had grown hot? "Whatever you call it, it is all the behaviour of a fretful matron. I'll not stand for it."

"You can barely stand at all, my friend."

That seemed grossly unfair of Chant to point out.

"Shall we go somewhere you can rest?"

"No," Gale said firmly. He forced his head up. "I... I will go home after this, but first, there are some things you must know."

"All right," Chant said, voice calm as ever.

Gale took a few shallow breaths against the shoulder of Chant's greatcoat. "Are you going to let me go?" he asked, his voice muffled.

"No," Chant said above him, his cheek pressing against Gale's hair. "If it's all the same to you, I'd really rather not.

CHAPTER 12

*A*ll told, Chant thought he did fairly well at schooling his manner and expression as he listened to Gale's story. Gale remained in his arms as he spoke, though he'd lifted his head again so Chant might hear him. This was a deserted enough spot Chant worried more about thieves than about gossip, but he did not wish to break the spell of Gale's trust by insisting they go to one of their homes. He knew his duty here was to listen. Still, he could not stop himself from tensing when Gale described being pulled into the abandoned house by de Cock.

"God," he breathed. "Gale…"

"Let me finish," Gale said.

He went on, and his description of the encounter left Chant queasy. De Cock had warned Gale to halt his investigation. That, Chant would have expected. The captain had drawn a line under his message by putting his dagger to Gale's throat. Chant could have gone off to find the man this instant and killed him without hesitation. Gale had attempted to get de Cock talking, but de Cock had not taken the bait. He did not confess to the murder of Howe, nor would he reveal whether he'd had a hand in Visser's disappearance. Not until their conversation was at an end, and de Cock made for the door, limping as he did.

The captain had told Gale there was a stone in his boot that had been bothering him all afternoon. Then he'd removed his boot, turned it upside down, and had shaken it.

What had fallen to the floor between them was not a stone, but a human ear.

The edge where it had been detached was rough and dark with coagulated blood. Gale had stared at it for a long while, even after de Cock left.

"It was Visser's," Gale told Chant now. "Who else's could it have been?"

Chant did not much care who the *fuck* the ear had belonged to. His arms eased from around Gale, and he swallowed several times.

Gale stepped back, out of the embrace.

"You told me you would not do this," Chant said. "That you would not put yourself in danger."

"I said no such thing."

"You said you would try. And you have not tried, even a little."

"This is precisely why I did not want you involved in any of this mess!" Gale swayed on his feet, and Chant almost reached out to steady him. But the man remained upright. "I tell you that de Cock has maimed Visser, and all you can think about is how you tried to extract a promise from me, and how I have not done as you wished. Here you are nagging at me like a disgruntled spouse!"

"Is that really what you think? I shall have no problem walking away if so." Chant shook his head when Gale did not answer. "You may know much that I don't, Gale, but I am beginning to see that you don't know the first thing about people, unless they have stolen a brooch or murdered a dockyard worker. You know on the surface why they do what they do, but you do not feel their motivations in your own heart."

"A good thing, I should think. To not feel in my heart the motivations of a murderer or thief, yes?"

"No. Do not deflect. You wilfully misunderstand my intention in condemning your behaviour."

"And you, sir, wilfully stand in the way of what I am trying to do."

"Stand in your way? I have wanted nothing but to help you since this began."

"Yet you hinder me!" Gale sounded surprisingly frantic. "I cannot clear my mind of you and focus on the investigation. I see you before me whether I'm awake or asleep. I cannot narrow my attention to any detail without being brought up short by the thought of your eyes, your lips, your—your bloody beautiful hands. Your hands are wonderful, Chant. I don't know why I have only just realised this. It was the eyes that had me before. You are a distraction, and a brutal one, and I need you to be *gone*."

Chant stared at him, stunned. Did he mean it? Did he really think of Chant so often without appearing to think of him at all? A mere day ago, Chant could have died of happiness to hear such words. Now, they seemed to strike his body like blows.

"I think you are very drunk," Chant said at last.

"What a very dull and obvious conclusion."

"Sometimes the obvious conclusions are the most accurate." He sighed as some of the furious energy left the air around them. "Let me see you home."

"Do not touch me." Gale jerked back as though Chant had moved toward him. "I mean it. I can stand on my own."

"I had no intention of doing so unless you asked. I learned my lesson last night." Chant hated himself for the bitterness of the words. It would have been satisfying to be able to brush Gale's ill humour away like so much dust on his coat. To smile and shrug and reassure Gale that nothing Gale could throw at him would rock him. Instead, he spun on his heel and began walking away.

"Do you think I was not frightened?" Gale called.

Chant stopped, then turned reluctantly. He should go. He should go now and have nothing more to do with Lord Christmas

Gale. Why was he allowing himself to be drawn back into this foolish argument? But this was the first time he had heard Gale admit to being frightened. He recalled what Warry had said about Gale being afraid. *Simply afraid.* "Yes. I imagine it was rather frightening to have a murderer threaten your life."

"I do not mean frightened of de Cock," Gale snapped. "All bullies are rather the same, and he is far from my first and only tormentor. I meant frightened to tell *you!*"

The words hung in the air between them.

Chant rolled his eyes heavenward. "What reason on earth," he asked, "have I ever given you to be frightened of me? I have tried gentleness, but you have mocked me for it. I have tried good humour, which you have met with disdain. I have tried at every turn to understand you, to excuse your rudeness as being of a piece with your brilliance, and I can do it no longer."

Gale took an ungainly step forward. "Not frightened *of* you. To —to *tell* you. To watch your concern turn to contempt. As it has!" he pointed out, with triumph in his tone.

Chant shook his head. "Contempt, Gale? Can you, with your brilliant mind, really not tell the difference between *contempt* and a fear for your safety that will consume me if I let it?"

Gale's mouth moved very slightly. His tongue ran along his bottom lip. "It is not my fault that you are fool enough to care for me."

"Yet it is my fault that you are fool enough to care for me?" Chant's temper blazed. He imagined it splitting the darkness around them like lightning.

"Yes!" Gale insisted. "I cannot prove it through any scientific method, but it is true nonetheless."

"Do not tease me now. I am in no mood for it."

"I am not teasing. I do not know what this is. I am drunk. I am angry. I am in awe of you."

"I am angry too. And I do not trust you."

"Tell me what you need from me."

"For you to *share* something of yourself, Gale!" He faced Gale fully, his mouth open, his arms arrested in a gesture that might have been a plea or a move to strangle the other man. "For God's sake, what I am asking is something most people give quite willingly!"

He let his arms drop slowly to his sides. Let his shoulders down from where they'd been hovering near his ears. He scoffed, and the sound became a sigh.

"I know," Gale said quietly. "But I have said it before, Chant, and it is you who have not listened. Is it not better that I know the limitations of my own character and make you no promises than to tell you what you wish to hear and then prove it false in the end?"

The words dropped through Chant's body like so many stones.

"I do not know," Chant admitted finally. "I think just once I might like to hear something from you that is not an excuse for why the words I'm hearing are not kinder."

There was no sound now but the wind guiding a low hush through the nearby trees. Gale had no answer for that, then? Very well. Chant ought to have known from the beginning that they were oil and water.

Very well.

"You deserve to hear kind words."

Chant closed his eyes. Shoved his hands in his pockets. No. He was not going to look at Gale again.

"There are so many I wish to speak to you, but I don't know where to begin. And I don't think I ought to begin now, for I am still approximately eight-tenths gin. I will not ask you to stay. You have shown me more consideration already than I have earned. But know that I admire you. And wish that I had done a better job of showing it."

No. God, no. Chant ought to press his hands to his ears and block out Gale's voice—though it would be rather like shutting the barn door after the horse had gone out.

Despite himself, Chant looked up. The ground seemed to shift under his feet as though he were a mouse on a rug and somebody had lifted the rug and given it a snap to dislodge him. As though he were the one in his cups.

"If that is true," Chant said, "then you have a decision to make. My affection for you is greater than it ought to be, and if you do not wish to share any part of your life, whether it be your investigation, your heart, your friendship, then I need to know that as soon as possible." He held up a hand. "Not tonight, for you are not clear-headed. But when you are sober, I will require an answer. Because I cannot do this again, Gale. Cannot feel one moment as though I matter to you and the next as though I am a presence you barely tolerate. I cannot bear another courtship with a man who needs me less than I need him."

Gale did not answer, and Chant's throat tightened.

"I would give everything to you in this moment." Gale said it with such naked sincerity that Chant was reminded just how disguised the fellow was. And yet Gale was steady on his feet, and there was no slurring of his speech. He looked rather like a child, alarmed to realise the full extent of the trouble he'd got himself in and desperate to make amends.

Once again in spite of himself, Chant gentled his tone. "That is precisely what I'm afraid of. That you would give it all to me now and then shut down again when next my affection seems too much for you."

"You might be right. I do not know what I can give of myself, for I have never tried to give anything. Not to someone like you."

And that, Chant realised, was complete honesty from Lord Christmas Gale. His to take or leave.

Somewhere in all this the distance between them had closed again.

"If you give me another chance, I would—I will—attempt to discover what I might—" Gale swallowed audibly. "What I might give."

Chant could not quite look at him. "I don't... know. I don't know."

When Chant did glance at Gale again, he saw the same expression he'd seen yesterday when he'd started to kiss Gale, then shied away. Such a complete and gentle understanding on a face that was all sharpness and angles. "You have made your choice. I see it now. Please forget I said anything. Please go and let yourself have the peace you deserve. Free of me."

Chant could barely swallow. He bit his lip hard, anchoring himself with the small, sharp pain. And then he forced out the words: "I do not wish to be free of you. And could not be, even if I walked away and never spoke to you again. But Gale? 'Try' has to mean more than it has meant so far."

"I do hear you, sir. And you will not like what I have to say next, but I will say it." Gale sounded quite sober now, and Chant braced himself, for he knew Gale could wound with precision whether he intended to or not. "This fear that Reid has left you with. The fear that you will be abandoned, that nobody cares quite enough for you to remain steady by your side? You have my sympathy. But you do not have the right to ask me to be what I am not in order to allay your own fears."

Chant stared at him.

Gale's mouth thinned and then twisted wryly. "I am not so dense as you might suppose on the subject of human feeling. I have not asked for your gentleness, your good humour, your understanding. There have been moments I've appreciated all three and admired your ability to offer them freely. But I rather think the street goes both ways when it comes to sharing ourselves. I want those things from you only when you truly wish to give them—not when you fear losing my company if you are not gentle enough, kind enough, or if you do not feign good humour in the face of all life hurls at you."

Still Chant could make no reply.

"I said as much to you last night. But perhaps I did not make myself clear. I have seen you angry. I have seen you afraid. I have caught glimpses of your grief. And all those things, more than the promise of whispered reassurances, drew me off the pier tonight and into your arms. I did not truly fear your contempt in telling you what I'd done. I feared that you'd care for me anyway. That you would offer me a second chance when it would be better for you to be rid of me. Do not offer me one now unless you mean it. For I cannot think straight. Indeed, I have not been able to for the past forty-eight hours since we stood on that terrace together. I cannot make the decision of whether I am worth the trouble for you."

Chant looked out across the river now. At the beauty of the moon's rippling reflection in the water, and the signs all around of human waste and industry, the bits of refuse that punctured the pool of silver light. What a fool he'd been to think Gale did not truly see him. And what a fool he was if he thought that being seen by the man would ever be the same as being loved by him. But Gale was right. Chant had made himself out to be the victim of Gale's guarded heart, when in a sense, he had guarded his own even more closely.

"All right," Chant said at last. "If you wake tomorrow and find you still mean what you've said tonight, then… then tell me."

"I am not so drunk now," Gale said quietly.

"Still. Let us take the night to think."

If they agreed to try again, they must knock down at least a section of the wall between them. And yet, how could he ask a man who lived such a private life to reveal his secrets? Especially when he could only imagine what Gale would say if Chant were to reveal his own. If he were to let Gale see, truly, that his gentleness, good humour, and understanding were no more than a convincing illusion.

If he were to tell Gale what he'd done, all those years ago.

ale awoke with a pounding head and a taste in the back of his throat he imagined one could only get by sucking the bristles of a street sweeper's broom. He groaned and blinked into the unwelcome morning light, slowly bringing his surroundings into focus. It took a moment for him to realise where he was, and that it wasn't the familiar paper hangings of his room in Russell Street that his blurry gaze fixed upon. Instead, he realised, with mounting horror, he was at home. Good Lord. He had a vague memory from the night before of being somewhat rescued by Chant, but any relief he might have felt—although, if he were honest with himself, there was not much relief to be found in such abject humiliation—was drowned out immediately by the fact that Chant had apparently delivered him home into the care of his *mother*. Such a sin felt unforgivable—even more so when Gale hadn't even managed to rise from the bed before she was bustling into his bedroom, flinging the curtains open wide.

"Christmas, darling," she said. "Do get out of bed. Your friend is here for tea."

"I don't have any friends," Gale muttered. "Besides, who invited him?"

"I did, of course," his mother said.

She opened his bureau and began to dig through it for clothes.

"Am I allowed no privacy at all?" he grumbled.

"Oooh," his mother said. "Is this where you've hidden your copy of *The Maiden Diaries*?"

"I certainly have not," Gale said, shoving his bed clothes off and sitting up. His head ached and throbbed like a fresh bruise. "I'm much more depraved than that, I'm afraid. You may find there's a copy of *Justine* tucked away under my cravats."

His mother laughed brightly.

Gale stared at the floor for a moment as he was assailed by memories of the previous night.

Oh, it was all coming back. With far too much clarity.

He was to make a decision with his head clear—there seemed no chance of him achieving that state anytime soon—about whether he and Chant were to try again. Try again at what, precisely? He and Chant had yet to do anything more scandalous than embrace. A line of Chant's from last night hit him: *"I cannot bear another courtship with a man who needs me less than I need him."*

Gale's heart pounded in time with his head.

Well, if it was a courtship Chant wanted, then Gale must tell him no. Obviously. They were not courting, they had never been courting, and they never would court. Gale would never court anyone. Had Chant felt that was what they were doing? Or were headed for? Gale must disabuse him of the notion at once.

Oh, yes, there it was: a memory of raging at Chant for occupying all of his waking thoughts and for ruining his investigation. Calling Chant's hands beautiful—his *hands*? They were very nice, but they were hardly the part of Chant's anatomy that intrigued him the most—and eventually telling Chant he would give him everything.

Gale drew a shuddering breath. What in the *hell* had got into him?

Was this what it was like to be in love? Did it make a man stupid?

It had certainly made Hartwell stupid, but if love was a plummet into idiocy, Hartwell had only been standing on a step stool to begin with. Gale was standing on a chimney sweep's ladder and had a lot farther to fall.

He glared at his mother's back as she went through his bureau. "Why did you invite Chant for tea?"

His mother sighed and turned, holding a dressing gown. She tossed it to him. "I suppose it's too much to ask you to dress correctly, but I am old fashioned enough to believe one ought to at least cover one's nipples before taking tea with friends."

Gale yanked his gaping shirt closed with a huff, and then stood and shrugged on the gown. "You are avoiding the question."

"I am getting to it in my own time," she replied with an airy smile. "And I invited Chant because he was kind enough to bring you home last night when you were so deep in your cups you almost drowned and because the girls and Elise like him. I also like him. I think he is a very pleasant young gentleman indeed."

Gale tied the gown closed and tugged his fingers through his unruly hair. "I suppose I could do with a cup of tea."

"Even some cake, if you can keep it down," his mother agreed.

He glared at her again. "I was not so deep in my cups as you think by the time I got here."

No, by the time he had accused Chant of not being fully honest with him, his drunken fog had lifted somewhat. At the point where he'd suggested Chant walk away for his own good, he'd been very nearly sober. And after Chant had refused to walk away and instead had hailed them both a cab, Gale had been in something of a trance. So much so that he hadn't noticed Chant was taking him to the family house until it was too late to protest, to demand to be taken to Russell Street instead. So much so that he scarcely recalled getting into bed.

"No, you were certainly yourself enough to tell me my new nightjacket made me look as though I'd skinned a zebra."

"Oh God," Gale said, recalling the garment. "I may lose the contents of my stomach just thinking of it."

She lifted an eyebrow and one side of her mouth, then headed for the door. "Hurry down, dear."

Just to spite her, he made his way to the door as slowly as possible.

When he reached the drawing room, he heard stifled giggles—never a good thing. He noticed Chant first because, apparently, his mind would not let him notice anything else. Chant looked well in a coat of deep blue, a silver-and-black waistcoat, and breeches that were, it seemed, just a bit tighter than they needed to be.

Gale swallowed.

And then he noticed his sisters.

They were standing in a line—now was probably a good time to take a formal count so he would know precisely how many he had —rather than sitting, as would have been natural for tea. All of them were smirking. At least two were outright snickering. They wore their usual day dresses, but their accessories were preposterous. Gaudy jewellery that could only have belonged to their mother. Satin sashes in colours that made his head resume its pounding. Half of them had their hair in piles atop their heads; the other half had their locks curled tight as springs. Elise was most definitely wearing rouge, and Eugenie's face had been powdered into oblivion.

"What on earth is going on?" he demanded. His voice was too full of gravel to make much of an impression.

"We are putting on a production!" Clarissa announced. Her sash was the colour of a lemon, and she'd pinned jewelled brooches to her bonnet.

"No," Gale said at once. "No, you are not."

"Prepare to be entertained!" Helene entreated.

Gale turned to his mother helplessly. "Mother…?"

"Don't look at me. Your father's fault. All of you."

Chant came and stood by him, and then all Gale could concentrate on was the slight shiver that went across his skin, and the heat that crept up the back of his neck. "I do love to be entertained," Chant said in a low voice.

"It is a tale of depravity!" Anne-Marie declared, striking a pose.

"Oh, absolutely not," Gale said.

"Of murder!" Cordelia ran to the pianoforte and began to play what Gale supposed was meant to be spine-chilling music.

"Cease at once." Gale knew his protests were futile. He took the cup of tea offered by a servant and wished it were sherry.

"Of a girl what's called Lady Mirabelle Sapstrom," Elise said in her high voice, gesturing to Eugenie, who sashayed into the centre of the room, then collapsed onto the floor. "Who was *murdered!*"

"I wish I *had* drowned last night," Gale hissed to his mother.

"You might consider enjoying yourself," she whispered back.

"Did anyone stop to think that the subject matter is insensitive to Elise?"

"The whole thing was her idea," his mother replied.

"And *you!*" Helene pointed to Gale, their mother, and Chant. "You're all the investigators who must figure out which of us committed the dastardly crime."

Gale groaned. Beside him, Chant laughed and clapped. "All right!" Chant said. "We are ready."

No, Gale thought. *We really aren't.*

One by one, his sisters stepped forward and introduced their characters and their relationship with the deceased. One had always been jealous of Lady Sapstrom's jewels—here, Elise plucked a number of surprisingly tasteful accessories off Eugenie—a sapphire necklace, a ruby bracelet, an opal ring—who was trying unsuccessfully not to laugh.

"Be *quiet*, Eugenie!" Anne-Marie hissed. "You are a corpse!"

Another was a neighbour who'd been annoyed by Lady

Sapstrom's barking dog. Here, Clarissa provided altogether too-convincing barks.

Another had been the lady's chemist, and so on, and so on…

Gale might have walked out of the house if not for the warmth of Chant beside him. Chant had been bitterly disappointed in him last night, of that Gale was certain. Yet the man seemed as genial as ever, casting Gale a smile as the girls continued their performance.

Would Chant want to know, immediately after this debacle ended, whether Gale meant what he'd said last night?

"I cannot bear another courtship with a man who needs me less than I need him."

I do not need you at all, Gale wanted to say. Yet that suddenly seemed as feeble a protest as telling his sisters to stop their pageant at once.

"All right, the time has come!" Clarissa said at last, her face flushed with such exhilaration that Gale nearly smiled without realising it. A pang of regret hit him. He had never been good at playing games with his sisters. Had never understood the point of such frivolities. Chant had said last night that what he wanted from Gale was something most people gave willingly. What if Gale was never "most people" enough for Chant?

"Investigators!" Helene waved at them. "Who do you think did it? Who murdered Euge—I mean, Lady Sapstrom, and why?"

"Which person in this room could be such a devil?" Elise demanded, giving her little peg-toothed grin.

Gale sighed and said in a bored tone: "Lady Forthright, clearly, but with Miss Camden, the chemist's help. Her alibi doesn't hold up as her pianoforte lessons were on Thursday nights, not Wednesdays. The medicine drops she brought over earlier that day that would help Lady Sapstrom calm her dog were actually poison, bought from Miss Camden. She added some to Lady Sapstrom's scone, and voila. A recipe for death."

Chant nudged him and spoke to the group. "I disagree. Miss

Bellwether, the pianoforte instructor, said earlier that she had to change the day of Lady Forthright's lesson due to illness, so Lady F was not lying about her alibi. Miss Bellwether herself visited the chemist to get medicine. I put forth that she was never ill. You said she was an actress in her younger days? I think she only feigned illness as an excuse to visit the chemist where she bought the poison. She sent tea cakes to Lady Sapstrom to apologise for missing their luncheon date, and the tea cakes were laced with poison."

A cheer went up from the performers. "That's correct!" Anne-Marie said. "Mr. Chant, you are a better investigator than our own Christmas."

"Well," Chant said modestly. "I don't know about that..."

Gale rolled his eyes and kept them rolled back until his head throbbed again.

"Delightful!" their mother said. "And here I was thinking Lady Sapstrom had faked her own death as her corpse could not seem to keep still."

This sent Eugenie into another fit of giggles.

Helene ran up to them. "Did you like it, Mr. Chant? We only wrote it yesterday."

"That surprises me not at all," Gale muttered.

"It was excellent," Chant said. "I've not had such fun in a long while."

Cordelia stepped out from the pianoforte, grinning. "Could you really not solve it, Christmas?"

"I suppose I am... distracted," Gale replied. He felt Chant tense beside him, then heard the rumble of Chant's laughter, which tore at him in a way he did not wish to explore.

Elise approached a bit shyly.

"This was your idea, Elise?" Chant asked. Elise nodded. "Splendid."

"I thought you and Lord Christmas might like it, sir."

"We certainly did!"

Gale said nothing, and Chant nudged him again, less affection and more elbow this time.

"Yes, it was delightful," Gale forced himself to say. "We must only hope that Mr. Chant keeps this a secret. With the spotlight thrust onto our family recently, the last thing we need are rumours spreading that such well-bred young ladies spend their time putting on ghastly theatricals." He set his tea cup aside. His sisters were maddening, the whole bloody lot of them.

He realised with a faint start as he gazed at the girls that somehow he had included Elise in that mental assessment and had since the moment he'd entered the drawing room. What madness was that? Elise was not a Gale, and yet somehow the thought of sending her into the care of the parish once this was all over was distressing to him. It made his stomach clench in the same unpleasant way it had when de Cock had confronted him yesterday. Gale was *fearful*.

He stared at his tea cup for a moment, wishing to pick it up so that he might have something to do but also wary that the rattle of the cup against the saucer might give away the sudden tremble in his hands.

Gale was not unused to fear—he had been in many situations in the past where a sudden burst of it had given his body the speed to escape—but he could not recall ever having been afraid of losing another person before. This was Chant's fault too, no doubt. He had weakened Gale's heart to the point that even a small child could squeeze it uncomfortably hard.

Gale felt the sudden urge to reach out and take Chant's hand, just to reassure himself the man truly was flesh and blood. How could a mere man do this to him? It seemed impossible, and yet there he was, all these awful, useless *feelings* churning inside him.

He realised there was something he needed to do, even before he talked to Chant. He leaned down. "Elise? Could you come with me for a moment so we can talk?"

She eyed him warily but nodded. "Yeah. 'Course."

He led her into the empty dining room and pulled out a chair for her and then one for himself. He placed his hands between his knees and drew a deep breath, wondering where to start. "I'm sorry we haven't found Flum," he began.

Elise chewed her lip, swinging her legs. "Maybe he doesn't know where to find me because I been here so long. When I go back to my house, maybe he'll come then."

"Maybe," Gale agreed, deciding that the matter of Elise going "back to her house" was a conversation for another day. He wet his lips and tried again. "Elise, I think I know who killed your papa."

She didn't fall down wailing like a banshee like she had the night Gale had announced her father's death, so that was something. She stared at him with her disconcertingly wide-set eyes and waited.

"We think it was the captain," he went on cautiously.

Still she stared. "Will he hang?" she asked.

"He certainly ought to. Mr. Chant and I want to make sure justice is served to anyone responsible for your father's death. But we need more... evidence, you understand? Proof."

"You could make him confess," she suggested.

"Right. We could, possibly. But first we need proof enough to have him arrested. And I think the key to this whole thing is Flummery."

"You need to find Flum? I told you that."

"You did. What I need, though, is to know if there was anything unusual about Flum. Any reason at all the captain might have wanted him so badly."

Elise's eyes seemed to grow even more strange. There was something almost ghostly about them, as though if Gale looked into them, he wouldn't see his own reflection. He was so close. He could feel it. She was holding something back, and if he could just manage, for once in his life, not to say the wrong thing...

"I need the truth, Elise."

"He was a good dog," she whispered. "Maybe that's why the captain wanted him."

"I'm sure he was. But the captain is not a good man. I don't know that he would care about having a good dog."

Not a muscle moved in Elise's face. But there was a fierceness in her eyes that, for a second, scared Gale more than the prospect of loving Chant.

Chant.

He'd told Chant that honesty went both ways. He supposed that was true whether he was speaking to a lover, a friend, or an orphaned child.

He took another deep breath. "I know it can be hard to tell the truth if we think it will hurt someone or… or hurt us, I suppose. I myself cannot seem to find a middle ground between telling harsh truths much too bluntly and keeping important things to myself. But your father is gone now. And all that's left is to prove this captain killed him. If I promise to protect you from whatever comes of it, could you tell me the truth?"

Elise's chin wobbled slightly. Gale would have missed it if he hadn't been searching for some sign that she understood.

"What is it, Elise?" he asked softly. "What's valuable about Flum?"

Just then, a footman slipped inside the dining room. Gale could have bashed him over the head with the table's centrepiece. The spell between himself and Elise broke, and she was swinging her legs again, watching the footman.

"My lord," he said, bending close to Gale's ear and speaking in an undertone. "A message has arrived from a Mr. Fernside. He says a corpse has been recovered in Rotherhithe and that you would wish to be informed."

Gale rose. A corpse? Well then, yes, he must go to Rotherhithe at once. But…

He looked back at Elise, who didn't meet his gaze. "Pa was a cheat at cards," she said to the table. "Maybe he cheated the captain."

He'd asked her that first morning if her father's death might be related to his gambling. She'd been adamant that they weren't in debt. He hesitated, wondering if he should stay and do whatever it took to get this confession out of her. Then he remembered trying to call Flum to him. He didn't have the necessary skill to persuade children or dogs to do as he asked.

And he was not going to bully a child who was scared and hurting.

He and Chant didn't need Flummery at this point.

They needed de Cock.

"Maybe so," he said.

Elise looked up. "He's a good dog. The best dog. When you meet him, Lord Christmas, you'll see. Anyone would want him."

CHAPTER 14

*C*hant had never been in a cab that rattled as much as the one he was currently in did. He felt like a cork bouncing on a storm-tossed ocean as they headed for Surrey Quays. His knees kept banging into Gale's, and the cab smelled of both cheap perfume and the stench of unwashed bodies, sickly sweet and sour.

"You talked to Elise?" Chant ventured.

"I did. I didn't traumatise her, if that's what you're worried about."

"It wasn't. But I'm glad to hear it all the same."

"Whatever she's holding back, she doesn't feel she can tell us. So we're going to have to proceed without her help."

"Do you have any theories about the corpse?"

"I won't until I see it."

"Very well. Then might we speak about last night?" Chant asked.

Gale stared out the window. "I'm not sure we have anything to speak of, sir."

Chant tried not to let his frustration transform into anger. "Last night you talked of us sharing ourselves. Do you remember?"

"Last night I was drunk," Gale said and pressed his mouth into a tight line.

Chant huffed out a short, sharp breath. "Then we will speak no more about it."

Gale turned his head quickly and stared at him, and Chant imagined a thousand regrets in his suddenly wide, desperate gaze. For a moment, his heart pounded fast, and he imagined Gale's walls crumbling in beautiful defeat, and Gale falling into his arms—but Gale did not. He simply looked out the window again and paid Chant no more attention at all.

Chant had thought—foolishly, as it happened—that last night had been a turning point in their relationship, an acknowledgement that they were attracted to one another, and that they could have more than a friendship. But it seemed Gale did not feel the same. And Chant was weary. He'd hardly known Gale any amount of time at all, but already the man had wrung him out. He'd be damned if he'd live every day in the hope that Gale might offer him a scrap of affection if only the planets all aligned in whatever complicated pattern they had to for Gale to admit he cared. And he'd be damned if he'd be with any man who could only admit he had a heart when he was drunk.

The rest of the trip to Rotherhithe passed in silence.

It was drizzling when they arrived in the street outside Fernside's house, and Chant tugged his greatcoat around himself peevishly while Gale, for some reason, squinted at Fernside's dour little house and paced back and forth outside it for a while. He appeared to be counting his steps. Then he paid close attention to the houses on either side of Fernside's.

"What the devil are you doing, man?" Chant asked at last.

Fitz, Fernside's assistant, stood watching from the open front door, his expression clearly asking the same question. He was an odd little fellow, Chant thought. He could have been as young as a teenager—his face was unmarked by wrinkles, but there was a bleak, ageless quality about him too as though his face had been cast in porcelain. He leaned in the doorway and watched Gale stride back and forth along the wet street.

"Gale!" Chant called again, and Gale heeded him at last. He stopped his pacing and joined Chant at the front of the house.

They entered, and Fitz shut the door behind them.

"Door to the cellar is just ahead to your left," Fitz said. "The body's down there."

Chant shivered as they took the stairs down. It was colder down there than upstairs, and in the lamplight the walls shone a little with moisture, and Chant remembered how close they were to the river. There was a peculiar smell lingering; lye and vinegar over-laying something unpleasantly reminiscent of a butcher's shop. The chill in the air thankfully took the edge off the worst of the smell, but Chant pressed his cuff to his nose in any case.

There were three long tables in the cellar, and two were occupied.

"Ah," Fernside said, turning his attention away from the corpse on the table in front of him. An elderly man, Chant saw before Fernside drew a sheet up over him, his lined face pale and pinched in death, his jaw tied shut. Fernside moved to the next table. "He was pulled from the river this morning. Visser."

He drew the sheet back.

Visser was bloated, discoloured, and missing an ear. Worse, he had been slashed down the torso, from throat to belly, leaving an awful, gaping wound behind.

"Dear God," Chant managed, bile rising in his throat. "What kind of a monster…"

"Oh," Fernside said, looking startled. "No, that cut was mine. I was checking his lungs to see if he'd drowned."

Gale stepped forward to inspect the body more closely. "And did he?"

"There was no water in them," Fernside said. "He was dead before he hit the river." He gestured to the corpse. "I can take them out again if you would like to see."

"No!" Chant exclaimed. "I am sure we can take your word for it."

He turned away.

Gale, quite unexpectedly, slapped him on the shoulder. "Courage, man."

Chant resisted the urge toward some snide response. Yes, Lord Christmas Gale would know all about courage, wouldn't he?

He checked himself. If Gale did not wish to court anyone, then he did not wish to court anyone. He had as much right to desire an unpartnered life as Chant did to desire a partnered one. And truly, a man was dead. Why was Chant still thinking about his own unrequited affection? He forced himself to focus on the corpse, which only served to turn his stomach again. And so he forced himself to focus on the far wall of the cellar instead, fixing his gaze on the uneven brickwork as he listened to a series of peculiarly wet, squelching sounds as Fernside and Gale poked around in Visser's chest cavity. The sounds reminded him of Wellington boots being sucked into mud.

He was heartily relieved when the inspection was over, and Fitz led the way back upstairs to the kitchen and set about making tea while Fernside and Gale washed their hands to get rid of the stench. Chant sipped his tea and listened to Fernside and Gale discuss animalcules and something they called Kircher's little worms of the blood. Chant preferred not to imagine that every surface in the world was teeming with poisonous creatures so ubiquitous that they even lived inside people's bodies, and he wasn't enough of a scientist to follow much of the conversation. He wasn't sure what consensus was reached, if any at all, only that Fernside and Gale both washed their hands a second time before they took their tea.

Gale did not drink his tea. He stared at it for a moment as though it might have been holding all the mysteries of the universe and then set it down and strode out of the kitchen. A moment later Chant heard him pacing along the hallway, stopping every few moments and making a soft thumping sound, as though he was kicking the baseboard mouldings.

Fernside and Fitz exchanged a concerned look, and then both gazed at Chant.

"I cannot explain." Chant shrugged. "Gale defies explanation."

Gale leaned around the doorjamb. "How long have you owned this house?"

"I do not own it," Fernside said. "I rent it. I've been here for…" He furrowed his brow. "Eight months."

"Ah," said Gale, and vanished again. And then, "Here it is!"

Fernside, Chant, and Fitz crowded out into the hallway to find Gale inspecting a section of wall just beside the stairs to the cellar.

"I thought a priest hole at first." Gale nudged a section of the baseboard with the toe of his boot. There was a faint clicking sound, muffled and distant, and then a narrow section of the wall creaked open. "But what priest would hide on this end of Rother-hithe? Torture and death would be preferable. Also, there are ships right there to take you to France or Spain or some other papist sanctuary."

Chant stared in astonishment at the dark space behind the wall.

"But of course it's for smugglers," Gale said. "Astonishing the lengths men will go to avoid paying excise." He gestured into the darkness, and Chant saw a set of steps that led downwards. "I'd wager this passage leads to somewhere very close to the docks, and that it's common knowledge in certain circles. This is certainly how Visser escaped your custody, Fernside."

"Good Lord," Fernside said mildly.

"Well, bugger me," Fitz said, much less mildly.

Gale turned to Chant, an expression of almost childlike glee on his face. "Well, come along, Chant! Fetch a candle, and let's go!"

And then, without even waiting for Chant or the candle, he dived eagerly into the darkness.

～

*T*he passage, as Gale had known, brought them out at the docks, close enough to the *Condor* for Gale to feel a real chill. De Cock's threat still hung over him heavily, and he was aware that if de Cock was watching him, the captain would see that Chant was with him still, blinking dozily in the sudden light of day and making unhappy faces at the mud on his shoes and breeches.

"Come now," Gale said briskly. "We shall take a cab to Bucknall's. I am in need of a drink."

They dodged around a group of men conversing in a cloud of pipe smoke in the street.

"And are you in need of my company too?" Chant asked.

"I have no need of any man's company," Gale said. "But I find yours more tolerable than anyone else's."

Chant opened his mouth, and then closed it again. And then he laughed, a short, bitter sound, and shook his head. "Good day, sir."

"What? Are you not coming to Bucknall's with me? We have much to discuss."

Chant reached out and grasped his wrist gently. "Gale, perhaps the fault is mine in hoping for more than you are able to offer, and I hope it does not ruin our friendship, but for today? No, today I will not join you for a drink. You might find my company tolerable, but I fear I cannot say the same at this moment."

Gale's breath caught in his throat.

Chant smiled. The smile was brittle, but his eyes were still kind. They were always kind. "I am tired and in bad spirits. I think I would prefer to be alone for a while."

Gale didn't know how to respond to that; he didn't know how to feel about the sudden unease in his chest, as though Chant's words had caused a black whirlpool to begin spinning in the place his heart should be—a dizzying, sickening sensation of drowning.

"Call on me tomorrow," Chant said. "I shall be glad to see you, I promise. And please do not seek out danger on your own in the meantime. Will you swear it as my friend?"

"As… as your friend," Gale said numbly.

Chant squeezed his wrist. "Good day."

Gale watched him walk away, and then leaned against a wall and brooded for a while. Then, because he would rather brood with a drink in his hand, he looked for a cab and brooded all the way to the Bucknall Club.

Gale made directly for Hartwell at Bucknall's, as there was no sign yet of Soulden. "Where is young Warrington?" he asked, surprised to find Hartwell alone and without a drink. The fellow was eating a pie and reading a news sheet.

He looked up as Gale approached. "Gale! Are you feeling quite all right?"

"Well enough," Gale said shortly, taking a seat by him.

"We were worried about you."

"You needn't have been."

"Ah, well." Hartwell set the news sheet aside. "I know what it's like to be…"

"To be what?"

"To be in my cups."

Gale looked sideways at him, then down at the news sheet. "Still pretending you read?"

"I'll have you know, I am up to volume three of *The Maiden Diaries*, and Gale… there are certain objects that I simply do not feel should be put up one's orifices."

"That's probably true."

"And yet it all turns out so well for those characters."

"It's just fantasy."

"Yes, but *can* a shallot—?"

"You're reading the news today, though?"

Hartwell waved a hand. "I don't know what the world is coming to. Murder and mayhem, everywhere you look. That Dutch fellow, the governor's brother? One of the papers provided a gruesome description of his stabbing wounds—unfit to print, they're saying, and now the printer's in all sorts of trouble because, well, he did print it. The wounds were *gaping*, so the story went. Great holes, rather than cuts. And all over a few jewels. I nearly lost my breakfast."

Gale had all but stopped listening. He was thinking of Chant once more. And he was feeling *guilt*, which did not sit well with him. Guilt, over hurting a man he had never invited into his life. "Would you say that you ever chide Warry?"

"Chide?" Hartwell repeated.

"Yes, chide."

"Are we on to a new subject?"

"We are. Do you chide him?"

Hartwell sat back. "Why, certainly."

"Under what circumstances?"

"Er… well, nowadays, it is more often he who chides me, for I have the baser manners of us two. I used to chide him for being a nuisance and an irrepressible whelp. But now if I chide him, it is usually for being a temptation."

Gale tilted his head, trying to understand. "A temptation?"

"Yes, you see, it doesn't seem to matter what he is doing. Whether he is standing or reclining or eating or reading or talking of scabies in sheep, I find myself thinking unseemly thoughts. So I chide him for habitually tempting me down the path of darkness, which used to have the delightful effect of turning him bright red and causing him to stammer, but now, the cheeky fellow, he grins. Or worse, continues on with whatever he was doing, but in an even more lascivious manner."

"I feel I am receiving more information than I bargained for."

"Do you know—I would never have thought this of Warry, but he can eat any food, and I do mean *any* food, in a manner suggestive of playing a fellow's pipe? Just last week I watched him eat a boiled egg and nearly spent in my drawers."

"This is definitely more information than I bargained for."

"You asked."

"And I am sorry I did. But you are... you are only teasing him in these circumstances. Do you ever chide him in earnest?"

Now Hartwell was staring at him with open curiosity. Gale struggled to keep his expression neutral. "Are you recently chid?" Hartwell inquired.

"It is of no consequence."

"Ah! Now you have turned nearly the colour Warry used to."

"Don't be ridiculous."

"Was Mr. Benjamin Chant unhappy with your drunken behaviour?"

"No. He was... he was very good to me," Gale admitted. "But prior to indulging, I had... done something rather dangerous. And I just wonder why on earth he felt it his business to weigh in on the foolishness of my actions."

Hartwell drummed his fingers on the table, then crossed his outstretched legs at the ankle. "It sounds to me as if he cares for you."

"Then it is I who should chide him for his foolishness." Gale paused. "He said he must know whether I... whether..."

"Yes?"

"Whether I think myself capable of sharing any part of myself with him."

Hartwell did not speak.

"He wants a courtship," Gale continued flatly.

"And do you want a courtship?"

"Of course not!"

"And you told him that?"

"Of course not."

"But you *will* tell him that?"

Gale pressed his forehead into his hand. "I don't know. I don't know what to do. This case has me all out of sorts."

"Did you just call it a c—"

"*Yes*. There was a drunk fellow who was murdered, and I took his orphaned child to my house, and today, I thought of her as a sister, but she may hold a secret she refuses to share with anyone that could help me solve this riddle. Chant wants something from me I am not prepared to give, and he *chided* me... Hartwell, am I losing my bloody mind?"

"Good Lord. You and I need to dine together more often. I feel I am always about eight steps behind in the story of your life."

"But am I mad?"

"I don't think so." Hartwell's voice remained quiet. "And while I would never suggest making a commitment you do not wish to make, I can't help thinking perhaps Chant would want to help you bear the other burdens you mentioned."

That was precisely what Gale feared. "I do not require his assistance."

"Perhaps not, but it might be nice to have it."

Gale wished he had never begun this conversation. "I treated him badly. Today. Well, several times. But most recently, this morning."

"Well, then he ought to have the sense to stay away from you. But if he does not, you might try apologising and not treating him badly in the future."

How could Hartwell make it sound so simple? Apologise, and then do what? Make some sort of promise he was not sure he could keep?

Gale was relieved beyond measure when he saw Soulden pass through the room. At a nearby table, Loftus Rivingdon, his near-silver blond hair shining in the lamplight, looked up from his conversation and followed Soulden with a gaze as hungry as a wolf's. Gale got up, determined to reach Soulden before Rivingdon did.

He caught up to him in the next reading room, touching him on the shoulder and causing him to startle.

"Oh, thank God," Soulden said when he turned, his shoulders slumping. "I thought you were someone else." He narrowed his eyes. "Why do you have mud on your breeches?"

"Secret passage," Gale said.

"I do love a secret passage," Soulden said.

"Is that a euphemism?"

"Not at all. I love secret passages, and also pert arses, and I never mix the two of them up."

"Yes," Gale said. "I remember from school."

"Yours was much perter then." Soulden appraised Gale with a narrow gaze. "You aren't forgetting to eat again, are you?"

"You are not"—*Chant*, he wanted to say—"my mother," he decided at last.

"I am not," Soulden agreed. "Tell me about this secret passage. Where in blazes did you find it?"

"Rotherhithe. The surgeon's house," Gale said. "For smuggling, of course."

"Of course," Soulden agreed. "Was it filled with skeletons and treasure and the ghosts of pirates?"

Gale rolled his eyes. "It was filled with mud, primarily. But it led to a spot at the docks very near the *Condor*."

Soulden's eyes narrowed. "I have heard whisperings," he said in a low voice, "about de Cock and a certain murder that is being blamed on the French, that de Cock may have had a hand in."

Gale felt a thrum of anticipation as heady as alcohol. "Tell me."

Soulden looked around the room and then drew Gale closer to the bookshelf. "De Cock is a Dutch privateer, working with the blessing of his king, and of course, with the blessing of ours because the enemy of our enemy is our friend."

"Our enemy and their enemy both being the French, of course," Gale said, cocking a brow.

"Of course," Soulden said, a smile pricking the corners of his mouth.

"Despite the fact that England has restored the Bourbons *twice* now."

"Despite that," Soulden agreed. "King Louis ought to be more careful with that throne of his. He keeps losing it, only to have us return it to him."

"I care not for politics. Tell me of de Cock."

"Well," Soulden said, "you have heard of Claude de Brouckère, yes?"

"Yes," Gale replied. "The brother of the governor of Limburg. Murdered by the French at sea. You have heard otherwise?"

"Whispers, as I say." Soulden ran his fingers down the spine of a book. "*If* de Cock is the one who killed Claude de Brouckère, then he murdered his own countryman, and he is most certainly a pirate and not a privateer."

Gale frowned, his mouth turning down. And then it hit him. Hartwell rambling on about murder and mayhem. 'That Dutch fellow,' stab wounds like holes rather than cuts. De Cock's work without a doubt. "Does the Dutch king know? Did he perhaps order the murder? If so, will de Cock ever face justice at all, or will he be allowed to slip the noose at the last moment? There may be political machinations and entanglements here we shall never uncover, or perhaps the plain truth is that de Cock is mad and greedy, and de Brouckère was simply an unfortunate victim of that. There were missing jewels, were there not?"

"Yes," Soulden said. "I believe the news sheets have that part correct."

Gale hummed. Surely the jewels were sold off when de Cock disembarked, perhaps. Buried before the *Condor* ever reached the Thames, even. Or possibly they were not lost at all, and they were still hidden aboard that black ship someplace. Or…

No.

"I can see your brain ticking over like clockwork," Soulden said. "It's just a rumour, remember."

"What is it, Elise? What's valuable about Flum?"

Please, please don't let de Cock have hidden stolen jewels up that damn dog's arse.

"Of course," Gale said, attempting to keep his expression

neutral. "And yet we both know that you, my dear Pip, have your ear to the ground in some very high up places."

Soulden smiled. "That's just another rumour, Christmas. Now, if you'll excuse me, I must make myself scarce before that little Rivingdon fellow finds me. I suspect that if he gets close, he shall be harder to dislodge than a tick."

"I suspect you are correct," Gale said.

"Ah, but before I do…" Soulden took a letter from the inside pocket of his waistcoat, and held it out to Gale. "Good day, Christmas."

Gale slipped the letter into his sleeve. "Good day, Pip."

Soulden clapped him on the shoulder and hurried away.

CHAPTER 15

"It is technically tomorrow," Gale said when Chant, sleep rumpled and confused, opened the door to him. He stepped past Chant into the house, all elbows and sharp angles. "You said you would be pleased to see me if I called on you tomorrow. Why don't you have a footman or a butler to open your door?"

"I have a butler," Chant said. "Also a footman, and a cook, and a scullery maid, and a hall boy. And I am sure they are all asleep as God and nature intended us to be when the sun isn't even up yet!"

"Hmm." Gale swept through into the parlour, where the glow from the embers of the fire that had burned down overnight still illuminated the room. Chant had fallen asleep here several hours before, a book in hand, only to be awoken by the knocking on the door.

"Do you make a habit of nocturnal visitations?" he asked, tugging his shirt straight and dragging his fingers through his hair.

Gale didn't answer him. He only stared in astonishment at the creature snoozing in front of the fire. "Why is there a dog in here?"

"The boys tried to catch her again to remove her from the house once we had established she wasn't Flummery, but she was not inclined to be caught."

Gale curled his lip. "At least it isn't the crow-pecked one, I suppose."

"You liked that one," Chant said.

"I did not."

"Well, it liked you."

Gale snorted.

Chant stood and gazed at him for a moment, utterly at a loss to understand what the man was doing here a good hour before dawn. He wondered if Gale sometimes simply forgot to sleep the way he forgot to eat. "I'm calling her Miranda."

"*The Tempest?*"

Chant nodded blearily, stifling a yawn.

Miranda woke then and realised they had a visitor. She growled suspiciously and let out a low, gruff bark. "She already hates me," Gale said.

"You might kneel and let her sniff you. Or give her those scraps on the table there, then she'll be your friend forever. Or if you have more bacon in your pocket…"

"I do not want to be her friend forever."

"Suit yourself."

Gale glowered at Chant for a moment, his dark eyes catching the first grey light coming through the window, and Chant tried not to laugh. Then Gale slowly bent and placed his hand nearer to the floor. He did not stick it in Miranda's face as Chant often saw people do with dogs—a sure-fire way to get bitten. Miranda took a few steps forward, then skittered back with an uncertain growl. "You see? Animals despise me. People too. But it is rather brutal, I must admit, to be hated by dogs."

"She does not hate you. She's only shy."

"So shy she refused to be parted from you."

"What can I say? She and I got on." Chant smiled as Miranda stood and stretched, then made her way over and stood protectively beside Chant. Chant stroked her great hairy head.

"Yes, well," Gale said brusquely. "I have come with two pieces of news. I am torn as to which to present to you first. But I gave it some thought on the way over, and the news pertaining to the investigation can wait. First, I wish for you to have this." He handed Chant a twice-folded piece of paper.

Chant eyed him as he slid the paper open. "What on earth is it?"

"Read it." Gale looked uncharacteristically... proud?

Chant gazed down at the paper. It was too dim for him to make out the words, and he moved closer to the window. Miranda sighed and flopped down again. On the paper was written an address. In France. A woman's name—Sylvie Babin. Dates spanning two years... "I don't understand."

Gale stepped closer. "I asked Soulden to make some inquiries. He's very well connected. He was able to ascertain where Reid has been living and for how long. Sylvie, that's the girl he married. That second address, that is where he teaches. All in all, it sounds as if Reid is safe and well. And quite happy with his life in France."

The bottom dropped out from Chant's stomach. He stared at the paper, his hand beginning to shake, and then he stepped away from the window and dropped onto the settee. He let the page fall to the floor. "What have you done?" he asked softly.

Gale stepped into his line of vision, but Chant did not dare look at him. His light-headedness turned to an awful pounding on the inside of his skull. "I found out what became of Reid. You do not have to wonder anymore."

This couldn't be happening. That paper—the information on it —that could not be real. It could not be true that Gale was standing before him, having handed him that page as though it were a bottle of poison that he were cheerfully asking Chant to drink.

"I never asked for this!" Chant's voice came out high and ragged. "When did I ask you to—to spy upon Reid?" It was as though a private corner of his heart had been invaded by gunfire and cannon blasts. He wished to cover himself somehow—physically and psychologically. But there was nothing to do but sit here before Gale and let a thousand old hurts rush back to him at once.

"Good God, man. You said you wanted to know what had become of him!"

"I didn't mean for you to send one of your *spies* to find him!"

"I thought to do a good thing for you! I thought..."

Chant took a deep breath. How could the man possibly be so brilliant and so dense at the same time? "Gale... I don't know how to explain this. How invasive it feels. I am attempting to leave Reid in the past where he belongs. To move forward. Seeing this... it *hurts*. It rips all those old wounds open again."

"I do not think they ever healed," Gale said bluntly. "You have not left Reid in the past. He is with you all the time. I wanted you to have... Chant, I wanted you to have peace."

Chant almost laughed. *Peace?*

He glanced down again at the paper on the floor, trying to put his thoughts in some sort of order. Hearing the sincerity in Gale's voice, he realised this was not quite the betrayal it had first seemed. And yet he wanted to shout. Not at Gale, necessarily. Well, perhaps at Gale. But just... shout until his throat was raw, until the weight on his chest lifted. Reid was married. Reid, who could not make a commitment to Chant, who in fact had gone across the ocean without a word in order to get away from Chant, was happily married. And Gale had thought this would bring Chant peace? He shook his head. If he could just have a few minutes to himself... But Gale was here, and—and it wouldn't help anything to shout him away. "I understand that you didn't do this to hurt me."

"Of course I didn't."

"No, it is not that simple, Gale. 'Of course you didn't.' It is not so obvious to me. This *feels* like it was done to hurt me. That may not be logical on my part, but it is how I feel."

"I didn't think. Chant, I am sorry. I do not always understand... Well, it is as you said. I do not always understand people's feelings. I do have feelings of my own, believe it or not. But I always seem to be walking a path parallel to the one the crowd takes. And it is as if there is only a small stretch of grass separating the two paths, but it might as well be leaping flame for all I can get across it to join everyone else. I am… sorry."

Chant sighed wearily. Perhaps he was too forgiving. Perhaps he always had been. Perhaps Gale behaved the way he did in part because he was entitled, indulged, and had never been asked to behave any other way. But Chant knew there was at least some truth to the man's words. This was how he perceived the world—as not having been designed for someone like him. If Gale's expression was anything to go by, what he had just confessed to Chant was not a bid for sympathy, or an excuse, but a difficult admission and as close to the truth as Gale could come.

Chant ran his hand over his forehead. "I should not have said what I did last night about your inability to comprehend people's feelings. I was angry and frustrated. Your mind is unusual, Gale, but you are not deficient. We may just need time to learn to understand each other." He closed his eyes and tugged at his own hair for a moment, then forced his eyes open again. "Reid is happy?"

"It seems so," Gale said awkwardly.

"That's good, then."

Gale approached the settee warily and sat on the other side—as far from Chant as possible.

Chant blew out another breath. "Gale. There are things you don't know about me. You were right when you said the sharing of ourselves must go both ways. I have never had to tell this story aloud, and I don't know what it will feel like to tell it."

"You may tell it to me," Gale said quietly. "If you trust me with it."

"I fear you'll despise me."

"I will not." Gale turned to him, looking mildly alarmed. "How could I? I have just hurt you—very badly—and you are letting me sit with you, and you are offering explanations instead of breaking my jaw, and I… If you think I could ever despise you, you are—you are just—very wrong."

There was a long silence.

"So you may tell me. I wish very much that you would. But only if you want to."

Chant dug his teeth into his lip. How to start? How to arrange the mess of his past into something presentable to Gale? He realised there was no way to do so. He would have to show Gale the whole disastrous spill of it.

"My sister," Chant began, "was… odd. That's what my parents called it at least. She would have fits where her body would jerk and she would lash out. She might shout obscenities or nonsense. But, Gale, she was sweetness itself when you knew her, you must believe me. My parents called it an affliction. Her doctors too. And I suppose it was. But I also think that, were the world more receptive to the idea that we are all made differently—that it is not really for any of us to say what is normal or right—perhaps her character would not have seemed such a burden to my mother. My father loved her so very dearly. My mother too, in her way. But my father was especially bonded to her. He was a busy man, and I don't think he fully understood the toll it took on my mother to care for Jenny in a society that thinks those with 'afflictions' ought to be locked away and only spoken of in whispers. Jenny's prospects lay in marriage. But my mother took her to a rout one Season, and it was such a disaster that we attended no more events. Gradually I noticed my parents were keeping Jenny inside more and more. Not even trips to the pie shop or the bookstore were permitted. Jenny became all but a captive within those walls. And I did very little to try to free her." Chant heard his voice lose its steadiness. He took a breath, then forced himself to continue.

"She was eighteen when she died. I was fifteen. I had never known grief before, and even in my wildest imaginings, I had not realised how terrible it would be. Perhaps my father had not realised either. He took to sitting in his armchair in our parlour, day after day. My mother would cajole him to eat, but soon he would barely do that. He would drink sherry but had little use for food or water and even less use for company. Still, I would sit with him each day and talk to him about... about whatever came to mind. Every once in a while he would respond, and my heart would lift, and I would think surely, any day now, he will come out of his stupor and be my father again.

"And then he stopped speaking altogether." Chant paused again. He could feel Gale's gaze on him. "That was the end of things for my mother. She left, and it was just my father and me, alone in that great house. I... I have older brothers. My father had been married before. But they did not care to see him. We had occasional visitors, but mostly, we were fodder for the rumour mill. I cared for him—if you could call it that. We had some servants who stayed and helped, but most of the household vanished. I forced him to eat. I tried to limit his drink, but you see, he would not eat at all unless I poured him a sherry first. So I watered it down, for his sake.

"I grew... Oh God. Gale, I... I grew unkind to him after the first year. This... anger descended on me, and I could not shake it. At first I let it out in my own room. I would shout and swear, bash my fist against the wall until my knuckles were bloody. I thought maybe that would finally pull him from the fog. That he would be unable to stand the noise and would speak at last, if only to order me beaten. But he remained in his chair, silent, staring at the wall. Even when I began to shout and curse at *him*. The things I said..."

He could not go on for several long moments. "And then I became silent too. As much a ghost as he. For five long years, I was very quiet. I behaved myself; I really tried. I thought perhaps if his mind was unburdened by my presence, he would... be well."

Chant tensed as Gale shifted nearer to him. "Do not come closer," Chant said hoarsely, "until you have heard it all. I cannot bear to see you recoil in disgust."

Gale ignored that and put his hand on Chant's hunched back. Chant closed his stinging eyes, his throat too tight to protest. Gale's voice was low. "I have not recoiled these last three days from corpses, ghastly leg wounds, or severed ears. I shall not recoil from you."

Chant drew a shuddering breath. He could not deny how good Gale's touch felt, how much it steadied him. What a desperate, pathetic creature he was.

"Needless to say, my silence did not save him. Things continued much as they had, except now I rarely ate either. And sometimes I drank. The rumour mill had begun to call my father the old mad earl, and I'm sure there were things said about me as well, but I didn't care. I did not feel like a person at all. I didn't even really hurt anymore, and perhaps that should have been a mercy, but it was the scariest thing of all. To feel that I had been shrunken down and put in a little box somewhere and that the only safety I would ever know again lay in feeling absolutely nothing. And then I met Reid." Chant smiled in spite of himself. "I was out one day, and I—I meant to go and buy a new shirt for my father, but I ended up at a stationer's. I don't know how. And the stationer could not get me to speak, to say where I lived, but Reid was in the shop, and said he'd get me home. I don't know to this day how he did it. But he stayed with me until I could speak again, and he made sure my father and I had supper. And after that, he visited regularly and helped with my father. He took me out on excursions, drew me from the twisted mess I had made of my own mind."

Gale's hand moved gently down his back, then up again. Chant stared straight ahead at the vases.

"I loved him so much. He seemed to love me in return, and at the time, I could not imagine that, Gale. I could not. Someone who could love the ruin of me.

"But he started to talk of how we would travel. How we would go sailing. How we would visit France one day. It was as though he no longer remembered that I had an invalid father to care for. He was so caught up in dreams of our future together. I was caught up too. But one day, I brought up the issue of my father, and he spoke seriously to me, saying I could not devote the whole of my youth to caring for a man who would not ever lift a finger to help himself. He said I had a choice to make." Chant paused again, wondering how his ribs had suddenly become iron bands. "I chose Reid. I left my father in the care of a live-in nurse, and I found this place, this house with the churchyard view. For the first time in my life, I felt like a whole person. Reid visited nearly every day. I have never known such lightness. Such freedom. If Reid could sometimes be difficult—prone to brooding and silence, I overlooked it. Even though at times it filled me with terror—as though Reid might become a ghost like my father. Eventually, Reid and I began making plans in earnest to travel. But then a letter came from my father's house. He was growing worse. He was having fits and outbursts of violence. The nurse could no longer manage him alone. I was devastated and planned to go to him at once.

"But Reid told me I should not. That if I did, that house should have me in its grip again, and this time I would never get free. I believed him. He said to let him take care of the situation. Of me. It had been so long since anyone had... had taken care of me. I am ashamed, but I let him do what he felt we ought. And after a week, he came to me with the name of a hospital. It was a fine place, he said. Not one of those dreadful institutions you read about in Gothic novels. My father would be well cared for. All I had to do was sign a form."

He gave Gale space to speak. To draw back. To condemn him. For surely Gale knew the end of the story by now. But Gale said nothing, just kept his hand, warm and solid, on the back of Chant's dressing gown.

"I did." Chant was weeping quite suddenly, but did not have the energy to be ashamed of himself. He put his face in his hands, hoping to at least muffle the terrible sounds coming from him. "I signed it."

"And Reid left," Gale said softly.

Chant nodded into his hands. He forced his head up slightly so he could be heard. "He left not two months later. My father died the year after that. And then I had no one. You see, even after I'd left my father's home, I… I was so very wrapped up in Reid I made no friends to speak of."

Gale's hand continued moving slowly up and down Chant's back.

Chant let out a bitter laugh turned at once to a sob. "I did not believe at first that Reid had left. I thought something must have happened to him. Drowned, murdered. Kidnapped. Eventually I did locate the man who had arranged Reid's passage to France. So I knew he had gone willingly. But even years later, I would still think, maybe a body will turn up. Maybe there will be some clue showing how he was coerced onto that ship. And then I will know it was not me who drove him away."

Gale made a soft sound of sympathy.

Chant was afraid to breathe, afraid he'd choke on the air.

"So when I told you he was happily married in France…"

Chant attempted a few ragged breaths. "I suppose I am glad to know. How could I have wanted him to stay, me being what I am? If I'd truly cared for him, I would have sent him to France myself."

"What are you?" Gale sounded confused.

Chant swallowed hard. "Have you not heard anything I've said? I put my father in an asylum so that I might travel to the Continent with a fellow I liked."

"There is far more to it than that," Gale said firmly.

Chant wished he had a handkerchief. Was surprised when Gale handed him one. He wiped his eyes and blew his nose. "You must think me astonishingly soft. Which I am. But I assure you, I have not wept in many years."

"I think no less of you for weeping."

"I should have stayed with him. My father. And been the son he needed."

"No. Chant, listen to me." Gale's voice was impossibly calm, and Chant quieted somewhat in response. "You did the very best you could."

Chant wept harder then, fool that he was, and Gale tightened his arm around his shoulders, drawing Chant into him.

Chant could not have resisted if he'd wanted to. He leaned against Gale, sobbing brokenly until the rhythm of it took him over and blocked out all thought.

~

*G*ale did not have time to reflect on what a bloody fool he'd been. His only priority right now was Chant. He held the other man as the weak grey light grew stronger, and dawn came.

"I'm right here," he whispered at one point. Which seemed, perhaps, the least comforting thing he could say. For what good did it do anyone to have Gale there? More often than not, Gale's presence did outright harm.

But, he reflected, Reid had disappeared on Chant. As had Chant's sister. And for all intents and purposes, Chant's parents. So perhaps Chant would like to know that Gale was not going anywhere. That the whole knobby, useless, uncomforting bulk of him would remain right here with Chant for as long as Chant needed.

He rubbed Chant's back in slow, steady strokes, relieved and a bit awed at how Chant calmed for him.

"You are a good man," he said, hardly aware of what he was saying, "who was put in a very difficult situation. It's all right now. I promise. It's all right."

Chant let out another breath in a rush and leaned hard against him. "I am not kind. I am not good."

"You are both. I know many things. You must believe me on this."

"You said I feel what I feel with good reason. And so you don't begrudge me an expression of those feelings. But what if I don't have good reason? What if I want to punch and kick and tear this whole bloody place apart for no other reason than that I imagine it would be satisfying?"

Gale glanced down at him, his chin resting on the top of Chant's head. "Then I shall assist you in any way I can. I shall spectate silently, cheer you on, help you tear things apart. Or leave if you should rather commit this act of destruction on your own."

Chant snorted through his tears. "I shall not commit such an act."

"Why not?"

"It does no good." Chant straightened, looking at Gale. "I should know that by now."

Gale did not know if what he was about to propose would be of any use to Chant at all. But he supposed it was worth a try. "I'll tell you what. In my private apartment in Russell Street, I have a decorative jug, given to me by the Earl of Someplace or Other. Several weeks ago, something quite terrible was done to it—not by me, mind you. By a friend. I am loath to disclose names, but it was Lord Hartwell. I will spare you the details, but suffice it to say I have not been able to look at this jug the same way since. And I never will." He paused. "Should you like to break it?"

"Break it?"

"Yes."

"But…" Chant appeared to consider this. "Now?"

"Well, yes."

"We would have to go to Russell Street."

"It is worth the trip, I'd say. To kill two birds with one stone like this. You shall be rid of some of what you're holding in, and I shall be rid of the desecrated jug forever."

Chant laughed softly. "You are mad."

"Oh, that should have been obvious to you from the start."

Chant smiled, though he didn't look at Gale. He stared at his hands, trapped between his knees. "It was."

"So, to Russell Street?"

Chant stood slowly, and Gale with him. He scrubbed his hands over his face. "I look a fright, I'm sure."

"It is very early still. No one of consequence will see."

Chant snorted. "Please don't hasten to reassure me that I in fact look quite lovely."

"Well, you do," Gale said, frowning. "It's just… If I may?" He extended a hand slowly toward Chant's face, giving Chant time to grant or deny permission, just as Gale's mother had done for Gale as a boy.

Chant nodded once, and Gale cupped Chant's jaw, brushing his thumb under the man's eyes and flicking away the wetness there. Then, on an impulse—perhaps the strangest impulse he'd ever had—he kissed the matching spots where he'd wiped away tears, salt clinging faintly to his lips. He stepped back so he could see Chant's face. It was still red and damp, and his eyes shone with unshed tears, but he was indeed lovely. And there was need in his gaze. Gale might not have been brilliant at interpreting emotions, but Chant's longing was as plain as if he had spoken it. Chant began to lean forward, then stopped, a question in his eyes. Gale stepped forward again and kissed him softly on the mouth. It seemed such a natural thing to do. Chant kissed him back with a cautious hunger that Gale answered with a sigh and a nonsensical murmur against the other man's lips. Chant closed his eyes, and Gale tasted salt again as Chant's tears spilled over. He stroked the side of Chant's face. The man's eyes remained closed, his pale lashes darkened and stuck damply together. Gale ran his thumb back and forth along one elegant cheekbone until Chant at last opened his eyes. He met Gale's gaze with a shyness Gale had never before seen from him.

Gale said, "You do not have to do anything right now except break a jug. And you do not even have to do that if you don't wish. I will get us to Russell Street. You may sleep there after the jug-breaking, as I have ruined any hope you had of a good sleep tonight. Or I will take you back home. You need think of nothing else except how good it will feel to watch an exceptionally ugly piece of pottery shatter at your feet. All right?"

Chant nodded. "All right," he whispered.

"No murders, no missing dogs, no orphaned children—"

"You are making me think of all of those things by saying them."

"Right. I'm sorry."

Gale kissed him again, this time on the forehead. How could he not have realised, until now, all that he felt for this man? What did one do when one had firmly rejected the world again and again and then found himself too proud to ask to be let back in? Gale had never meant to stray so far from kindness. Just that it had been so much easier to barricade himself in, to invite others to try to hurt him so he could experience that small satisfaction every time they could not get close enough to do so. It had felt like a victory when in fact it was a self-inflicted wound deeper than any Society might have laid upon him. It was so stunningly easy now to do what he should have done all along and take Chant's hand.

"Come on then, my friend. Let me take care of this."

Of you.

But he didn't say it.

～

*C*hant found Gale's rooms in Russell Street to be tidy if a bit stark. The woman who'd chased him away from the building two days ago was nowhere in sight.

"The place is quite pleasant. Though it does not look entirely lived in." Chant straightened his coat. He'd tried to dress well, at least, to make up for his swollen face and dishevelled hair. He'd had some practice over the years in dressing without the help of his man. But he'd been so out of sorts as he'd pulled on his clothes he was not sure he looked at all put together. His front was already covered in dog hair from his goodbye to Miranda, and he'd forgotten his greatcoat entirely—an oversight Gale had remedied as soon as he'd noticed it by lending Chant his own.

Gale nodded. "It is a bit like your home in that regard. Or rather, no. Your home does look lived-in. It just looks like you are afraid to live in it fully."

Chant's mouth hung open for a second. "Whatever do you mean?"

"Only that your house has much of you in it, but there is also a palpable sense of your own fear to occupy it entirely, perhaps because you think that doing so means you are edging out the memories of the loved ones you've lost, when in fact it means nothing of the sort, and it is slowly draining you, in a nearly imperceptible way, to pour so much of yourself into your memories as though you fear their very ghosts will return to those memories to find you absent from them, gone to live in the present. You fear that seizing the happiness you are entitled to will be somehow disrespectful to those you have grieved for. Am I close?"

Chant could do nothing but gape.

"Oh God. I have hurt you again." Gale looked genuinely horrified. "Please, Chant, I didn't mean to. I am absolutely terrible at offering comfort and at everything to do with conversation, really. You may break the jug over my head if you wish."

Chant gazed at him with more interest than affront. Gale's skin was red-gold in the lamplight, and he... he meant it. He was sorry. He was afraid of offending Chant. He cared what Chant felt. Gale had kissed him—he could still feel Gale's lips on his—and Gale had brought him here to break a jug. "You're right," Chant admitted. "Though I wish you weren't."

Gale said nothing.

"Oh God." Chant drew a breath, willing himself not to weep again. Gale surely wouldn't have the patience for another round of such childish behaviour.

"It's all right," Gale said again. And once again Chant's entire body relaxed.

Chant stared at the floor. "They're not coming back."

"No."

"Even if I break the jug."

"Even if you break the jug."

"But it might… feel good to break the jug."

"It might," Gale agreed. "And to scream. Or cry some more. You may punch me if you like—though not very hard. My frame is rather insubstantial."

"Will you tell me what happened to the jug to make you hate it so?"

"No."

"All right. Where is it?"

"Here." Gale brought it to him. It wasn't as ugly as Gale had made it out to be. It was stout and earth-coloured, a good two feet high, with a deep lip that tapered to a small spout on one side. A deep red glaze ran over the rim and about halfway down its sides. Chant took it from Gale. It was unexpectedly heavy.

"What if the neighbours hear?"

"They're quite deaf."

"You are lying."

"I would not tell you to break it if I felt there would be any serious consequences."

Chant drew a deep breath, feeling suddenly foolish. And yet, Gale was looking at him as though he were anything but foolish, as though this moment they were about to create together was as intimate as any they might share in a bed.

Chant dropped the jug.

It hit the floor with a *thunk*, toppled to its side, and rolled across the floorboards, unharmed.

"It is very well made, Chant. You are going to have to put some effort into breaking it." Gale picked the jug up and handed it back to him.

Chant hurled it downward this time. He did not give himself time to think. He simply threw it.

It shattered into several large shards and a few smaller pieces. Chant stamped on the smaller pieces, grinding them to dust. He could not seem to stop. But when he finally did, he stared at the mess, a sick shame washing over him.

"It is only a vase. It is not them."

"Don't you think I know that!" Chant snapped.

"I do," Gale said. "Go on and yell at me. I am not them either. I shan't go away."

"Oh God," Chant choked, putting his fist to his forehead and squeezing his eyes shut. "I'm sorry."

"You are not allowed to apologise. It is the one rule here. That, and do not piss and vomit into my jugs."

Chant opened his eyes. "Piss *and* vomit?"

Gale held out his arms as though he were quite accustomed to embracing people, which Chant did not think he was. And Chant stepped into his arms as though it were a familiar routine between them, broken pottery crunching under his shoes. "I'm sorry. I had no wish to upset you further, but yes."

Chant laughed, a bit hysterically, into Gale's shoulder. Gale's hand never stopped moving up and down his back. His answering chuckle bumped his chest against Chant's in a way that was incredibly reassuring.

"In quantities you cannot fathom."

Chant clutched at the back of Gale's coat, twisting fistfuls of the fabric in a childish effort to assure himself Gale really would not vanish. He drew in a deep breath, then loosened his grip. Exhaled.

"Good man," Gale whispered.

Chant had no wish to be anywhere but Gale's arms. But he was exhausted, and Gale's patience was unlikely to last forever. "I can see myself home," he said into the wool of Gale's coat. "Thank you for being so kind to me."

"You may sleep here as I said. Or I will take you home."

"No, truly." Chant stepped back. Gale's arms loosened around him but did not release him, and Chant could not bring himself to take another step back and break the embrace entirely. "You've done more than is necessary. I—"

"This is not a favour I am doing out of a sense of obligation," Gale said seriously. "Tell me what you wish."

"I… I am very tired. And I feel embarrassed. And strange. And very… tired."

"Then might I suggest we get you out of your coat and shoes and into the bed?"

"What about the investigation?" It came back to Chant suddenly. "You said you had other news."

"The investigation can wait." Gale's voice was still soft, but he spoke with utter certainty. He drew the heavy curtains until only a thin strip of light remained on the floorboards.

"I…" Chant could scarcely believe this was happening. He didn't feel at all nervous that Gale would grow impatient with him for needing comfort, that Gale would expect anything of him in return. He felt entirely safe here. "Very well."

And then Chant let Gale remove his coat, cravat, and waistcoat, as though he were a small child who could not do such things without assistance. The shoes he managed on his own, and he pulled his stockings off too.

Gale hesitated. "I have slept in breeches before. It is not terribly comfortable. Should you wish to remove yours and sleep in your shirt, I shan't be offended. I have already seen you in half dress, after all."

Chant snorted. "At least I had a gown on then." He hesitated. "Are you… staying? You seem not to have slept at all."

Gale shrugged. "I could do with a rest. If that doesn't bother you? I can sleep in the chair if you prefer. Or we can share the bed. I promise to be a gentleman."

"You are not sleeping in the chair, Lord Christmas. I forbid it."

"Ah. Well then." Gale shrugged out of his own coat, unbuttoned his waistcoat, and yanked free his cravat. His shoes and stockings went next, pushed into a pile beside Chant's. "If you forbid it, I daren't go against you." He stepped toward the bed.

"You find breeches uncomfortable to sleep in," Chant pointed out.

Gale stopped. "I do."

"If you wish to remove them, I shan't be offended." He managed a ghost of a smile in response to the lift of Gale's brows.

Gale hesitated only a second, then began to unbutton the fall on his breeches.

Chant worked on his own buttons, though he could not keep himself from watching Gale as the man stepped out of his breeches and stood before Chant in just his shirt, which hung to his thighs.

"If you've looked your fill," Gale said with a hint of imperious annoyance that Chant knew was a tease. "Might I have my turn?"

Chant grinned and finished removing his own breeches. He tossed them on top of Gale's. His breathing was not entirely even. Gale was gorgeous. Gale was always gorgeous, and especially so half-stripped of his clothing. But Chant had not the energy for anything carnal right now. He didn't even know if the interest was there on Gale's part. Though, if the front of his drawers was anything to go by, Gale was at the very least not *un*interested.

"I have fantasised so often about you taking off your clothes in front of me," Chant confessed. "It is every bit as delicious as I imagined. I only wish that tonight I were not so..."

"Tired?" Gale supplied gently.

"I'm sorry."

"What is the one rule?"

"Don't piss and vomit in your decorative pottery."

"The other one."

"Don't apologise," Chant murmured.

"Precisely. Benjamin Chant, if you think this was all some ploy to get you into my bed... well, you're not wrong. But the object was to get you into my bed so you might rest. Anything else we might do in a bed will happen if and when we are both eager for it. You may believe me."

Chant looked at Gale, words snaring on one another in his throat. Finally, he simply said, "Thank you."

Gale gestured to the bed, and Chant climbed in slowly, every part of him aching as though he'd just been in a brawl. Gale climbed in beside him and pulled the covers over them both.

Suddenly, Chant was wide awake.

"Later, might we break the vases in my house? The ones Reid left."

"Certainly."

"Good," Chant said. "I'm ready to be rid of them." He paused. "Will you not tell me the other news?"

"No," Gale said simply. "Later."

Chant sighed, but it was relief he felt, not frustration. He shifted, attempting to get comfortable.

Gale set a hand on his shoulder. "Sleep now, my friend. Nothing bad happens in this room."

Chant could very well believe that was true. He could imagine this place becoming a sort of sanctuary as long as Gale was here with him. Could imagine it starting to look lived-in. "Except to jugs."

Gale's laugh was unexpectedly loud in the near-darkness. "Except to jugs," he agreed.

CHAPTER 16

*C*hant awoke to watery sunlight glinting on the fraction of windowpane he could see exposed between the dark curtains. His eyes itched, his throat was raw, and he felt wrung out like a piece of wet cloth pulled through a mangle. He was too tired to even berate himself for unburdening his soul to Gale last night or to feel the sting of humiliation for doing so. Perhaps that would come later, or, he thought, blinking up at the ceiling, perhaps it would not.

He turned his head and looked at Gale in the faint light.

He had thought that Gale might look younger in sleep, softer somehow, but he had failed to take into account Gale's contrary nature. Instead of wearing a mask smoothed out by slumber, Gale's forehead was pinched and his brows were drawn together. His mouth was downturned stubbornly.

"Of course you scowl in your sleep," Chant whispered to him fondly. "Of course you do."

A part of him longed to touch Gale's forehead to smooth away the furrow in his brow, but at the same time, he was unwilling to risk waking him. And so he lay there instead, warm and weary, and simply watched him.

"Why are you staring at me?" Gale's voice was gravelly with sleep, and he did not open his eyes.

Chant did not know how to respond. Perhaps he ought to pretend to be asleep. But before he could make a decision, Gale cracked one eye open. Chant regarded him, still unsure what to say. As more of last night came back to him, his stomach tightened, and yet, the humiliation still did not come. He felt curiously calm, and what he recalled more than anything was the sensation of being in Gale's arms. Even as the darkness of the past had washed over him, had made him feel broken and ashamed in a way he had not for many years, some part of him had felt anchored by Gale's touch.

Gale had not recoiled. Had not thought him a terrible person.

"Are you all right?" Gale opened both eyes.

Chant smiled slightly. "I am."

Gale sighed and closed his eyes again, pulling one arm out from under the covers and placing his hand on Chant's shoulder. Chant hardly dared move. After a few minutes, Gale's hand slid down to the middle of Chant's back. Gale pulled lightly, and Chant shifted closer, his head fitting beneath Gale's angular chin, his face pressed to the man's neck.

And then Gale whispered sweet words of romance…

"De Cock may have murdered Claude de Brouckère and stolen his jewels. If that is so, I do not know whether he sold them off at once when the *Condor* docked or whether they are still hidden somewhere, but I think the jewels have something to do with why Visser is dead and de Cock is chasing a dog he doesn't even like."

Chant did not particularly want to leave this bed. But Gale's mind was clearly back on the investigation.

"It is a theory I should like to explore in more detail, once you and I have had a conversation."

Chant blinked against Gale's neck. He did not lift his head. "A conversation?"

He was suddenly nervous. Perhaps this was the point where Gale told him that yes, he'd been happy to help Chant through a

singularly horrible night, but he had no wish to maintain an associ-
ation with a man as cowardly as Chant. Chant, who had done
terrible harm to his own family and then wept about it in Gale's
arms like a child. Well, he could hardly blame Gale for that,
could he?

Yet still he kept his face pressed to Gale's skin, inhaling its scent
—hints of bergamot and musk from his cologne, and a note that
was uniquely Gale—and imagining that this did not have to end.

Gale's Adam's apple moved as he swallowed. "I don't imagine
you will easily forgive my transgression yesterday, but I am sorry."

"Your transgression?" Now Chant did lift his head, settling it on
the pillow once more so he could see Gale's eyes.

"In obtaining information about Reid."

Chant gazed at him for a long moment. "You are already
forgiven. It is I who must apologise to you. I have likely strained
your patience, both with my behaviour and my tale of woe. But I do
thank you for your concern last night. You have been very kind."

Gale slowly drew in a breath.

Here it comes, Chant thought.

"How anyone could have you and leave you is beyond me."

"What?"

"Whoever is lucky enough to have you for a husband or a lover,
may they appreciate every good thing you are. Don't ask me how
seldom I say that of people. I doubt I have ever spoken such words
before in my life."

Hope and disappointment warred in Chant. Gale was praising
him and with no prompting whatsoever. But he was not saying that
he intended to be Chant's husband or lover.

"You said you wished us to be friends, no more," Gale said. "I
presume that is still true?"

"I don't know." Chant's voice was soft. "It seemed to me, when I
said that, you were not willing to be more than that to me."

Gale's dark eyes flicked upward, and his gaze moved slowly
down Chant's face, as if taking in every detail. Chant hardly dared

breathe, wondering what Gale was seeing, what he was thinking. He longed to reach out and use his thumb to smooth one of Gale's black brows where the hairs had been forced every which way by the pillow. To run the backs of his fingers over that sharp cheekbone and see if Gale would close his eyes and drink in the pleasure of the caress.

Gale spoke at last. "I have thought about what you said by the river. I should like to try, Chant. To be… something more to you. But I cannot promise I won't make horrible mistakes. You have already been hurt, and I don't want to be the one to do it again. And so I don't know that it is fair for me to make any sort of pledge to you."

Chant wanted to say he didn't care. That if Gale was willing to try, that was all Chant wanted. That he would forgive any mistakes Gale made if only Gale would do the same for him. But he forced his racing mind to slow. What Chant wanted was somebody who would remain by his side all his life. Someone secure in himself and secure in his love for Chant. It would be folly to compromise on this, no matter the attraction he felt to the man beside him. That was the far-from-simple truth of it.

"You are honest with me." Chant's throat was tight. "I appreciate that. I know I owe the same honesty to you, and so I will say this. I wish to be loved. I have always wished that. I understand it is not an easy thing to predict how you may feel in a week's time or in a month or several years. But if you are in doubt right now, I think it best we make no pledge." He gave Gale a gentle smile. "I do not know that my heart can take another pummelling."

The words, sincere though they were, tasted like a mouthful of ash. He could still feel Gale's lips against his. That kiss—so gentle, no demand in it at all, nothing but tenderness. One could not fake the feeling behind a kiss like that.

Gale nodded slightly against the pillow. He still had his arm draped around Chant, and he didn't take it away. "All right." He looked slightly relieved, and that made Chant feel all the worse.

Had Gale been hoping Chant would free him of any obligation to attempt a courtship?

Chant sighed.

"You are not happy," Gale murmured.

"I am content enough."

"But not happy."

Chant hesitated. "No."

Neither of them said anything for several minutes.

Chant finally offered, "Over the past few years, I have learned to play with whatever hand life deals me. To accept my lot with good nature and not to take anything too personally. It has worked out well in a way. But I have also been in a sort of fog. It is as you said... I am not entirely honest, with myself or with others, about what I feel. You have lifted that fog. You have made me feel so many things and so deeply. Frustration, anger, affection, desire... I cannot pretend anymore that nothing hurts me. I cannot pretend to smile at all I see. And that is a good thing."

Gale's throat made a soft sound as he swallowed again. "As your friend," he said, "I can promise you do not ever have to pretend around me."

Chant's heart ached even more terribly at that. He did not want to ask anything else of Gale. Did not want to admit that he *needed* anything else from the man. Yet... "May friends still embrace?"

Gale nodded and pulled Chant close again. Chant wrapped his arms around the long, lean frame, and Gale tightened his grip and rolled them both so that Chant was nearly on top of Gale. For a moment, their bodies pressed together full-length, and the heat between them was almost unbearable. Chant's shirt had pulled so tight in places that it seemed the fabric might rip, but he didn't care. He hugged Gale tightly, feeling Gale's stand against his through their shirts. Gale wrapped his legs around Chant's and squeezed even tighter until Chant shivered. He had not known contact this complete for years. He wished he could be held like this every day, and he thought, with frustration, that life had been so much simpler a few days ago when he had not allowed himself to crave such things.

Gale eventually eased them both onto their sides again, facing one another.

Chant reached out and stroked Gale's hair, running his fingers through the soft strands, pleased when Gale sighed and let his eyes drift closed. "De Cock awaits us," Gale said eventually.

"Precisely what I was thinking," Chant murmured, rubbing his groin lightly against Gale's.

A chuckle from Gale was followed by a brush of lips against Chant's forehead. "We must see this through."

Chant nodded. "All right. I'll dress."

He climbed out of bed before his regret could worsen and located his clothes. He could feel Gale watching him as he bent to pick up his stockings, and his stand hardened further, which was most inconvenient. He pulled on his right stocking with determined haste. Then his left. And then his breeches. But before he could button them, he heard Gale leave the bed. Chant stilled and listened to the soft footsteps as Gale came to stand behind him. Chant straightened slowly. Gale's breath was light against his shoulder, and he turned, meeting Gale's eyes for just a moment—and then he lifted onto the balls of his feet and pressed his lips hard against Gale's. Gale wrapped one arm around his waist and the other around his shoulders, cupping the back of his head. He kissed Chant as though he had been starving for him, meeting every hungry thrust of Chant's tongue with one of his own. The hand at Chant's back ran down to cup his arse and pull him closer, and Chant, unable to help himself, ground the swell at the front of his breeches against the matching bulge under Gale's shirt.

Gale made a soft, high noise of what sounded like mingled surprise and pleasure. Chant ran his hands down the man's sides, counting ribs through his shirt, until his hands rested on Gale's hips. He was quite dizzy. In the years since Reid had left, he had learned to seize any moment he wanted, to take joy and pleasure where they could be found as long as doing so did not hurt anybody. But a more sensible voice in his mind pointed out that he ought not to be doing *this*. That he and Gale were complicating things in a way that would be difficult to untangle once they both came to their senses. But each time their lips met, there was a pull in the very pit of Chant's belly, a rush of pure heat between his legs, and he realised he did not care at all about the sensible voice. The sensible voice could go to hell.

Gale's hand slid from Chant's back to his front, and he tugged lightly at the waistband of Chant's unbuttoned breeches. Then he hesitated, and even his kisses faltered as though he thought he might have gone too far.

Chant could not have that.

He grabbed Gale's wrist and guided the man's hand down the front of his breeches, and Gale complied with such urgency that Chant smiled against his mouth. He tangled his other hand in Gale's hair and gasped as Gale stroked his stand through his drawers. He let go Gale's wrist and clumsily sought Gale's prick. The warmth of it in his hand, the way it hardened further at his touch, made him groan as he tried to rut against Gale's hand, his hip, anything.

Gale let go of Chant's hair and gripped his arse again, kneading there while he continued to grope down the front of Chant's open breeches. Chant cried out and suddenly braced both hands on Gale's sides, resting his head against Gale's shoulder as his hips jerked convulsively, and Gale held him steady as he spent.

Gale continued to hold Chant as Chant shuddered against him, panting hard. Gale tipped his head down and kissed the crook of Chant's neck.

Chant felt quite as if all the bones had been removed from his body. But he moved his hand between the two of them and trailed his fingers lightly down the front of Gale's shirt. He was surprised to find that Gale was no longer hard. Then he noticed how damp the fabric was.

"I spent," Gale whispered. "Watching you. Feeling you. That has never happened to me before."

Chant draped his arms around Gale's hips and leaned against him once more.

"Is this also what friends do?" Chant murmured after a moment.

Gale's breathing was still ragged. "I... Yes. There is nothing strange about a bit of physical affection between friends."

For a few seconds, there was no sound in the room but their harsh breathing, and then they both began to laugh.

They laughed rather harder than the situation called for, and Chant relished the rare sound of Gale's uninhibited amusement. Eventually, he kissed Gale again, soft and slow. And when they parted, Gale leaned forward and pressed his lips to Chant's forehead. "I cannot resist you," he whispered.

"Nor I you," Chant replied.

"It is confounding."

"I don't know what to do," Chant confessed.

"Nor I." Gale pulled back so they were looking into each other's eyes. "I do not ever wish to hurt you again. It pains me that I have done so before, and that was just what I managed in three days' time. I fear what I might unthinkingly say in the future."

"But if we... if we continued to learn each other... might'nt we both figure out how not to do harm?"

"I would hope so. But I fear this is the one area in which I have little competency."

"Only one, is there?" Chant chuckled.

Gale squeezed his arse. "Yes. I am a genius, you know."

"You scarcely let me forget."

Gale's expression grew sober. "There are also many times—many, Chant—when I cannot stand to be touched. When I feel I shall crawl out of my own skin if someone lays a hand on me. What sort of lover could I be to you or to anyone?"

Chant recalled the night in front of Gale House when Gale had pulled away from him. Not a rejection, then. If only Chant had known. "You think I should care for you any less on those occasions?"

"I honestly don't know." Gale was standing so the band of light coming in between the curtains fell partially on his face, illuminating the flush in his cheeks.

"I will not," Chant said. "If there are times when you cannot stand to be touched, tell me, and I will not touch you."

Gale narrowed his eyes as though searching for a trap in his words. "You say it as though it is simple, as though you would not tire of my inconstant moods if you were subjected to them every day."

"I think there is no answer I can give you that will satisfy you," Chant said. "I could tell you of the cat I loved deeply as a child, who blew hot and cold with me, or I can tell you that I fear my own imperfections of character will ruin whatever it is we build between us, but the only way we shall know for certain if we can be together or not is just by *trying*. Do you see?" reached up and tugged a twist of Gale's auburn hair, relishing the way Gale's eyes half closed in pleasure at the sharp sensation. "And I believe we both want to try."

Gale's breath slipped out of him on a sigh. "Yes," he said at last, "I believe you are correct."

Chant leaned in quickly and kissed the cold tip of his nose. "Then perhaps you are not the only genius in this room, Christmas Gale."

Gale fixed him with a haughty stare. "Let's not get too carried away, Chant, for God's sake."

Chant laughed, and kissed his nose again. He glanced down at his open breeches. "I suppose I ought to return home and change before we make any further plans for the day."

"No," Gale said softly but firmly, and Chant tilted his head, confused. Gale then began to do up the buttons on Chant's breeches with remarkable efficiency. Chant tensed as the man's knuckles brushed a highly sensitised area, and Gale kissed him briefly as though in reassurance. Then he cupped the front of Chant's breeches. Chant let out a sharp puff of air, followed by a gasp. Gale rubbed with his thumb so Chant felt all the damp stickiness of his own spend against his skin as well as a dizzying rush that encompassed arousal, mild embarrassment, and an extremely pleasurable sense of being possessed. Gale snaked an arm around him and clapped his arse—none too gently either. "I rather like the idea of the Honourable Benjamin Chant sitting down to breakfast with me with a mess in his drawers and that very becoming blush on his cheeks."

Gale let him go and strode for the door without another word, and Chant stood there, his face heating and pleasure snaking up his spine.

~

They breakfasted at the Bucknall Club, in one of the more ornate rooms that Chant usually avoided. Gale, however, didn't seem to mind eating his cake and drinking his tea surrounded by the sort of overwrought neo-Classical architectural flourishes that made Chant feel as though he might at any moment catch a glimpse of a Neronian orgy. But despite the vastness of the dining room and the fact they were not the only occupants, it felt strangely intimate, as though their closeness from the night before had been carried with them out of the rooms on Russell Street, and they were still wrapped in it like a comfortable, soft blanket.

One night with Christmas Gale, and Chant was entirely soft-hearted. He felt like a fool, but a happy one. He had not felt like this since his time with Reid, and he was older now, certainly, and hopefully wiser too. He wasn't the same starry-eyed boy who thought the man sitting across from him could do no wrong. He was well aware Gale could break his heart, and that love was not a happy ending where all day-to-day travails simply ceased to be, drowned under a sea of a pure, unchanging joy. There was no room in Chant's heart for fairy-tale endings these days, but when he looked at Gale and saw him—his imperfections, his contradictions, his trepidations—it did not diminish his happiness. Just because he knew the road ahead of them was not without its potholes and wheel ruts didn't mean he believed it wasn't worth taking.

"We must go back to Rotherhithe," Gale said, picking a caraway seed off his breakfast cake and examining it thoughtfully as though it contained all the mysteries of the universe. Then he ate it.

"To do what?" Chant asked. "To search for Flummery?"

"Flummery clearly has no interest in being found," Gale said, "and I have no interest in being bested by a mutt. Again. So, no, not to find Flummery." His expression grew serious. "To find de Cock."

Chant felt an unpleasant thrill in his gut. "Gale…"

"He is the key to it all," Gale said. "I believe the stolen jewels might have, at least at one time, been hidden on Flummery."

"On Flummery?"

"On, or in, or through…"

"*In?*"

"Let's not dwell on prepositions, Chant. But if Flummery had, or has, the jewels, it would explain de Cock's obsession with finding him."

"But we don't know for sure de Cock stole the jewels."

"No. That is why he is now our key. And what use is knowing the key exists unless we possess it?"

"Leaving aside all ideas about"—Chant lowered his voice—"possessing de Cock—"

Gale choked on a sliver of ginger cake.

"Would now not be an excellent time to speak to your friend the Runner?"

Gale narrowed his eyes. "Your face."

"What about my face?"

"Something about it twitches when you mention my friend the Runner," Gale said. "It's barely there for a second, just a tiny ripple, but I saw it. Good Lord. You're jealous, aren't you?"

"No," Chant lied.

"You are," Gale said, "and there is no point in denying it. Darling is an acquaintance, I suppose, and that is all."

"I should think he is very much your friend since you brought him to dinner at your family home."

Gale tilted his head and regarded Chant curiously. "I invited him to dinner that evening because we had spent the entire day chasing down rumours of Balfour's fraudulent financial dealings, and his stomach was growling louder than a lion. That is all."

Chant felt slightly mollified, yet he couldn't help but ask, "Is he a handsome fellow?"

"He is quite comely, yes," Gale said. "And his face also did the twitchy thing whenever I chanced to mention Teddy around him, so I suspect that, had I asked him, he would have agreed to be my companion."

"And did you ask him?"

"I did not," Gale said. "He's not like one of the boys who lingers in the salons, content to catch the eye of a swell and be kept by him. And one certainly does not court a man from the lower classes. Darling is a decent man, for all that we do not see eye to eye, and an affair might ruin him."

Chant's nascent jealousy was washed away by a wave of admiration. Gale wanted to believe himself a misanthrope. Chant knew better.

"Why do you smile?" Gale asked.

Chant shook his head. "But do you not think we ought to speak to Darling? Or perhaps one of his superiors, even. Why, there are several members of the House of Lords within spitting distance, any of whom might be able to offer us assistance. Why must we go and speak with de Cock when there is probably someone here inside Bucknall's this moment who could send the navy instead?"

"Because de Cock is an enemy of the French," Gale said, "which makes him a friend of ours. Without any evidence against him, we would be advised, very strongly, to leave Admiralty House and not return."

"The Runners, then?" Chant pressed.

Gale looked at him sharply. "Do you think there is a man among them who could be trusted to make the same observations I can? I swear this isn't vanity speaking, Chant, only the truth."

"Gale, the man has already threatened your life!"

"And I do not intend to get close enough to allow him to do it a second time," Gale said. "I mean to observe his movements only, and to see where they might lead us. Once we have more information, I will go to Darling."

Chant felt his face twitch.

"Or any Runner," Gale added. "It need not be Darling."

A trickle of unease ran through Chant's gut, but he held Gale's gaze and nodded. "Only to observe then."

"Of course," Gale said, arching a thin, aristocratic brow. "To observe."

~

*C*hant took a cab home to Mayfair, having wrested a promise out of Gale that he would not go dashing madly off to the dockyards alone. He did not like Gale's plan a whit, but, having found himself at a loss to provide an alternative, he had agreed to accompany him if only he could first go home. The wind off the river could be cold, and Chant wanted to fetch his greatcoat. And, he could not deny it, he had hoped that the detour to collect his greatcoat would allow him some time to come up with an opposing strategy to offer to Gale, but as he alighted from the cab in front of his house, he still had not come up with one.

He paid the driver and then stood for a moment in the street, pinching the bridge of his nose, until some compulsion drew him not to his door, but around the corner to the churchyard he could view from his window.

It was a neat little churchyard, restful and pleasant, decorated in the fresh green shoots of springtime. Chant headed for the angel, brushing his fingers against the planes of its marble face as it wept over a grave.

It was not Jenny's grave. Jenny's grave was not in Mayfair, and it had no angel. Yet it was there that Chant felt closest to her. It was there that he sometimes came to speak with her, imagining he could hear her responses.

"He is mad," he told the angel, his mouth quirking as he thought of smashing the jug the night before. "And he makes me quite mad as well. He is… he is not like Reid. He is like no one I have ever met before. You would like him, I think."

He listened for her answer in the faint clatter of traffic on the street beyond the churchyard wall and the chatter of a pair of sparrows. He heard the crunch of boots on the gravel path behind him and turned in expectation of having to explain his presence to some parson or rector.

Instead, his vision was filled with a man so tall and broad he was almost a giant—a giant with a shock of white-blond hair that appeared as coarse as twine, eyes a cold, flat sort of blue, and a mouth that, as Chant recognised him, pulled into a gruesome smile.

Chant's blood ran cold.

De Cock.

There was no hope of bolting, but Chant tried anyway. De Cock caught his arm and spun him so his back was to the captain's chest and put his blade to Chant's throat. The steel was brown in places —dried blood, Chant realised, his gorge rising. When the captain spoke, his voice was higher than Chant had expected. Softer. "You're going to take me into your home, Mr. Chant, and you'll give me that fucking beast you've been harbouring. And anything you might have taken off the mongrel as well."

It took Chant a moment to understand.

Miranda. He tried not to breathe too rapidly for every breath pressed his neck harder against the blade. Glancing down, he saw the two globes on the dagger's hilt and had the absurd urge to laugh. De Cock thought Miranda was Flummery. *Anything you might have taken off the mongrel as well.* He believed *Chant* had the jewels. The thought of the captain harming Miranda was enough to break through Chant's terror and prompted him to raise his arm, then ram his elbow backward into the captain's stomach.

CHAPTER 17

*A*n ugly clock ticked away in the Blue Room of Bucknall's, its pendulum swinging underneath a darkly polished case. Gale glanced at it and wondered how long it would take Chant to get back with his greatcoat. He thought about going home to collect one for himself. Then he thought about running into his mother and sisters and decided against it.

He drummed his fingers on his knee.

"Gale." Soulden slipped into the room, looking as suspicious as an alley cat.

"Soulden," Gale said with a nod.

"You look dreadful. Did you *sleep* in those clothes?"

"Yes," Gale said and lifted a hand in a vain attempt to straighten his cravat. "You're not looking terribly chipper yourself. Are you still being pursued by that Rivingdon fellow?"

Soulden sighed and collapsed in the chair opposite Gale's. "There are two of them now, can you believe?"

Gale raised his eyebrows.

"Rivingdon and also Warry's cousin Notley." Soulden made a face. "They're like two little puffed-up bantam roosters shaking their feathers at one another, and for some reason, they've both set their ambitions on me."

"Don't be modest, Pip," Gale said. "It doesn't suit you. You're wealthy, titled, and unmarried. You must be the most eligible bachelor in all of London now that Hartwell's taken himself off the market."

"You think Hartwell was more eligible than I?"

"Your father is an earl. His is a duke."

"I'm more handsome though."

"If you insist."

Soulden cast a narrow look at the doorway as though he was expecting one of his unwelcome paramours to burst through it at any moment. "How are things going with you?"

"With my what?"

"Well, with life in general," Soulden said. "Your investigation, of course, but also these rumours I'm hearing about you and Chant."

"Only one of those things is your business."

"The other is all of Society's," Soulden said. "And the fact you have been spending so much time with Chant since you danced together at the Harringdons' ball has not gone unremarked."

"Nothing ever goes unremarked by the *ton*," Gale said. "It's why I hate it. Unlike you, Pip, I am not comfortable wearing a mask."

Soulden took no offence. He only smiled. "I know, Christmas."

"Chant and I are going to watch de Cock's ship today," Gale said to change the subject.

"Do you think you will learn anything?"

"I have no idea," Gale said, "but it seems a better use of our time than doing nothing at all."

"I shall make no comment on your willingness to spend all day with Chant."

"Good. Please don't."

"Still, I'm surprised he's not here with you."

"He's gone to fetch his greatcoat." Gale glanced at the clock again. "How long does it take to fetch a damned greatcoat from Mayfair?"

One of the boys slipped into the room. He was an apple-cheeked little fellow, and Gale was fairly certain he'd last seen him wrestling with a dog on Chant's floor. "My lord," he said, hastening forward and holding out a note. "A message for you, sir."

Gale took the note and unfolded it. He read the words there, and felt the floor fall away from underneath him.

Chant.

De Cock had Chant.

~

"Gale?" Chant mumbled in the darkness some time afterwards and was suddenly overcome with the stench of something fetid and rank. "Good God, what is that *smell?*"

Gale's voice came to him, distant and strained. "That would be bilgewater, I believe. How is your head?"

"What?" Chant blinked, but it was still pitch black.

A warm hand found his shoulder, and long fingers squeezed. "Take a moment to catch up, my dear fellow. You've had quite the crack on the head."

"*What?*"

The last thing Chant remembered was breakfasting at the Bucknall Club. He'd had cake. It had been delicious. So what on earth was…

Oh.

He had gone to fetch his greatcoat, and he had been in the churchyard when de Cock found him. He remembered something —something about a *dog?* And then everything else was a mystery. His head throbbed, which gave him some indication as to what had happened.

And now he was in the dark with Gale but, unlike last night at Russell Street, the situation was not a comfortable one. Everything stank, and Chant's body ached in unpleasant ways, and it felt as though his head had been split open. He raised a hand to touch his jaw, somehow misjudged the distance in the blackness, and slapped himself in the mouth instead.

"Ow!"

"Did you—" Gale sounded startled. "Did you just strike yourself in the face? To what end? Have you gone mad?"

"Days ago, I think," Chant muttered. "When you first appeared on my doorstep in the middle of the night and asked me to come with you to find Elise. Yes, I think I was most certainly mad then."

He sensed Gale moving, rather than saw him, and felt the press of lips against his forehead. "Yes, you are probably mad. If we escape from this, we will certainly both end up in Bedlam."

Chant pushed him away, a chill running through him.

"I did not mean..." Gale's throat clicked as he swallowed. "Forgive me. I spoke without thinking. I meant it as a joke."

"They say madness is hereditary, do they not?" Chant murmured, his eyes stinging.

"Nobody dares say it much nowadays at all, actually," Gale said, his tone wry. "Not in front of the Prince Regent, at least."

Chant couldn't help his snort. He sought Gale's hand in the darkness. "I know you meant no offence, Gale." He drew a breath. "What are you doing here? You weren't with me in Mayfair. How...?"

"De Cock was good enough to send me a message telling me he had you," Gale said. "Such manners for a pirate. Or perhaps it's quite normal in his circles. I don't know. I can't say I've ever met a pirate before. I'm afraid he doesn't quite meet the expectations I set of them as a child, reading accounts of Blackbeard."

"I'm sorry for your disappointment," Chant said.

Gale squeezed his hand. "Perhaps next time you are abducted by pirates, you might pick one with the common decency to fly a flag with a skull on it."

"I shall keep that in mind," Chant murmured. "About the jewels… I think you're right."

"I usually am."

"He wanted Miranda. He thought she was Flum."

"Oh no."

"So I fought him."

"Over a *dog*."

"Mm-hmm. I think that's when he struck me. Did he get Miranda, though?"

"I couldn't say."

"Are we… are we on the *Condor*?"

"Yes. How is your head? Are you back with me?"

"Mostly," Chant said. "I think."

"Good," Gale said, and for the first time, Chant heard a waver in his voice. "Because I am not ready to lose you, Benjamin Chant."

"Even if you were, I probably wouldn't leave you alone anyway."

Gale's laughter was faint and breathy. "Good," he said again, taking Chant's hand and raising it to his mouth. He pressed his mouth against Chant's wrist, and Chant felt his pulse beat rapidly. "Good."

~

*G*ale's mind raced, which was nothing new to him, but the total lack of light in the little hold beneath the deck of the *Condor* made the sensation a bit dizzying. He was seated on the floor, his back pressed up against the damp, cool wall. Chant lay curled on the floor beside him, and Gale grasped his hand. Chant's hand was cold—he had lost his gloves somewhere en route to Rotherhithe, and Gale had left his at Bucknall's—but it was solid, it was real, and it anchored him in the darkness when his madly racing thoughts might have sent his mind spiralling into a fathomless pit.

There was a rhythm to being on a ship that Gale did not like. He was no fan of the water and no fan of ships. Everything seemed too precarious on a ship—even on the sheltered Thames where the *Condor* squatted like a black fowl—and the world lifted and sank, lifted and sank, as the river breathed underneath them. Wood groaned and creaked, and the bilge, the stench of it apparent from the moment Gale had been brought under deck, sloshed back and forth, back and forth. Gale heard distant shouts on occasion, carried down from the decks above them, and sometimes the creak of footsteps over their heads.

"You were senseless when I was brought aboard," he said, rubbing his thumb against Chant's. "It has been some time now, I think, although it is hard to tell exactly how much."

"Ah." Chant's slow exhalation was heavy. "And de Cock?"

"I haven't seen the man yet," Gale said. "But I am quite sure he will make himself known to us."

Chant shifted, his coat whispering against the boards of the floor. "I suppose now would not be a good time to remind you I suggested you tell Darling where you were going?"

"No," Gale agreed. "Now would not be a good time. Perhaps you can save your recriminations for when this is all over."

"Very well," Chant said. "My head is killing me. I feel as though I've been kicked by a horse." He blinked in the darkness. "I don't understand why you are here."

"I told you already," Gale said, his fingers finding Chant's hair and tugging a few strands gently. "De Cock sent a message to me."

"But why did you come?" Chant asked, and Gale hated the sheer disbelief in Chant's voice as though he honestly thought Gale could have made any other choice and perhaps should have.

"Well, I can never resist a fool's errand," Gale said. "I am eminently qualified for them, after all, as my mother often tells me."

"I am cold," Chant said.

Chant sounded half addlepated still, and Gale swallowed down his worry. When the sailors who had let him aboard had brought him under the deck and into this dank little storeroom and he had seen Chant senseless on the floor, his heart, an organ most of the people who knew him would argue he did not possess, had seized. "Yes. I am sorry."

"But what are you doing here, Gale?" Chant asked. "How did you come to be in their clutches too?"

"You fool," Gale said. "Did you think I could leave you to be abducted alone?" He pressed his finger to Chant's mouth. "Now hush a moment and let me think."

Gale listened to the rhythmic sounds of the ship again. He caught some of Chant's hair between the pads of his finger and his thumb and gently rubbed to tease the strands apart. Chant made no complaint.

When he'd been brought aboard, there had been no sign at all of de Cock, but his men were a menacing enough bunch that Gale had no doubt they did not intend for him and Chant to leave the *Condor* alive. De Cock's sailors were a motley collection, but all of them narrow-eyed and closemouthed. When they spoke amongst themselves it was in Dutch, in short, sharp undertones and with none of the joking and ribaldry that Gale had overheard before from sailors. They were cognizant, he supposed, that they had just abducted two Englishmen on English soil, and that a noose awaited them if they were caught.

And all for a damn dog.

Well, no, not for the sake of the dog, and yet somehow the dog was the key to the whole business. If that poor wretch Howe had not seen the beast to begin with and decided to take it home to Elise, he would have been alive today.

No.

Gale exhaled.

No, it was not as simple as that, was it? Gale remembered how enthusiastically Howe had approached him, and how delighted he had been to discover him that night on the banks of the river. And how his daughter followed all of the stories about Gale in the news sheets. No, this wasn't just about Howe looking for Flummery at all. This was about the fact that he'd got Christmas Gale involved, and de Cock must have been following him and witnessed their meeting and thought that Gale had agreed to help him. De Cock might not have cared if some old drunk was searching for his dog, because how could such a man be a threat at all to him, but *Christmas Gale*? Christmas Gale was exactly the sort of man who would begin by searching for a lost dog and end by uncovering treason.

Or did de Cock think Howe had the jewels?

No. De Cock had killed Howe and continued searching for the dog. He must have had reason to believe that Howe was ignorant of the dog's value.

Gale's mouth curled into a self-satisfied smile. "Oh, I think I almost have it now, Chant."

"Have what?" Chant asked faintly.

"I almost have de Cock where I want him," Gale said. "And, for the love of God, please do not ask if that is in my arse."

Chant laughed softly in the darkness. "Gale, are we really to be murdered over a dog?"

"Of course not," Gale said. "Well, it's very likely we're to be murdered, but it's certainly not because of a dog. It's because of jewels. "

"That is not very comforting, you know."

"I know."

They were both silent for a long time.

When a faint glowing line appeared in the darkness, Gale at first wondered if it was some trick of his mind, a sort of delirium brought on by sitting in the pitch black for too long. And then, as the line brightened and sharpened, Gale heard the creak of footsteps, and realised that someone was approaching, and lighting the way with a lantern or a candle.

A moment later a latch scraped, and the door to the dark little storeroom was pulled open.

Gale held up a hand against the sudden shocking glare of the light. It took a moment for his eyes to adjust, and then he was blinking a teenage boy into existence. He had dark curls, glinting eyes, and was barefoot and rather ragged like some artist's inspiration for an Arcadian shepherd boy; lovely and innocent in a rough, uncultured sort of way. He was, more importantly, slender enough for even Gale to attempt to fight, and he was unarmed. He had a jug in one hand and a lantern in the other.

Gale shifted, ready to push himself to his feet, when the narrow doorway behind the boy filled with a man who had the same bodily proportions as a brick: he was big and square with no discernible neck, and he gave Gale a very knowing look as he squeezed into the room. Gale thought of the only biblical character his mother could name: Goliath. He was a big, blond Goliath.

Gale sank down onto the floor again and showed the boy and Goliath his palms.

"Water," the boy said and held out the jug.

Gale reached out and took it and then set it on the floor. He knelt over Chant. "Chant, sit up. There's a good fellow."

Chant groaned but allowed Gale to help him into a seated position and then lean him back against the wall. Gale held the jug for him until he took a sip of water.

Goliath said something in a rush of words.

"Teube says sorry," the boy translated in heavily-accented English. "No food, sorry. Just water."

Goliath—Teube—turned the corners of his mouth down.

"An apology from pirates for a lack of cake and crumpets, Chant," Gale murmured. "Astonishing."

"No, no," the boy said, sounding suddenly anxious. "Privateer, not pirate. We have letters. From the king."

"It won't save you from de Cock though, will it?" Gale asked.

The fear in the boy's dark eyes was palpable.

"It didn't save Visser," Gale said.

Even Teube flinched at the name.

The boy's mouth trembled.

"Kees," Teube said, his rumbling voice pitched low. He squeezed the boy's shoulder.

"You liked Visser," Gale said softly.

"Was funny," Kees said. "Very funny."

Gale couldn't recall anything particularly amusing about the fellow, but Kees didn't strike him as a sophisticated audience.

"He would dance and sing," Kees said. "Do silly things."

"De Cock killed him," Gale said.

Kees nodded, his eyes wide. "For... silly joke."

"What silly joke?" Gale asked keenly.

"Visser put..." Kees paused for a moment as though trying to find the word. "Jewels. Put jewels on the dog's collar and made him dance. 'Oh, look at me! I am very important man! I am de Br—'" And then he clamped his mouth shut on his sing-song voice and shook his head.

But he didn't need to finish.

I am de Brouckère, he'd been going to say. Claude de Brouckère, brother of the Governor of Limburg, presumed murdered by the French but actually murdered by his countryman de Cock. And there was no letter from the Dutch king that would save de Cock from a noose if that could be proven. And Visser, stupid, drunken Visser, had put the jewels on the dog as a *joke*.

"The dog was still wearing them when he fled the ship?"

Kees glanced at Teube, then nodded. "We were at the dock. De Cock came in while the dog is... dancing. He was very angry and tried to get the dog, but the dog is fast. Off the ship he goes, down the... the gangplank. De Cock tried to chase him, but Visser, he is trying to escape. So de Cock stabbed him in the leg"—Kees pantomimed it—"told men to tie Visser up, keep him here, and went to find the dog. But too late."

Good Lord.

"Why just Visser? Wasn't he angry at you two or whoever else was present for this *joke*?"

"Visser was only one who knows where the jewels were. So de Cock knew he is the one who is taking them to dress the dog."

"But Visser eventually escaped. Did he have help?"

Another glance between Kees and Teube, and Kees translated for Teube. "We must not tell you," Kees said.

"I rather think we're past the point of no return with regard to this confession."

Kees tilted his head, looking confused.

"Get me and my friend off this ship," Gale said, "and I'll vouch for you and Teube. I'll make certain you are both spared the noose."

"No," Kees said, his voice almost breaking on the word. "No, is too late. Is—"

Gale heard new footsteps approaching, boots this time instead of bare feet, heels clicking on the boards of the ship.

It was too late.

De Cock was here.

Gale rose to his feet. He was a Gale. He had no wish to meet his fate sitting on his arse. Chant... well, Chant had taken a blow to the head that had clearly rattled his brain. Gale would not judge him harshly for staying seated. But Chant stood too, on legs that appeared as wobbly as a newborn calf's, but with a determined jut to his chin that made Gale wonder how he'd ever denied to himself that he was in love with this man. Loose strands of golden hair had escaped his queue, and they glittered in the lamplight.

De Cock filled the narrow doorway in a way that even Teube hadn't been able to, and Gale didn't miss the way that Teube moved forward to give him room, keeping himself between de Cock and Kees. His instinct about the sailors had been right. They were afraid of de Cock, which meant that loyalty, built on a foundation of that fear, wasn't as solid as perhaps de Cock thought. It was an assessment and nothing more. Gale doubted de Cock would allow him enough time to try to drive a wedge into those narrow cracks.

"Christmas Gale," de Cock said, his ugly face split with a

murderous smile, not unlike the one he'd shown Gale the day he'd tipped Visser's ear out of his boot.

"*Lord* Christmas Gale," Gale corrected haughtily.

De Cock laughed and gave a mock bow. "*Lord* Christmas."

The *Condor* shuddered suddenly, and Chant staggered against the wall. Gale put out a hand to steady him.

"What's that?" Chant asked.

"We are leaving, Mr. Chant," de Cock said. "*That* is my men rowing the *Condor* out into the river, away from the dock."

Gale hated the water. He hated it even more when he had no doubt that the only reason de Cock was moving them farther into it was so he could dispose of them unbothered by any witnesses and unhampered by any attempt rescuers might make via the gangplank. But it occurred to him that if most of de Cock's men were manning the oars of the pinnace pulling them out into the Thames, then what remained aboard the *Condor* at the moment was only a skeleton crew. Another assessment, not a plan by any means but backed by the burning knowledge that Gale had to get Chant off this blasted ship.

"You murdered Claude de Brouckère," he said.

"You have no proof of that," de Cock said, "and nobody to tell."

"You think I was the one who put all the pieces together?" Gale asked, genuinely curious. "No, I might have known the dog was the key to this whole business, but your treason to your king is already the subject of much speculation in certain circles. And if the English suspect it, you can be damned sure the Dutch do too."

Kees shot a worried look at Teube. Teube, whose English was perhaps not good enough to follow along, simply looked solemn.

"Killing me," Gale said, "would accomplish nothing."

"Perhaps not, Lord Christmas," de Cock said, "but it will feel so very good."

"Why kill Howe?" Gale was aware the longer he kept de Cock talking, the farther they got from the docks and the harder it would be to get back. But he did have to know. For Elise's sake.

"Howe?" de Cock laughed. "Ah! You mean the drunken fool. I went to his home days ago to find the dog, but the dog ran from me. I pursued, but—" He held up his empty hands. "I began to… *observe* Mr. Howe. I saw him speak to you. I approached. Asked him very politely where the dog was. He said the dog was missing. I said he had better find it. He didn't like being given orders, and I didn't like being spoken to with such… disrespect." He planted the tip of his ballock dagger firmly in one of the floorboards and left it there.

"You still don't have the dog," Gale pointed out.

"Gale," Chant whispered.

"No," de Cock said, his pale eyes seeming to grow dark. "But do you know… I don't think the jewels are on the dog anymore. Lord Christmas, I really don't. I don't even think that fool Howe ever knew about them. It has taken me some time to realise where they must be, and I have just now sent some men to… test my theory." He grinned, the lantern light painting his filthy teeth a sickening red. "Do you know who I think has them?"

Gale did, and he would be damned if he would let de Cock say the name.

He moved quickly, bending down to grasp the handle of the lantern. Then, swinging it in an upward arc, he smashed it soundly against de Cock's face. The light flared for a moment as de Cock howled, his visage wreathed in flames like a demon's, and then the storeroom was plunged into inky darkness.

Gale gripped Chant's wrist and hauled him toward the door. Someone caught at his greatcoat—either Kees or Teube, he suspected, because they were halfhearted about it at best—but Gale pulled free and burst into the narrow corridor below decks.

He shoved Chant in front of him, pushing him toward the bright rectangle of light that indicated a door to the deck. Chant stumbled and slipped on the steep steps that were pitched as sharply as a ladder, but Gale shoved again, and Chant miraculously continued to climb. They both spilled out onto the deck, into watery sunlight that seemed to blaze after being locked in the darkness for so long.

Behind them, Rotherhithe receded. To the north, the docks and warehouses of Limehouse clustered at the edge of the muddy river.

Someone yelled, and Gale twisted around to see a man standing at the ship's wheel, looking down at them in shock as they bolted like rats out of the *Condor*'s dark belly.

Still pushing Chant, Gale headed for the ship's stern. He pulled Chant over to the edge of the deck, and peered down at the river. It felt as though it was miles beneath them, and Gale grew faint for a moment.

"Gale," Chant said, wild-eyed. He gripped the taffrail. "You must be mad!"

Gale shrugged out of his greatcoat. "Nonsense. Ducks land on the water all the time."

"Ducks have *wings*!"

"You can swim, can't you, Chant?" Gale asked, cocking an eyebrow.

"Yes," Chant said. "Of course, I—"

"Excellent. You'd best go first then because I can't."

"What?" Chant exclaimed, his eyes wide and horrified. "Gale, what do you mean you—"

And then, since time was of the essence and de Cock was approaching them with a dagger in his hand and a murderous look in his eye, Gale took hold of the back of Chant's coat and the seat of his tight breeches, and pitched him over the side of the ship and into the filthy Thames.

And then, holding his breath, he followed him over the side.

"ale," someone said roughly and slapped his face.

"Chant?" Gale rasped and then pushed away from the

hands holding him so he could vomit up half the Thames onto the filthy stones of... of wherever the hell he was.

"No," said the voice.

Gale squinted up at the man. "*Pip?*"

Soulden hauled him upright by his coat. "You fool," he said.

"Eh." Gale's heart raced. "Where is Chant? I—"

"He's fine," Soulden said, and Gale caught a glimpse of Chant through a forest of men's legs. He was wet and bedraggled, but someone had put a blanket around him.

"You took long enough."

"I prefer to arrive in the nick of time," Soulden said dryly. "It's much more dramatic, I find." He rolled his eyes. "It takes a moment, Gale, even for me, to commandeer the *navy*."

"The navy." Gale twisted to try to see the river, and the *Condor*, but Soulden was in his way. "And de Cock?"

"On his way to meet a naval blockade at Greenwich," Soulden said. "Won't that be a surprise to him?"

Gale was almost disappointed he wouldn't see the look on the man's face. "Soulden!" he said suddenly, desperately. "My family. De Cock said..."

"It is all taken care of. Your friend Darling was able to apprehend de Cock's men before they reached Gale House."

Gale attempted to sigh out some of his tension but ended up choking.

"Did you find the jewels?" Soulden asked.

"No," Gale wheezed. "But surely the attempted murder of two Englishmen will be enough to hang him?"

"Oh, he'll hang," Soulden said. "But it would have been rather nice to have the jewels as well to prevent war between the French and the Dutch."

"Kees and Teube will testify against him. If you promise to spare them from the noose." He didn't want to tell Soulden just yet where he thought the jewels were.

"Good man," Soulden said and patted him on the back.

The gesture was perhaps not as comforting as he had intended. Gale went into a paroxysm of coughing and expelled even more water from his heavy lungs. By the time he had finished he was weak, his vision dark, and he was as dizzy as he had been when he'd leapt off the *Condor*.

He tried to push away Soulden's solicitous touch. He had a brief memory of cold, murky water all around him, his limbs heavy as lead as he tried to move them, his lungs tight with sharp, shooting pain. And then a hand had grabbed his coat, pulling him up, up...

"Chant?" he asked, his voice weak and tremulous, and then pitched forward into a faint.

CHAPTER 18

C hant found that pacing the Gales' parlour warmed him faster than sitting on the sofa shivering, and had the added effect of distracting him somewhat. He knew he would be fine. The ordeal had been frightening, but it had not ended as badly as it could have. He and Gale had been brought to St. James's Square where Lady Gale had, without even demanding an explanation, begun to bark orders. Gale had been whisked off to his bedroom, the family physician summoned, and two servants sent to attend to Chant in the parlour. None of Gale's clothes would have fit Chant, but he'd been given a shirt, dressing gown, and ludicrously soft breeches that must have belonged to Gale's older brother. He'd been offered cakes, which he'd been unable to eat, and tea, which he'd managed two sips of. One of the servants had noticed Chant was still shivering, even with dry clothes on, and had thrown more wood on the fire and practically flung a thick woven blanket over him.

Everything would be fine. He kept repeating it to himself. De Cock's cold eyes were just a memory now. But he worried for Gale, and the effort of trying to observe propriety when all he wanted to do was storm into the man's bedroom and see for himself that he was still alive was even more draining than that endless swim to shore had been.

He focused on the chintzy furniture—the sofa really was spectacularly ugly: red and gold paisley upholstery and carvings of creatures he couldn't identify on the arms—thinking of Jenny and her love for shining things. Thinking of Reid, who would buy decorations he knew were in poor taste just so he and Chant might laugh about them.

Chant had wanted to leave the past behind him, but now it seemed to collide with this horribly uncertain present, and guilt washed over him unchecked. He had put Gale in danger. He had nearly lost him. If he had been paying attention to his surroundings in Mayfair, if he had fought harder to free himself; for God's sake, if he had not insisted that he and Gale be honest about their feelings for each other, perhaps Gale would not have felt obligated to come to Chant's rescue. He shivered again, though he no longer felt cold.

He made himself take a breath, then gripped the back of the sofa and dug his fingers in, trying to remain anchored. He had not lost Gale. Gale was upstairs in his room being tended to, and he would make a full recovery.

He started as the door opened and turned to see Lady Gale standing at the entrance, looking impeccable as always in a violet satin gown with a square neckline and sleeves to the elbow. It felt disgraceful to stand before her in the borrowed shirt and dressing gown, his feet bare, his hair still damp and smelling of the Thames, knowing he had almost got her son killed. For a second, her face was drawn tight, but then she smiled gently and dipped her head to him. "Mr. Chant. I came to see how you are." She approached, glancing about the room. "Where are the staff I sent to attend to you?"

"I sent them away, my lady. I apologise. I wished to be alone."

"I know the feeling well," she said. "But this hardly seems like the time to be alone." She said it with a warmth he might not have caught had he not come to know her son these past few days. She seated herself on the sofa and patted the spot next to her. "Will you sit a minute?"

He wished to keep pacing until he wore a hole through the floorboards and down into the earth, where he might disappear. But he sat beside her. She glanced at the discarded blanket on the sofa arm, and he flushed with an embarrassment he didn't quite understand. He knew logically that what had happened was not his fault, but he still felt Gale's mother would be within her rights to despise him.

"Do you feel you don't deserve to be comfortable?" she asked bluntly.

His cheeks might well have been embers from the dwindling fire. "I am quite comfortable, Lady Gale. I mean, I am warm enough."

She reached out and put the backs of her fingers to his cheek, saying, "Forgive me" as she did. Chant was so surprised by the gesture he did not pull away. "You are as cold as a block of ice."

That seemed impossible when his face burned so.

"Would you resent me terribly if I were to put this blanket around your shoulders? I don't know how similar you are to my son in this regard. He hates to be mothered."

Chant smiled in spite of himself. *He doesn't,* he nearly said. *He only pretends to.* But of course, Lady Gale knew that. "I would not resent you, but it is not necessary..."

He trailed off, for she was already shaking out the woven blanket, and she draped it efficiently around his shoulders, smoothing it over him.

Such a strange feeling came over Chant then. His throat grew tight, and he hoped he would not be required to speak until he had got hold of himself.

Lady Gale sat there in comfortable silence. "He is sleeping," she said at last. "He's fine, Mr. Chant. He was his usual prickly self to the doctor. Just tired and a bit shaken, that is all."

Chant nodded. "I'm glad to hear it."

She glanced at him shrewdly, then faced forward again. "I owe you an incalculable debt. He told me the story, or most of it. You saved his life." There was the slightest waver in her voice, and Chant realised that for all her cool exterior, the certainty of her reassurances, she was shaken as well.

"It was I who got him into trouble in the first place."

"Nonsense. Christmas follows trouble like a hound trailing rabbits."

He tried to laugh. "All the same, it was he who saved me. Not the other way around."

"I have seen him try to swim, Mr. Chant. Only once, but the memory lingers with me. He needed you, and you were there." She drew in a breath, then seemed to stop herself before speaking. The hesitation lasted only a few seconds. "I am so very, very glad he came to your aid. I would not have been able to bear losing you."

Losing *him*?

His brow furrowed, and he turned to her. "My lady, that is kind, but I am as good as a stranger to you."

"Now that really is nonsense. The moment I met you, I could see what a kind soul you were. How lucky my son was to have found you."

Now Chant's chest seized as tightly as his throat. "There are things you do not know about me."

"Well, of course. I suppose that is true of all the people in all the world."

He swallowed with some effort. "Perhaps you have heard the rumours about my family?"

"I have heard enough to gather that you were put in a very difficult situation at a very young age. And I know enough of the world to realise people are often cruel and judgmental when their kindness is most needed."

That was giving Chant far too much credit, and he almost said so. But he had a sudden memory of Gale holding him, telling him that the whole mess of the past was not his fault. That he was a good man. In that moment, Chant had been able to believe it.

"You must have felt so very alone," Lady Gale said quietly.

"I sometimes think that I deserved to be. Still do. Deserve to be."

"Well, I know you cannot help thinking that, wrong as you are. Your thoughts are your thoughts. But you are *not* alone. And you are not a stranger to this family. My son loves you very much. He may do a terrible job of showing it at times, but it is as plain to me as the rather sharp nose on his face."

Chant stared at the rug, which clashed quite garishly with the sofa. Lady Gale was an unconventional woman, and there was something reassuring in that. The same characteristic was oddly reassuring in her son as well. They seemed better than most people at seeing the world in shades of grey.

"He would not settle down up there." Her gaze flicked to the ceiling. "You were all he talked of. He demanded that you be given anything you wished." She smiled. "I told him I would come see to you myself if only he would stop snarling and go to sleep."

Chant sank his teeth into his lip.

"Whatever the two of you choose to be to each other in the future, know that you have my love as well as his. And, from what I have gathered from my daughters, you have their enthusiastic affection too." She rested one hand on the arm of the sofa. "I cannot—nor would I ever intend to—replace the parents you have been separated from by circumstance. You may tell me if I am overstepping. But whether you wed Christmas or not, you do have a mother who is here for you whenever you might need one."

Chant could not breathe for a moment. His heart beat faster than it had when he'd been sure de Cock was about to kill him.

"But I should also warn you, as a mother, of the scolding you will get should you so much as *think* you are not deserving of such love. I can very nearly read minds, Mr. Chant. I will be able to tell."

He snorted, then swallowed hard on a great choking tangle of emotion. "Ben," he said hoarsely—though nobody had called him that since Reid, not even Gale. "If you… if you don't mind."

"Ben," she repeated with a nod.

When he could speak again, he said, "Thank you. I know this is an inadequate response and encompasses almost none of what I am feeling, but I don't know how to say it all right now."

"That's quite all right."

They sat a moment longer, and then Lady Gale said, "I have taken the liberty of having a chaise moved into Christmas's room should you wish to rest there."

He could not be in the same room as Gale and not climb into the man's bed with him to reassure himself Gale was still in one piece. And he was fairly certain Lady Gale knew that. Still, he appreciated the illusion of propriety.

"I should like that."

Before he could rise to be shown upstairs, the door burst open again, and this time Gale stood there, managing to look rather imperious for a fellow wearing a ridiculous red and black striped dressing gown with a gold medallion pattern overlaid on it. His hair was still damp and disarrayed, and he scowled as only Gale could.

"Mother, what are you doing? Do not harass Mr. Chant."

"He has asked me to call him Ben," she said primly.

"How ridiculous. His name is Chant. It's a fine, steady name."

"Well, maybe one day, if you behave yourself, he will invite you to call him by his given name as well."

Gale strode toward them.

"Aren't you supposed to be in bed?" his mother asked.

"I did not wish to sleep."

"Your physician did not ask what you wished. He told you to remain in bed."

"He is a quack. Do fire him at once. I needed to come down here to protect Mr. Chant from you."

Chant had not spoken yet, needing a moment to take Gale in, to remind himself yet again that the man was well. That perhaps—hopefully—he did not blame Chant for their ordeal. "Your mother has been incredibly kind to me."

"Really?" Gale said sceptically, not looking away from his mother. "The fire has nearly died. How do you expect him to stay warm? Where are the servants? I see no plates about nor tea cups. Has Mr. Chant not even been given any cakes? Or hot tea?"

"He was fed and given tea," Lady Gale retorted. "I will have Jones build the fire back up should Ben want it."

"Truly, I require nothing further—" Chant was swiftly interrupted.

"He has not even received medical treatment," Gale groused. "Look at his head wound! It is not bandaged."

"It is a scratch, nothing more," Lady Gale said dryly.

"Scratch. Scratch! Let me hear you say scratch when he dies of fever and infection."

"Goodness, that took a turn," Chant remarked.

"Get a physician," Gale said to his mother. "Not the quack. Somebody who knows what he's about. I wish to speak to Chant alone."

Lady Gale rose, flicking her hand dismissively at her son. "If I'd known you had such a penchant for drama, I'd have told your sisters to cast you in their play."

She squeezed Chant's shoulder through the blanket. "I'll see you at dinner, *Ben*," she said kindly.

"Lock the door," Gale told her as she exited.

Lady Gale turned, her lips parted. "Really, Christmas, whatever you are planning, it is most certainly not what your physician ordered."

"We have *business* to discuss, Mother," Gale snapped, exasperated. Chant bit back a grin.

"If it is anything like the 'business' your father and I discussed when I recovered from my fever in '91 after he had thought me lost, then I must remind you there are children in this house. And servants."

"Mother!" Gale was as red as Chant had ever seen him.

She gazed steadily at him. Then she rolled her eyes heavenward. "May God forgive me for aiding and abetting."

Gale sighed. "Please will you lock the door?

She continued to stare at him, her look of icy imperiousness putting Gale's to shame.

Gale softened and looked, Chant thought, genuinely contrite. "Please, Mother?" he wheedled.

She shook her head and looked at Chant. "You see? A good thrashing years ago would have done wonders for him."

"*Go!*"

"Anon, my darlings."

She turned and walked out, and Chant heard the click of the lock once she shut the door.

Gale shrugged out of his dressing gown. Beneath it, he wore dry breeches and a loose shirt that hung open. His feet were bare like Chant's. He dropped the gown on the floor and took a seat beside Chant.

"It is strange to see you in my brother's clothes," he remarked.

Chant nodded. "I'm sure it is."

A moment passed in silence.

Finally, Gale said, "I feel more than entitled to chide you, but you look so forlorn."

"You, chide me? It is I who ought to chide you. You were the one who rushed headlong into mortal danger to save a poor sod you ought to have let drown."

"Do not say such things." Gale sounded at once completely serious.

Chant glanced sideways at him. "You told me I should save my recriminations regarding your unwillingness to go to Darling, and Gale, I have saved them. I am prepared to offer them to you now."

"I did get Soulden, though. And the navy. They did far more than Darling would have done."

"I don't think I like this Darling very well," Chant grumbled.

"I thought you liked everybody."

"Everybody except Darling. And Teddy. And de Cock. And Visser."

"You've made so many enemies of late, Benjamin Chant. You are practically a misanthrope. I'm very proud."

Chant looked down at the floor. "All joking aside, I am sorry. I was foolish. I was not paying attention in Mayfair. I could have got you killed—"

"Do not apologise. And you're right. I rushed in headlong. There wasn't time to do anything else." He added softly, "There never could have been time with your life at stake."

The weight of that hit Chant hard. "The jewels…"

"Are, I suppose, either still tied to that damned dog, or—"

"Or what?"

"Or lost on the street somewhere. Who cares about the jewels, Chant?"

"De Cock said—"

"De Cock said a lot of things."

"I wanted you to solve your case."

"Do not call it a case. And anyway, it is *our* case."

A pause.

"Investigation. Endeavour."

Chant laughed. "You investigated a murder, Gale. You *endeavoured* to hunt a killer. Sorry, *we* endeavoured. I feel that qualifies it as a case."

"I do not wish to feel like a fellow out of some cheap novel."

"You are far from that." Chant's voice was faint, even to his own ears.

Gale put an arm around his shoulders. "Come here, my friend. You do not seem yourself at all."

Chant exhaled, relaxing against Gale. "I was so afraid to lose you. If he had killed you, I would have begged him to kill me too."

"Oh, he would have. But he probably would have done it slowly, and you would have lost a great many body parts before it was over. Better that he did not kill either of us."

"Well, yes, obviously. I just mean..."

Gale tugged him close. "Hush now. I am not the centre of the universe. Much as I might like to believe I am. I do care for you, sir. More than I can properly express. You will not lose me if I can help it. But I am not all there is. Do you understand? You are a wonderful man in your own right. You have much love to give. I hope that I may prove myself loyal so you may let go of some of your fear that I will vanish." He jostled Chant lightly.

"You worry that I will smother you if I do not let go of some of this fear?" It was an honest question.

Gale's lips twitched ruefully. "No, I do not think that. I simply do not want to see you tie your worth to how well you love someone else."

"But Gale, what if that is what I am made for in the way you are made for solving cases? Sorry, investigating crimes. Surely it cannot be an unheard of thing for someone to want to devote their life to loving. I know, based on my history, it may not seem as though such devotion is my calling, but—"

"Stop right there," Gale said firmly. "Do not speak ill of yourself. I will let it go this once and assume it is related to your untreated head wound, but in the future..."

"Are you chiding me?"

"Most certainly."

Chant exhaled, studying what he could see of Gale's bare chest through the open shirt. He should have liked to trace every line of muscle, every bone that shifted beneath the skin. But it seemed an effort to lift his arm. "I just want to be by someone's side."

Gale's fingers dug lightly into his shoulder. "You are. You have someone by your side as well. Don't forget it."

Warmth settled in Chant at that quiet order. Gale kissed the top of his head, and Chant closed his eyes. "You are very good at loving, my friend," Gale whispered. "You might consider saving a bit of that love for yourself."

"Such sweet words from a fellow who hates all of humanity." Chant attempted the joke, but it came out flat, and he turned his head and breathed Gale in. As he exhaled, he felt Gale pull him closer still as though even the slightest gap between them wouldn't do.

Then a whisper-soft, warm breath at his ear. "Well, I suppose you have proved me a liar on that front, Benjamin Chant. For I certainly do love you."

$\sim$

*P*erhaps—though Gale never would have admitted it aloud—he should have taken his physician's advice to rest. For while he had no wish to leave Chant's side for the foreseeable future, he was extremely tired. And with exhaustion came a restlessness that made him short-tempered.

He squirmed for perhaps the hundredth time in five minutes.

"Gale?" Chant asked. "Are you not comfortable?"

Chant had seemed to come back to himself gradually over the half an hour they had been sitting together. His eyes sparkled again with good humour, and he spoke with the easy confidence that Gale was accustomed to.

"I do not know how to be comfortable on this hideous sofa. I wish my mother would burn it."

Chant sat up so his weight was no longer on Gale. That made Gale even more churlish, for he had rather liked the feel of Chant in his arms.

"Are you hungry?" Chant asked.

"No," Gale muttered. His stomach took that opportunity to

growl. Chant laughed, and Gale rolled his eyes. "You are not always right, you know."

"No. That is an honour reserved for you."

Gale dug him in the ribs, and Chant snickered and pulled away.

"I wish you would do that thing with my hair," Gale said, trying to keep the peevishness from his tone.

"What thing?'

"You know very well! The thing. With my hair." He drew his long legs up onto the sofa, bending them awkwardly, and placed his head in Chant's lap. If Chant was too fool to understand what Gale wanted, well, there was nothing to be done for it.

He glanced up, seeking Chant's eyes. Chant smiled faintly down at him and placed his hand on Gale's head. "You are hungry," Chant whispered. "And it is making you disagreeable."

He began to stroke Gale's hair, very gently at first, and then with light tugs that made Gale's entire body prickle with pleasure. He let out his breath slowly and turned his head a bit to try to place a kiss on Chant's knee where he estimated it was under the borrowed dressing gown. Chant rubbed small circles at Gale's temple.

"You are good to me," Gale said softly. "Little as I deserve it."

"Now wait." Chant tugged a lock of hair, harder than Gale thought necessary. "If I am not permitted to speak ill of myself, then you are not either."

"But it is a lie when you do it."

"And when you do it as well."

"You may not forbid my speaking the truth. I shall say what I like, when I like—"

"Perhaps your mother is right," Chant interrupted with a laugh.

"That seems unlikely. About what?"

"That a sound thrashing would have done you good in your youth." Chant ran his fingers through Gale's hair, arranging a few still-damp strands into some semblance of order. "Might still."

There was nothing but warmth and amusement in Chant's eyes,

but Gale's heart beat wildly. His prick was stiffening, and he licked his suddenly dry lips. "I should like to see you try it."

"Mmm." Chant sounded thoughtful. Then, with no apparent effort, he rolled Gale onto his front and tugged him so he was over Chant's knees. Gale gave a strangled yelp of surprise. Chant ran his hand down Gale's back.

"Unhand me at once, sir!" Gale ordered, throwing an arm back to swipe at Chant while making no actual effort to get away. He had rarely played games like this before. He prided himself on being at least moderately adventurous at molly houses, but it was strange to do this with somebody he knew intimately without being entirely sure to what extent they were playing.

Chant ran his hand over the seat of Gale's breeches, and Gale's breathing grew shallow. "I cannot unhand you just yet. We are teaching you some manners. Don't you remember?" He landed a light swat to Gale's backside. Gale muffled a yelp in the crook of his elbow, though the swat did not hurt in the slightest.

Chant rubbed again, and Gale spread his legs as wide as he could without sliding off the sofa. Then Chant lifted his hand and delivered another swat. "What do you think? Are you learning anything?"

"Your efforts are tepid at best," Gale replied, his tone bored.

The next slap was just hard enough to sting a little bit. Gale moaned, shifting his hips, a fierce pleasure mixing with a sense of awkwardness and embarrassment. He felt overwhelmed, but he did not know why.

"You heard my mother," he protested. "There are children in this house."

"A fair point." Chant rubbed Gale's arse slowly, up and down each cheek, squeezing every now and again. He tugged the fabric of Gale's breeches a bit tighter. Gale muttered in frustration when he could not achieve the right angle to rub his cockstand against the sofa and pulled himself farther up across Chant's lap so he might grind against Chant's leg.

It took only a moment of squirming and shifting his hips, and then his breath shuddered out of him and he let his full weight rest over Chant's thighs.

Chant gave him another swat. "No more," Gale murmured. "I've learned. I do swear it, Chant."

"Good," Chant whispered. "Very good." Gale started to sit up, unsure about what he was feeling. There was such safety in being with Chant. But his stomach was twisting, and his heart still hammered. Instead of rising, He curled himself sideways around Chant, knowing how awkward his lanky frame must look balled up like this. He buried his head between Chant's hip and the back of the sofa, arms tucked ungracefully against his chest. The dampness of the spend in his pants was uncomfortable, but it was a welcome discomfort.

Chant rubbed his back. Occasionally, his hand travelled higher, fingers running through the hair at Gale's nape, and Gale's heart slowed until he felt almost at peace.

"I was not a well-behaved child," Gale said eventually, hoping Chant could hear him, for he did not wish to repeat himself. It was hard enough to speak as it was. "I gave my tutor, Marsh, a great deal of trouble. I didn't necessarily mean to. But I found my lessons very dull. I think he resented me for knowing more than he did and took satisfaction in finding my weaknesses and making sport of them. My mother thinks the story of me avoiding a whipping from him is quite funny, but I was humiliated, in truth, by the way he treated me, though I feigned arrogance and indifference at the time. The topics I was extraordinarily knowledgeable about or interested in became topics he would avoid, and he would replace them with more... practical examinations, I suppose? Of my social skills or—or how people function in a society. Things I had an insufficient grasp of. And these were not lessons. They were tests, designed to draw a line under my deficiencies. I did not always understand what was being asked of me. And I was rather frightened of being... disappointing."

"Ah." Chant's touch was so steady and gentle, Gale could scarcely muster the energy to be embarrassed by his own words.

"It's not an excuse for how impertinent I was. And still am. I just... wanted you to know."

"That ought not to have happened to you. And I am very sorry that it did."

"It is past."

"I should not have teased you. I do not truly think children should be whipped. I hope you know. And I certainly do not think you should have been."

"No, it is fine. I... I suppose I like you teasing me about it. It is only a memory. I've not told anyone before."

Chant stroked the back of his neck. "You will not disappoint me."

"Perhaps I will." Gale swallowed, glad he had nothing to look at but the sofa's upholstery. "I'm certain I will, at times. But I do trust you will forgive me, and so I wondered... might I ask you, if there is something I don't understand? I know it sounds very silly, and I'm not even sure what an example would be. But if you, or someone else... oh Christ, I don't know. If you are clearly feeling some way, and I'm not sure why, but I can tell it's the sort of thing most people would pick up on intuitively... could I ask why, or would it upset you to be asked? Would it make you wish I were better at just... understanding and giving you what you needed?"

"It's not silly at all. You may always ask," Chant said. "And I will do my best to explain. But for what it's worth, I think you understand what I am feeling quite well. Much of the time."

Gale exhaled.

"You are quite a wonder, you know."

Gale stilled. He knew Chant did not mean it the way the papers meant it. The way people on the street meant it. He did not mean that Gale's investigative ability was some circus trick that he wished to be able to see on command. He meant Gale. Gale himself.

How terrifying.

Gale rolled onto his back, gazing up at Chant. "I do know. And I'm glad to see you know it too." It was difficult to glare haughtily in this position, and by the time the smile spread across Chant's lips, Gale was laughing too. Openly and without reservation, putting his arms up to shield himself as Chant shifted out from under Gale, careful to keep Gale from rolling off the sofa. Chant straddled him, and Gale pushed half-heartedly at his chest.

Chant somehow wormed around Gale's shielding arms and kissed his neck, which made Gale laugh harder. "I'm sorry," Gale gasped. "I'm sorry."

"You hardly sound it." Chant nipped his throat, batting Gale's hands out of the way. They struggled, both laughing, until they tumbled off the sofa and landed in a tangle of limbs on the rug.

"Oh God," Gale said between gasps. "You're crushing me."

"Your extremely bony knee is somewhere very personal," Chant ground out.

A knock on the door startled them both. "Boys," Lady Gale called. "I'm sorry to interrupt your 'business' discussion. But we have a most unexpected guest."

CHAPTER 19

*G*ale stared first at the dirty-faced boy in the entryway and then shifted his gaze along the rope the boy held to the giant, shaggy mongrel at the end of it.

"My God," Chant whispered behind him. "Is that…"

"Flummery!" Elise cried, shoving between Gale and Chant. She dropped to her knees and hugged the beast, who wagged some part of himself Gale presumed was his tail, and then a great pink tongue snaked out from the other end of him and lapped at Elise's face.

Gale's sisters had all crowded into the hall and were talking so loudly Gale could scarcely hear himself think. The boy explained that he'd seen this great hairy dog eating scraps behind a pie cart in Jacob's Island, and he'd wondered if Gale was still in need of a great hairy dog. Gale gave the boy a coin and thanked him sincerely before sending him on his way.

He cringed at the amount of filth stuck in the dog's matted fur. He did not wish to interrupt the happy reunion, but he felt it quite important to figure out if de Brouckère's jewels still adorned the beast. So he crouched down. "Hello, Flum," he said, trying to sound casual and friendly. He could not tell if the creature was looking at him or not. "Hey, old fellow, come here now. Nice and easy. Nothing to be scared of."

Chant cleared his throat. "Perhaps Elise could teach you how to call a dog without sounding as though you are leading him to a chopping block to slaughter him for his meat."

Gale's sisters giggled.

Elise turned to Chant, scandalised. "Lord Christmas wouldn't kill a dog. Anyone who would is a nasty piece of work!"

"I agree, Elise," Chant assured her. "I am only teasing Lord Christmas."

"Well, if you're so good with dogs," Gale snapped at Chant, "perhaps you could call him."

Chant crouched down next to Gale and called to Flummery, who bounded over at once. Elise laughed with delight. Gale held his tongue and was quite proud of himself for it.

Chant began stroking the dog, feeling around the creature's neck for the collar the sailors had described. He shook his head at Gale after a moment. Gale tentatively put a hand out and parted the dog's fur, feeling around between the mats.

The dog didn't wear a collar at all. And there were no edges that would indicate jewels braided into the filthy locks. Gale was not surprised.

"How unfortunate," he said calmly. Flum stopped panting and glanced up at him. At least Gale thought he was glancing up at him. Difficult to say.

"What's the matter?" Clarissa asked.

Gale rose slowly, his knees popping. "De Cock's sailors wrapped priceless jewellery around this fellow's collar before he escaped the ship. All this time, we thought the key to finding the jewels was to find Flummery. But the jewels aren't here."

He helped Chant to his feet, and a moment later felt a tug on the leg of his breeches. When he looked down, Elise stood there, staring solemnly at him. He was fairly sure he knew what she was going to say, and he kept his gaze steady on hers.

"Flummery was wearing jewels," she said very softly. "When Pa brought him home."

Gale's eyebrows lifted. "Was he?"

"You couldn't see them through all his hair, but I was petting him, and I found them. They were so pretty. I was afraid Pa would sell them if I showed him. He's always trying to sell things, but he loses his money at cards."

The room had gone silent, and Gale hoped having an audience wouldn't discourage Elise from speaking. She went on. "I hid them. And that's why the captain wanted Flum. That's why he killed Pa."

"Where are the jewels now?"

"I had 'em with me, in my skirt, when I came here. You saw them once, Lord Christmas!"

"Eugenie was wearing de Brouckère's stolen jewels in the play." Gale said as steadily as he could. He thought he'd been prepared for Elise's confession, but hearing it out loud was a bit more painful than he'd imagined. "Right in front of me," he said out the side of his mouth. "It all happened right in front of me, Chant."

Chant placed a hand on his shoulder, and Gale forced himself to draw a breath before speaking again. "Where are they now, Elise? At this particular moment?" Elise hurried from the room, and Gale heard her pounding up the stairs. He turned to Chant, not quite able to meet the other man's eye.

"You knew," Chant whispered.

"I suspected."

"De Cock thought it as well."

"Yes." Gale sighed heavily. "She had them this whole time. I cannot," he said. "Chant, I simply cannot."

"There's no harm done."

"No *harm* done? You almost died."

"I would argue that *you* almost died, as you were the one who couldn't swim."

"I *asked* her. I practically *begged* her to tell me…"

"She had her reasons."

Gale sighed. "Who will give me strength since I don't believe in the Lord?"

"I will. Pull yourself together and be kind to the child."

Elise was back a moment later with a small velvet bag that rattled lightly as she handed it to Gale. Gale peered inside, then turned away at once as though the bag held a dead rat. "Good grief."

Chant glanced inside. "Astounding."

The sapphire necklace. The ruby bracelet. All the pieces Visser had wrapped around Flummery's collar. That Elise had volunteered to Eugenie for their pageant without telling her where they'd come from, but that she couldn't possibly have just... told... Gale... about.

"Elise," Gale said. "Why on earth didn't you say anything?"

Lady Gale stepped forward. "Christmas, don't shout at her."

"I'm not *shouting—*"

"I wanted to tell you!" Elise stared him in the eye. "But you said whoever was responsible for Pa's death ought to hang. If I hadn't ever taken the jewels, Pa wouldn't have got killed. It's my fault, what happened to him! And if you'd known what I did, you would've put me in gaol same as the captain."

Gale was genuinely blindsided. "How could you possibly think that?"

"It's my fault!" she shouted, her eyes wild. Tears streamed silently down her face accompanied by tiny, almost imperceptible hitches in her breath.

Gale knelt in front of her and took her hand.

"No," he said firmly. "Listen to me. Sometimes bad things happen, horrible things. And they make us feel so small, like we have no control over anything in the world. And so we give ourselves control by imagining we're the villain, the one who brought about these horrible things. We give ourselves that power, thinking it will make us feel safer, but all it really does is give us permission to eat away at ourselves with blame."

A slight movement caught his eye, and he looked up to see

Chant watching him. Chant gave him a tight-lipped smile, his eyes suspiciously glossy.

"You did not get your father killed by hiding the jewels. You did not make de Cock a cruel man by keeping that secret. De Cock is a man who hurts people. And I'm so terribly sorry it was your family he hurt. But it is not your fault."

Elise leaned forward without a word, and he did too, wrapping his arms around her.

"I think your pa would be very proud of you," he whispered.

He figured it was true enough. He might have thought her a more impressive child had she simply told him in the first place that her stray dog had come to her covered in stolen jewels. But Chant was looking at him with such pride and probably thinking Gale would be a far more impressive adult if he had simply told Chant in the first place that he was dreadfully in love with him. So Gale was not going to split hairs.

Flummery snuffled his way between them, and Gale let go of Elise so the dog could better lick her face. Elise laughed and wiped her nose with her fist. She looked at Gale again. "You mean that?"

"Every word."

"I never wanted you and Mr. Chant to get hurt. I really didn't."

His chest constricted. What was happening to him? It must be a heart attack brought on at such a young age by the unholy amount of stress he had been put through. By this child, by Benjamin Chant, by this blasted dog, by the entire world and its insistence on existing. "I know that."

Elise drew back and looked at him solemnly. "Are we going to give the jewels to your friend? The one who likes you even though you're in love with Mr. Chant?"

Chant snorted, and Gale felt himself colour up. "Yes, I suppose that is one possibility."

Elise was soon drawn into a conversation with some of Gale's sisters, who wished to know more about her discovery of the jewels on the dog. Chant and Gale watched the bedlam around them as

Helene stepped in a puddle of Flummery's drool so thick it pulled her slipper off, and Flummery chased Eugenie, trying to grab the ribbons on her dress, and Cordelia declared she would compose a new piano piece inspired by the stolen jewels. Chant said softly, so only Gale could hear, "Well, I guess there's no other recourse but for the two of us to wed and then adopt the girl. And the dog, of course."

He slapped Gale's shoulder, then walked off to join the girls in trying to corral the dog.

"Wed?" Gale called after him, horrified. And then it hit him. "*Adopt?*"

"Oh, good!" His mother was suddenly beside him. "I was hoping you would agree that adopting Elise is the only logical course of action. We simply can't take her to the parish, Christmas."

A moment ago, Gale had been sure his cheeks were scarlet. Now he felt all the colour drain from his face. "You can't be serious."

"So you would take her to the parish? Oh, and to think a devil like you is my own flesh and blood."

"No! I... But perhaps we could...place her with a nice family..."

"We are a nice family, Christmas. Well, perhaps that is being generous," she added as Cordelia screeched that Anne-Marie was a greater oaf than the dog. "But the girl could do worse."

Gale gestured desperately at the girls. "These are already more sisters than God ever intended any man to have."

"Then I suppose it's a good thing you don't believe in God, isn't it?"

"If I needed any further proof of His nonexistence, it is this conversation we are having."

"It's no use pretending you're not fond of her, love. You never were very hard to read."

"You are the only person who thinks that."

She twitched her lips and cut her eyes toward Chant, who had smoothed things over between Cordelia and Anne-Marie and was attempting to get Flummery to sit. "Oh, I don't know about that."

Gale's chest grew tighter. The end must be near. He wished his body would get on with the business of collapsing into a pile of twitching, spider-like limbs and black bile.

"I'm very proud of you, you know," his mother said softly.

"*Why?*"

"There's no one reason. I just am."

He ran the tip of his tongue along his teeth.

"I suppose your heroic rescue of the man you love from the clutches of a murderous pirate didn't hurt," she mused.

He turned to face her. "I didn't know what I was doing," he confessed quietly. "I just knew I couldn't lose him."

She smiled, fondly and perhaps a little sadly. "I know." She lifted her arms, "May I?"

Gale gave the slightest nod and stepped forward. She put her arms around him, and after a few seconds, he placed his arms around her too. And then squeezed a bit harder than he'd meant to. She always seemed such a tall, imposing figure, but in this moment, she felt slight and breakable, and he felt a new rush of panic at how easy it was to lose people. He breathed in her familiar scent, one he had known since his earliest days of awareness, and let his head fall against her shoulder. "I love you," he mumbled.

Her arms tightened around him. "I love you too. Have since the moment I laid eyes on you. Before that, even."

"I'm sorry I've been so much trouble."

She hummed softly into his hair, then drew back, taking his hands in hers. "I dare say I enjoy a bit of trouble almost as much as you do."

He tried to smile.

"I have never wanted you to be any other way than how you are," she said. "You know that, don't you?"

He turned away, not wanting her to see whatever was in his eyes at that moment. That was a mistake because his gaze landed instantly on Chant, who was sitting on the floor with an arm slung around Flummery, talking to Cordelia about her new piano piece.

"How do I make sure I don't hurt him?" he asked, and even knowing how foolish the question was didn't stop him from meaning it with his whole heart.

She squeezed his hands. "I rather think that's up to you. But you might start by trusting how fond you are of him and how little you *want* to hurt him."

He sighed and gently drew his hands away. "He said *wed*, Mother."

"He did."

"Why would he say such a thing?"

"I'm no investigator, but perhaps because he wishes to wed you."

"Don't be silly. It was only a joke. Wasn't it?"

"My dear, he cares for you deeply. He will not ask you to do anything you don't want. There is no rush to marry. It does not mean you love each other any less."

Gale rubbed a hand over his face and nodded, not entirely convinced. "He will want marriage, but I don't want that. He will think it means I am not fully committed, and then he will not trust me, and—"

"Don't assume, Christmas. You must actually talk to him."

"That is very difficult."

"Is it really?" she asked gently.

He hesitated, then shook his head.

"Society knows you two now as investigative partners. I dare say there is much you can get away with under the guise of such a partnership. But if any of your 'business talks' should get out of hand and should Society grow wise to you, you can always do what your father and I did and have a rather spontaneous wedding that ends up being such a splendid celebration people forget they were ever suspicious about the suddenness of it."

"I am both horrified you're telling me this and oddly reassured."

"You are hardly the first person in history, or even in this family, to talk business before marriage."

"Please let us end this heart-to-heart while I still stand a chance of getting these images out of my head sometime in the next decade."

"Oh, it's far too late for that, my dear."

"Yes, I am realising that more with each passing second."

She brushed some invisible speck of something from his shirt. "Do not dwell too much on how it can all go wrong. That way lies madness. Besides, there only one scandal that everybody is talking about right now. You and Ben could take off all your clothes and race through Hyde Park, and Society would only have eyes for Loftus Rivingdon and Morgan Notley."

"I could not possibly care less what those two fops are up to."

His mother shrugged, biting her lip mischievously. "I must say, it is jolly entertainment."

"Jolly is hardly my area of interest."

"Talk to him," she repeated. "It will all work out. You'll see."

"All right. But I will come complaining to you when I have broken his heart with the news that I do not wish to wed right away… or possibly ever."

"Oh, Christmas. Would you like to place bets?"

∼

*L*ater, when he and Chant were properly dressed and ready to go in to dinner, Gale stopped him outside the dining room. "You look…" That was as far as Gale's brain got.

"You also look—" Chant leaned in and kissed him.

Gale kissed back with a ferocity that rather contradicted the protests he made against Chant's lips. "Chant! My family is just through that door."

Chant pulled back and regarded him with that quietly amused expression. "And just how am I supposed to help myself?" he inquired.

Gale pulled him in for another fierce kiss, then released him and addressed the matter at hand.

"If I tell you I am unsure about marriage, you will doubt my love for you, and your resentment will fester between us, and I will hate myself for knowing that if we carry on as we are while remaining unwed, I put you at risk of a scandal. There is no way for us to avoid this calamity."

Chant simply stared. His lips were delightfully reddened, a bit puffy where Gale had nipped at him. "What the hell are you talking about?"

"If you are in love with me, as you say you are, then you will wish to wed. And I love you in return, but I don't know whether marriage is a good decision for me."

Chant looked as if he were fighting a smile. "Gale, we have known each other less than a week. I think we could stand to wait at least another before discussing marriage."

Gale hesitated, surprised. "But you will want it eventually, won't you?"

"I cannot say just yet. I do not doubt your love for me. And I certainly hope you do not doubt mine for you. Marriage is no more proof of devotion than attending church is proof of one's inherent virtue." That sparkle in Chant's eyes was damnably reassuring. As was the way he ran a hand down Gale's arm and tugged lightly on his hand before letting it go. "Come. I told you hours ago you were hungry. You will think more clearly after a good meal."

Gale remained in place. Why did his mother always have to be right?

"Come on," Chant urged again. "Afterward, perhaps we can go back to your place—or mine—and I shall show you just how committed I can be even without a ring on my finger. In fact, for what I have in mind it is probably best I am not wearing a ring."

He turned toward the dining room.

"Chant?" Gale whispered harshly. "What do you have in mind?"

Chant called over his shoulder, "You're the investigator, Lord Christmas. You figure it out."

From inside the dining room, Gale heard his mother's laughter and Anne-Marie telling off Flum for trying to grab food from the table. He could imagine Elise sitting at the table, one of the family, this girl who had lost so much but who still believed in good people and good things to come. And Chant, taking his seat among them all.

He supposed he could spend hours, weeks, a lifetime, wondering how this had happened. How a heart locked as tight as his own had been opened with the easy, effortless amusement that sparkled in a pair of deep blue eyes. He could wonder if he deserved such love, if it would last, if he would have to fight for it in ways for which he was unprepared.

Or he could simply have it. Because Chant gave it freely. He could have it, and cherish it, and return it. He could live in the light of Chant's kindness. And he could do everything in his power to let Chant know he was there. That he would not disappear.

Moments later, Gale entered the dining room, thinking it would surely be best to go back to Russell Street tonight rather than Mayfair. After all, it was the only place they could go without some great damned hairy dog watching as Gale rendered Benjamin Chant completely and utterly senseless.

And Gale intended to do that at least twice, possibly three times, before dawn.

AFTERWORD

Thank you so much for reading *A Case for Christmas*. We hope that you enjoyed it. We would very much appreciate it if you could take a few moments to leave a review on Amazon or Goodreads, or on your social media platform of choice.

ABOUT J.A. ROCK

J.A. Rock is an author of LGBTQ romance and suspense novels, as well as an audiobook narrator under the name Jill Smith. When she's not writing or narrating, J.A. enjoys reading, collecting historical costumes, and failing miserably at gardening. She lives in the Ohio wilds with an extremely judgmental dog, Professor Anne Studebaker.

You can find her website at https://jarockauthor.com.

ABOUT LISA HENRY

Lisa likes to tell stories, mostly with hot guys and happily ever afters.

Lisa lives in tropical North Queensland, Australia. She doesn't know why, because she hates the heat, but she suspects she's too lazy to move. She spends half her time slaving away as a government minion, and the other half plotting her escape.

She attended university at sixteen, not because she was a child prodigy or anything, but because of a mix-up between international school systems early in life. She studied History and English, neither of them very thoroughly.

Lisa has been published since 2012, and was a LAMBDA finalist for her quirky, awkward coming-of-age romance *Adulting 101*, and a Rainbow Awards finalist for 2019's *Anhaga*.

You can join Lisa's Facebook reader group at Lisa Henry's Hangout, and find her website at lisahenryonline.com.

ALSO BY J.A. ROCK AND LISA HENRY

When All the World Sleeps

Another Man's Treasure

Fall on Your Knees

The Preacher's Son

Mark Cooper versus America (Prescott College #1)

Brandon Mills versus the V-Card (Prescott College #2)

The Good Boy (The Boy #1)

The Boy Who Belonged (The Boy #2)

The Playing the Fool Series

The Two Gentlemen of Altona

The Merchant of Death

Tempest

The Lords of Bucknall Club Series

A Husband for Hartwell

A Case for Christmas

A Rival for Rivingdon

ALSO BY LISA HENRY

The Parable of the Mustard Seed

Naked Ambition

Dauntless

Anhaga

Two Man Station (Emergency Services #1)

Lights and Sirens (Emergency Services #2)

The California Dashwoods

Adulting 101

Sweetwater

He Is Worthy

The Island

Tribute

One Perfect Night

Fallout, with M. Caspian

Dark Space (Dark Space #1)

Darker Space (Dark Space #2)

Starlight (Dark Space #3)

With Tia Fielding

Family Recipe

Recipe for Two

A Desperate Man

With Sarah Honey

Red Heir

Elf Defence

Socially Orcward

Writing as Cari Waites

<u>Stealing Innocents</u>

<u>Hapi</u>

Printed in Great Britain
by Amazon

85561350R00161